PAPER
SON

PAPER SON

SON

S. J. ROZAN

PEGASUS CRIME

NEW YORK LONDON

PAPER SON

Pegasus Crime is an imprint of
Pegasus Books, Ltd.
148 West 37th Street, 13th FL
New York, NY 10018

First Pegasus Books hardcover edition July 2019

Interior design by Sabrina Plomitallo-González, Pegasus Books

ISBN: 978-1-64313-129-0

10 9 8 7 6 5 4 3 2 1

Printed in the United States of America
Distributed by W. W. Norton & Company, Inc.

ACKNOWLEDGMENTS

Josh Getzler, my agent

Gilroy and Sally Chow
Gene Joe

Jonathan Santlofer
Barbara Shoup

Steve Blier
Hillary Brown
Susan Chin
Belmont Freeman
Charles McKinney
James Russell

Ace Atkins
Reed Farrel Coleman
Margaret Maron

Craig and Karina Buck

Patricia Chao

Parnell Hall

The NYPL Chinatown Branch

And a special lift of the moonshine to
Eric Stone,
who started me off

For Nancy Richler,
with love, food, and a good long hike

1

"*Mississippi?*"

"Ling Wan-ju, please do not stare with your mouth open in this way. It makes me worried that I didn't raise you well." Reaching into her sewing basket, my mother took out the folds of fabric that were in the process of becoming a blouse for my brother Ted's wife.

"You raised me fine," I said. "Only now I think maybe my hearing's going. The Mississippi Delta?" It's not the easiest phrase in Cantonese, so maybe it wasn't what she'd said. Maybe I'd just been doing what she so often accused us of when we were kids: listening in English.

However, my mother's eye roll made it clear I'd understood her correctly. And actually, I knew nothing was wrong with my hearing. I thought something was wrong with my mind. I must be hallucinating, except I didn't know which part was craziest: that *my mother* wanted me to go to Mississippi on a case; that my mother wanted me to go to *Mississippi* on a case; or that my mother wanted me to go to Mississippi *on a case*.

I tried to recover my equilibrium with a different question. "Why didn't I know we had cousins in the Mississippi Delta?"

"You do not pay attention." My mother threaded her needle. "Your father used to get letters from his cousins. One of the wreaths at your father's funeral was sent by the Mississippi cousins. The wreath with the big white bow and the yellow chrysanthemums."

My father died fifteen years ago, when I was thirteen. He was a popular man; so many wreaths, sprays, and bouquets crowded the funeral home that it was remarkable bees weren't buzzing around the casket. That I didn't know who'd sent which flowers wasn't surprising. Nor was the fact that my mother did, and to this day could tell you. It was likely she also had a comprehensive list of people who'd sent nothing, but that was a different issue.

"Who are these cousins? And who's the one who's been arrested?"

That was what she'd just told me: that I had a cousin in Mississippi, which was a surprise; that he was in jail, which took me aback; and that she wanted me to hurry down and get him out, which rocked my world.

My mother smoothed the fabric. "Your father's grandfather's brother, Chin Song-Zhao, came to America as a boy in 1915." Her needle started flashing, making quick, even stitches. "He worked in the grocery store of a man from his village who had come earlier. In Clarksdale, in the Delta of Mississippi."

I left aside the Delta and the fact that a Chinese person a hundred years ago would go there—and that another Chinese person already had a grocery store there for him to work in—and focused on the family. Yes, Chin Song-Zhao's descendants qualified as my cousins. Something like my fourth cousins three times removed, but we don't cut it fine like that. Older relatives who aren't your grandparents are your uncles and aunties. Besides them and your nieces and nephews, everyone else is a cousin. And now, four generations later, behold, I have Mississippi cousins.

"So who's been arrested?" I asked again.

"A young man, Jefferson Tam."

"For what?"

She frowned in distaste. "The killing of his father."

"Ma!" I stared at her. "*Murder?* I—" I clamped my mouth shut before any words like *can't* or *don't* got out. I was in a real bind.

My mother's attitude toward my PI career has zigzagged from

disgust, disapproval, and attempts at deterrence to, on good days, a kind of pointedly exaggerated patience, a showy expectation that I'll get this out of my system and turn to a pursuit worthy of a good Chinese daughter. That she would bring me a case and demand I take it is something I never would've imagined five years, or five minutes, ago.

Many things about this profession escape my mother, though. One is that PIs generally don't get involved in homicides.

It's understandable she'd miss that point, on two counts. First, some of my past cases actually have included homicides. Once or twice, when the suspicious death showed up, I'd turned the whole thing over to the cops, but other times, for various reasons, I was in too deep by that point and I just stayed in.

Second, as far as my mother's concerned, homicide, tax evasion, and jaywalking are all as bad as each other. Criminals on every level are dangerous, unsavory people, and if I insist on getting involved with them, why draw the line at murder?

I watched her sew. In midwinter, the sun never quite makes it into our living room, so even though it was barely two o'clock, my mother sat in a pool of lamplight. This case could represent the first tiny thaw, the sharp edge of the wedge, the foot in the door. A change in her attitude toward my career. And it was a case I had no business taking.

"Tell me all about it, Ma."

"If I knew all about it, why would you have to investigate?" Her needle flicked. "Jefferson Tam is innocent. You will find things out. Then you will clear up this mistake."

"How do you know what happened?"

She gave me a look as disbelieving as it was disapproving. "As usual, you are not listening. I just told you I don't know what happened. But whatever happened, Jefferson Tam did not do this crime. He's your father's cousin."

Oh, right. A relative of my sainted father, and therefore incapable of such an act.

"I see. But that's not what I meant. How do you even know he's in jail?"

"His uncle called me. Captain Pete Tam. From Clarksdale, Mississippi. To ask me to send you there."

I digested this news. If this uncle knew I was a PI, it could only be because my mother had told him, something I thought she never did unless wild horses were dragging it out of her.

Then she dropped the capper on My Weird Day with Ma.

"But do not think for a minute, Ling Wan-ju, that I'll permit you to go to the Delta of Mississippi alone."

"Permit me? It's your idea!"

"Of course it is. You'll go help your cousin. But not alone. You will tell the White Baboon he has to go also."

2

"So let me get this straight."

My partner, Bill Smith, poured himself a cup of coffee. An hour after being more or less hired by my own mother (do you say "hired" when there's no possibility of turning the job down and you can't expect to get paid?), I was at Bill's Tribeca apartment, a big-windowed place above a bar on Laight Street. I already had my mug of oolong tea and was curled up in the easy chair by the piano. There's lots of tea at Bill's place, not that he has any idea what to buy in that department. You'd think after all this time, starting from our sometimes-coworker days up to our current full-partner situation, he'd have caught on, but no. So I stock his shelves out of self-interest.

"Your mother not only wants you to go to Mississippi, to work a case," Bill said, settling on the sofa, "she wants me to go with you."

"Do you think I need to get her a mental health exam?"

"Maybe so. Maybe she's got some weird dementia that makes you sane in your old age. What exactly did she say?"

"She said I had to go to the Delta—which has never been on my radar as a destination and which, by the way, I don't think she even knows where it is—to straighten things out because a cousin I've never heard of is in jail. But I can't go alone, and I should tell the White Baboon to come with me."

"Oh, wait, she called me that? Then don't worry, she hasn't lost a step." He took a contemplative sip. "In fact, I think we should leave before the echo comes back and she hears herself."

"Seriously? You're willing to go?"

"Why wouldn't I be?"

"Who wants to get involved in Chin family business if they don't have to? Especially for free?"

"You underestimate the enduring fascination of other people's problems. And there's more than one kind of compensation. Your mother wants me to go. If I do, she'll owe me. She'll have to be nicer to me."

"You know that'll never happen."

"Then I'll have the moral high ground. And anyway, the Delta? Where they eat grits three times a day and drink moonshine with their barbecue? Where they play the blues deep into the starry night? Where we'll stay in a Motel Six on Highway Sixty-One with a connecting door between our rooms?"

"That won't happen, either."

"And your mother's right, you need me down there. I speak the language. Y'all are fergittin' ah'm from Kin-tucky. Born 'n' bred below th' Mason-Dixon lahn. Ah kin talk South'rn with th' best of 'em."

"Please don't do that, it's creepy."

"Someday you'll be glad I have that skill. But back to this cousin you've never heard of."

"Jefferson Tam, twenty-three. Arrested yesterday in Clarksdale, Mississippi."

"For?"

"Murder."

Bill stopped mid-sip. "Is that true? Or you just said it to see if I'm paying attention?"

"No, true, and worse: patricide. They say he killed his father, Leland Tam. He says he didn't. My mother says he didn't."

"Who says he did?"

"I'm not clear on the details, but he seems to have been found kneeling over his father in the family grocery store, with blood on his clothes and his prints on the knife."

"I see. And what makes your mother so sure he didn't do it?"

"Because." I looked straight at him. "No one related to *my* father could have done such a thing."

Bill raised his eyebrows. "Well, if that's her thinking, I've got to say she's entirely compos mentis in her own inimitable way. What's your sense? You think she's right?"

"About my father's relations? I doubt it." I sat back. "About this guy, I'd have to meet him to say. Like I told you, I never even knew these people existed."

"Okay. And what is it we're supposed to do down there?"

"For one thing, be Chinese."

"I'm not very good at that."

"Har har. I think my mother's idea is, there might be things he's not telling a white lawyer but he'll tell me, his Chinese cousin."

"Did he grow up down there?"

"Yes."

"Then Yankee might trump both Chinese and cousin, and he'll freeze you out, too."

"I guess. The whole situation's a little unclear to me. Not to my mother, though—Jefferson Tam's related to my sainted father, he's innocent, go get him out of jail."

"It's sweet she still thinks of your father that way."

"Yes, well, it gave her an unfair advantage after he died. She invoked him all the time. We half believed he was standing beside her, watching us from the other world."

"He probably was. He's probably here right now. Hi there, Mr. Chin. Could you remind your daughter how much she loves me? She forgets all the time."

"He can't do that, dummy. Ghosts can't lie. So you're really in?"

"Come on, you didn't actually think I'd turn you down."

"I thought you might turn my mother down."

"See aforementioned forlorn hope of nicer treatment. But speaking of forlorn hopes, there's your mother's, about Jefferson Tam. Mississippi justice has a bad rep, but even a blind squirrel sometimes finds an acorn."

"Is that a Southern saying?"

"They have an endless number of those, just wait. The point is, this kid might not be a saint like your father. Your mother might find herself disappointed in him."

"And by extension, in me, you mean?"

"If you have to be the messenger bearing the bad news, yes."

I sighed. "I thought of that. But the thing is, my mother's never asked me to take a case before."

"A milestone, I agree. Showing a good deal of faith in you."

"It's more even than the faith. It's that she's finally sort of admitting this is my job." I looked for the words to explain it. "My parents were thrilled when I was born. They didn't want a fifth son. They wanted a daughter. My mother made all these flowered dresses. But I could look around the schoolyard and see who was having all the fun. When I turned out to be a tomboy, my father kind of enjoyed it. We went to ball games and he signed me up at a dojo. My mother's always been disappointed, though. She doesn't like it that I'm a PI, but the problem goes deeper than that. It's my—" I waved the mug at my jeans, my boots, my short hair. "My whole unmarried, non-girly-girl self."

"You sure she's disappointed? Not just worried about you?"

"Why should she worry?"

"Because where she came from, an unmarried woman was potential prey to every man who came along, likely to be misused, abandoned, and, in the end, starve to death."

I stared. "That's not only extraordinarily feminist of you, it's bizarrely empathetic toward my mother."

"She's not always wrong. Just about me."

I drank my tea, which I was grateful to find tasted just like I thought it would, seeing as how the rest of the world was upside down.

"So," Bill said. "When do we leave?"

"You're sure?"

He didn't dignify that with an answer. If it had been Bill asking me to do something like this, I wouldn't have, either.

"Tomorrow morning," I said, and smiled. "Thanks."

He returned the smile, our eyes met, and I went quickly back to business. "The closest airport's Memphis," I said. "There's an eight A.M. flight—"

"Ugh."

"Ugh, Memphis?"

"No, I love Memphis. Ugh, eight A.M."

Bill's a night owl. I'm an early bird. I shrugged.

"You know that means we have to leave for the airport at six?"

"We can watch the sun come up."

He nodded slowly. "Maybe that connecting door's not such a hot idea."

"Told you. Anyway, when we get there, we rent a car and drive to Clarksdale, which I understand is about an hour south, and meet the client."

"Wait. I thought your mother was the client."

"Technically, no. She might never have known about this murder if a guy named Captain Pete hadn't called and asked for her help. Actually, my help. Generally, when people come to my mother asking for me, she tells them to go fry ice, but I guess because this is family, it's different."

"I'm having a little difficulty following this part of the story. Do I get in trouble if I ask who Captain Pete is?"

"Pete Tam. Uncle of the victim and great-uncle of the suspect. He's the cousin who sent the flowers to my father's funeral."

"Okay, now explain something else. If these are all male relations on your father's side"—he paused; I nodded—"how come they're Tams, not Chins?"

"Because," I said, "the original one, Chin Song-Zhao, came here as a paper son."

3

Throughout the middle of the nineteenth century, thousands of Chinese men headed for America—*Gaam San*, the Gold Mountain. They farmed, panned for gold, and were indispensable to the building of the railroad. But when the railroad was finished, white people began to see them differently. Suddenly they were the Yellow Peril. Dangerous, devious, out for your jobs and your women. It happens to many immigrants—Bill's people, the Irish, coming over around the same time, weren't exactly welcome, either—but against the Chinese, and us alone, Congress passed a law: the Chinese Exclusion Act of 1882. It pretty much choked off immigration. The Exclusion Act and its extensions made landing on the shores of *Gaam San* illegal for most Chinese, and it stayed that way until the 1940s.

Congress did not, however, take the further step of shipping home the Chinese already here (though their neighbors in the West often found it expedient to beat them up and burn their homes to drive them away). And this being America, the law had loopholes. Merchants and scholars—who were few, and who had money, as opposed to laborers, who were numerous and needed it—could still come. The Exclusion Act also didn't affect the right of an American citizen, natural-born or naturalized, to bring his foreign-born family in.

Thus was created the paper son.

Many of the original immigrants had families back in China that they'd go home every few years to see. A man who'd been naturalized could register any children born in China and then bring them to America. A young man wanting to come over would make arrangements with—meaning, pay off—one of these citizens and for immigration purposes claim to be his son.

On, um, paper, being a paper son seems simple enough. In reality, it was arduous and anxiety-filled, because immigration officials were onto the scam. Questions about the weather and geography of the home village, relatives' names and ages, and neighbors' occupations became standard. Paper fathers had reams of information to provide, and paper sons had hours of memorizing to do. Many hopeful paper sons got sent back, but many made it through.

Apparently, my great-grandfather's brother was one of those.

He got to stay. But he lost his name.

I told Bill all this as the last traces of sunlight slipped off the building façade across the street.

"A lot of immigrants change their names," Bill said. "It can be a way of shedding baggage, starting over."

"Not for us. In Chinese culture, your family name is who you are. It's a big deal. Our family records go back a dozen, twenty generations. We have ancestor tablets and family altars. Just because someone's dead doesn't mean he's not kept up-to-date on relatives' affairs and consulted on important decisions."

"Like your dad. Hi again, Mr. Chin."

I raised my tea mug. "Hi, Baba." To Bill, I said, "I mean, I've known about paper sons since grade school, but I guess I never really thought about what it must have been like to be one. I didn't know I had one in the family."

Though, I thought, considering that one of his progeny had now been arrested for killing another, my great-grandfather's brother in the other world might be just as happy that he and his own ancestors, stretching back through the mists of time, were seeing all this happen with someone else's family name attached.

4

I walked across Canal, through the December afternoon. In Tribeca things were quiet, but once I hit Chinatown I had to slip sideways through the bustle of Christmas shopping, Chinese New Year shopping, grocery shopping, and, among the tourists and uptowners, knockoff shopping. Chinatown's famous for luxury-brand counterfeits, though Chinese people won't buy them. The real thing means you've arrived; a fake, even a good one, is an admission of failure. For tourists, it's the opposite: a knockoff indistinguishable from the real thing proves you're a savvy shopper. Among the Chinese merchants, the ability to peddle phony goods without getting pounced on by the law proves you're a sharp shopkeeper. In this little ecology, everyone wins.

I watched a man fold a grass-leaf spider for a little girl. His table showed his wares: bugs, birds, and animals, made from long sprays of dried grass like the ones he no doubt used to pick by the stream in his home village and now bought wholesale from a grower in New Jersey, to work into marvelous shapes and sell for a dollar on a Chinatown street.

Behind steamy restaurant windows, young men hefted bins of dirty dishes or took cleavers to roast ducks. These men, like the grass-leaf folder, probably spoke neither English nor Cantonese. Unlike the old days of Chinatown, when everyone came from Guangdong, a lot of the new immigrants' hometowns were in farther-flung provinces: Fujian, Henan, Xinjiang. If they had a common language, it was Mandarin, but some only spoke their home dialect because, as always, the immigrants were the poor, the least educated. Those who, in coming across the ocean and starting over, had nothing to lose.

Climbing the stairs to the apartment I shared with my mother, my thoughts were far away: on leaving home, on starting over. In a way, that was the situation here. My four brothers and I grew up in this apartment. I still lived here, so my mother wouldn't be alone, and my brothers paid the rent, did the repairs, and covered whatever else my mother needed, until we could persuade her to move in with Ted and his family in Queens. My mother, so far, had ignored all our highly reasonable arguments. She didn't want to start over, even at her son's home, and that was that.

I slid off my shoes and walked into the living room, unprepared for my mother's next move in the Can I Top Myself? game.

"I've found the letter," she called. The air was full of the gingery scent of snow fungus soup. I had to smile; this soup was always her send-off, her way of fortifying a family member before a trip.

"What letter?"

"The letter your father sent me when he went to Mississippi."

I walked into the kitchen. "Ba went to Mississippi?"

She looked up from stirring the pot. "I just told you that, Ling Wan-ju." She opened a cabinet and took out a jar of rice. "He rode the Greyhound bus. You were eight years old. His cousin Leland Tam was operating his family's grocery store."

"Leland Tam, the man who got killed? Jefferson Tam's father?"

"Yes. At the time, Leland Tam was a young man, with great responsibilities. Your father thought perhaps we would move to the Delta of Mississippi. He would become partners with Leland Tam in the store."

"Us? Move to Mississippi?" This was news. I wondered if my brothers had known that was being considered. I certainly hadn't.

"Ling Wan-ju, do you only talk in questions now?" My mother pursed her lips. "It's because of your job. Asking questions all day long about things that are not your business."

"Ma, you're the one sending me to Mississippi because of my job."

Her expression made it clear I'd missed something. "This is for family. This *is* your business."

The rice made a crisp slide into the electric cooker. My mother turned the dial with a firmness that dared it to come out any way but perfect and walked back to the living room. On the side table was an envelope bearing my father's unkempt handwriting and a thirty-two-cent stamp. She picked it up and held it out to me. "Here."

"It's okay if I read this?"

She lifted her eyes to the ceiling. All right, in view of the fact that she had put it in my hand, it was a dumb question.

I sat and took two sheets of yellowing, character-covered paper from the precisely sliced envelope. That would be like my mother, to open a letter from my father with delicate care. And like my father, to write rather than call. Partly to save money; but also, I could picture him at the end of the day, at a table in his cousin's house. He'd be smiling to himself as he thought of my mother, choosing his words with care, because they were for her.

My father's handwriting in Chinese was more under control than in English, but it took me a moment to get used to reading the vertical columns. Chinese today is written horizontally, left to right, but my father learned it top to bottom, and he never made the switch. Surrounded by the aroma of my mother's soup and the staccato chopping of vegetables, I began to read.

My dear wife,

I hope you are well. Before I left I made it clear to the

children that they are not to misbehave while I'm gone. I
trust that command has tempered their natural exuberance so
that you don't find them too much of a handful.

I smiled. The most naturally exuberant member of our family had
been my father, an energetic, generous man, full of jokes and ideas. In
truth, my brothers and I were always more likely to misbehave if he
was around. Alone with our mother, we were pretty sure we'd never
get away with anything.

I arrived here safely after a tiring but not unpleasant
journey. It happens that another Chinese was on the bus,
returning home to Greenville (a town larger than Clarksdale,
south of here), where his family also has a grocery. I shared
with him your char siu. Also your ho fun. As usual, after
filling me full of snow fungus soup, you sent me away with
more food than I could eat in a week! He was grateful,
proclaiming you a most excellent cook. His own wife was
born in Greenville as he was. Therefore, he says, although
she's Chinese, she's more partial to deep fry than stir-fry.

"Ma," I said, "Ba met another Chinese man on the bus. Another
grocer. From Mississippi."
"I've read the letter."
Practically read the ink off it, I'd bet. "Okay. I was just surprised."
She didn't answer, so I went back to reading.

Our conversation gave me much to think about, preparing
me for my visit here. My new friend, Ro Tung, whose slow,
strange English is still better than his odd-sounding Chinese

(I suppose that must be the Mississippi accent I'm hearing),
is planning on closing his family's grocery in the coming year.
The neighborhood, he tells me, has become dangerous. Also,
profits have gone down as stores such as Walmart have opened
outside the city. He thinks the situation in Clarksdale might be
different, as there were fewer Chinese groceries to begin with,
in a smaller, more self-contained town. However, he warned
me that all over the Delta, the Chinese stores are closing.

I put the letter down. "Ma, I don't get it. Ba's talking like Chinese
grocery stores in the Mississippi Delta are a . . . a *thing*." I had trouble
saying what I meant in Chinese, but my mother's face as she peered
around the kitchen doorway made it clear she wasn't having any trouble
understanding me, just trouble understanding why I was having trouble.

"Each store is a thing," she said. "Of course it is. If it weren't a
thing, it wouldn't be a store, only the idea of a store." She spoke as
though that were a clarifying comment.

"That's not what I mean. There are lot of Chinese grocery stores in
the Delta? How many?"

"I haven't been to Mississippi to count them, Ling Wan-ju."

"Are they like a chain?" I persisted. "Some Chinese family went to
Mississippi and started a chain of stores? Ba's cousins?"

"I don't believe that's what happened, but really, Ling Wan-ju, these
questions won't help you solve your case. I gave you that letter to read
because I hoped you would learn things from it. Instead of constantly
questioning me." She pulled her head back into the kitchen like an
annoyed turtle.

My cousin Leland Tam (he doesn't use his Chinese name,
Lo-Liang, at all) is a respectful but harried man who's taken

on a good deal of responsibility. His father, Jonas, who also prefers his American name (I can see you frowning, Yong-Yun, but our children do the same), no longer involves himself in the store's daily operations, as Leland told us in his letter. This isn't because he's elderly or infirm. I'm sorry to tell you the reason: Jonas gambles. Not in the way of so many people, like his own younger brother Pete, enjoying pai gow or mah-jongg (or following the horse races with excited friends at the OTB—come, you're frowning again!), but in the consuming fashion with which we are unfortunately familiar. Jonas spends days on end at the casinos while Leland works. Your opinions on gambling differ from mine, Yong-Yun, but when it becomes a devouring disease, we agree.

Tomorrow I'll take Jonas aside to demand that he look around: at his wife, his son, his daughters, his business. I'll insist he acknowledge where his responsibilities lie. I'll do this because it's my duty, but Leland is sure my words will have no effect. His own have not, nor have Pete's, nor those of Jonas and Pete's eldest brother, Paul, who has left Clarksdale for Jackson but continues to admonish Jonas for his irresponsibility. I'm afraid, though I've known Jonas for only a day, that I agree.

As to our coming here to become partners with Leland, I'll need more time to explore the situation. We'll speak about it when I return.

Tell the children I'm watching them!

Your loving husband.

Dinner prep complete, my mother came into the living room and sat on the sofa, picking up her sewing again. She almost never just relaxes. "He who waits for a roast duck to fly into his mouth must wait a very long time," is her response when someone suggests chilling out.

I put the letter down. "Ba said to say he was watching us."

"He always wanted me to tell you that, when he was away."

"Is that why you still said it, even . . . years later?"

"It was what he wanted me to tell you."

I stood. "Do you want some tea, Ma?"

In the kitchen, I plugged in the kettle. Fifteen years is a long time, and I'd gotten used to my father being gone. But every now and then, something reminded me how much I missed him.

I made jasmine tea and brought a mug to my mother. I sat back down on the sofa with my own tea and asked, "Did you want to go?"

"To Mississippi? If that had been your father's decision, we would have gone, of course."

"That's not what I asked. I know you would have. You'd have made a big success of it, too. But did you want to?"

She looked at me for a long moment, then went back to her sewing. "These questions will not help you investigate this case, Ling Wan-ju."

"We didn't go," I said. "So Ba must have decided not to. It won't be like you're disagreeing with him"—a cardinal sin, policed by my mother, though Ba had enjoyed argument and debate—"if you tell me you didn't want to go."

She sighed. "No, Ling Wan-ju, I did not want to go. Leaving China to start a new life in Hong Kong, leaving Hong Kong to start another new life in New York, that was enough. Your father had worked hard to make a good life for our family here."

I thought about the long days my mother had spent in Old Lun's sewing factory all through my childhood, doing the hand finishing.

After my father's death, she also brought piecework home in the evenings and sewed while she watched, eagle-eyed, to make sure my brothers and I did our homework. *My father and you made a good life for us,* I thought. But I didn't say anything. My mother's not a particularly humble person, the notable and enormous exception being when it comes to my father.

"In Mississippi," she went on, "we would have had a house with a yard. A garden to grow our vegetables. You children could have played in the grass, fished in the river, instead of riding the subway to classes at the YMCA. It was a pretty picture. But there are not many Chinese people in Mississippi. Who would I exchange recipes with? Who there plays mah-jongg?"

I wondered if I were the first person she'd told this to. Had my father known how she felt, before he decided?

Glancing down at the letter, I said, "There seem to be a lot of Chinese grocers."

I'd been joking, but she answered me seriously. "The Delta of Mississippi is not like Chinatown," she said. "Even if there were other families, they would be far away, like your brother in Queens. They have no subways there to take you places."

My mother grew up in a small Guangdong village, spent years in Hong Kong, and then came to Chinatown, which she rarely leaves except to go visit one of my brothers. She's never not been surrounded by Chinese people.

"So you told Ba you didn't want to go?"

"Of course I didn't. It was your father's decision to make."

I sipped my tea. "What does Ba mean about the kind of gambling you're 'unfortunately familiar' with?" I made air quotes around "unfortunately familiar" before it occurred to me my mother probably didn't know what air quotes were.

"Really, Ling Wan-ju—"

"Really, Ma, you gave me the letter to read."

My mother took a long pause. From the way she didn't look at me I knew she had something to say.

"I came from a poor village in China," she said. "Your father, from a poorer one. To have a good future for our family we decided to come to America." More silence. "In my poor village, my family was the poorest. This was because my father, your grandfather, could not stay out of the *pai gow* parlors. My mother raised geese, my brothers worked from the time they were small. Myself, my sister, also. None of us finished school. Because Ba bet on *pai gow*, on mah-jongg, on whether the brown duck would swim under the bridge before the white duck did. He had a sickness." She stopped, lifting her mug. I waited without speaking until she was ready to continue.

"After our marriage, we put off leaving China for two years," she finally said. "American visas were expensive. We wanted to have the price of them with us when we went to Hong Kong. Finally, we had saved enough. As poor as they were, our families gave us a farewell banquet. With all our possessions in two suitcases, we got on the train for the border. The ride was long, dusty, bumpy, but we were going to America. I was pregnant with your brother." Hot red spots glowed on her cheeks. Not being particularly modest, my mother has no false modesty, either, so I wasn't sure why mentioning her pregnancy embarrassed her. But as it turned out, that wasn't it. She went on to say, "It was only at the border that we discovered my father had taken our money."

"Oh, Ma," I breathed.

"We talked about going back. But we already had visas to Hong Kong, which had taken some time to get. We decided to remain there. My cousin, who was our sponsor, had offered us a place to stay while we waited for our American visas. We went to her apartment. Instead of leaving for America we found jobs, then a tiny apartment of our own. I cleaned rooms in a hotel. After your brother was born, I left him with my cousin on her days off. She left her two children with me on mine. When your second brother was born, the same." Surprising me, my mother smiled. "It was a hard life, but not an entirely terrible thing. Your father got a job washing dishes in a restaurant. He was hardworking, dependable. Always cheerful. Soon he was promoted to vegetable chopper, then to under-chef. In Hong Kong, your father learned to cook."

My father had been a chef in great demand in Chinatown, restaurants always trying to poach him from each other, until finally he opened a place of his own.

"Also," my mother said more slowly, "in Hong Kong, we learned to live in a city. In a tiny room in a tower, without grass, or rivers. We cooked in the hallway, with five other families. At first, I hated it. Then I became used to it. By the time we came to New York—to an apartment with its own kitchen, a great luxury at the time in Hong Kong—I was at peace with cities."

"Ma," I said. "About your father. I had no idea."

"Of course you didn't. Why would I tell my children such a shameful thing?"

"Did he ever say anything? About the money?"

"He said he'd taken it to double it for us, to give to us as a surprise. But things had not happened as he had hoped. The money was gone. He said—" She looked through her pale tea at the flowers painted on the inside of the cup. "He said that he was sorry."

5

Bill at the wheel, our rented Chevy Malibu rolled down the highway between dry yellow hills. Skeleton trees waved tangles of branches against charcoal clouds skidding across the sky. I gazed out the windows at the bleak midmorning. I'd stuffed my Uniqlo parka into my carry-on before the flight but now that we were here, I found I still needed a sweater over my shirt.

"Where's the magnolia? The, what's that stuff at the Botanical Gardens that smells so good? Bougainvillea—where's the bougainvillea? And the cotton, for Pete's sake, aren't we way down south in the land of cotton?"

Bill glanced over at me. "It's December."

"They have winter here?"

"They do."

"And strip malls. They have strip malls."

We were heading down Highway 61, like in the Bob Dylan song, from the Memphis airport to Clarksdale, Mississippi.

"And what about those big plantation houses?" I said. "With the white columns and the wraparound porches to drink your mint juleps on? Where are they?"

"In Alabama, Georgia, Louisiana. Other parts of Mississippi, even, but not here. The Delta has some big plantations, but the mansions you mean are from before the Civil War, and the Delta wasn't cleared and planted until after it. That war, by the way, is the War Between the States down here. That's if people are being polite to

Yankees. If they're among friends, it's the War of Northern Aggression."

"Seriously? Still?"

"That's white people, of course."

"How do black people feel about that?"

"It's complicated."

"How can it be complicated? That was actually a rhetorical question. Racist is racist."

"And Yankee is Yankee. Loyalty's a thing that can be hard to pin down."

The land began to flatten out. After another couple of miles, Bill turned the car off the highway. The new road was curvier and smaller, going through towns and areas of scattered houses, but there were still strip malls. And the trees were still bare.

"This isn't what I expected," I said.

"One thing about the South. Generally, even when you get what you expected, it turns out not to be what you thought."

I watched out the window as the houses and malls slowly coagulated into suburban blocks on the outskirts of Clarksdale. "Look," I said as we rolled down a residential street, passing lawns decorated with penguins, Santas, and oversized snow globes. "That yard sign says 'Tam for Governor.' You don't suppose he's another relative of mine?"

"You think if you had a cousin running for governor—even of Mississippi—your mother wouldn't have told you?"

"At least fifty times. Good point. His name's probably been shortened. It used to be Tamowitz."

"Or Tam O'Shanter."

"That's not a name, it's a hat."

"Stetson. Bowler. Fedora. Panama."

I narrowed my eyes at him. "Pith helmet."

He laughed.

"Anyway," I said, "there's a sign that says 'Vote Mallory for Governor.' So Tamoshanterwitz isn't a shoo-in."

"And he may be in trouble, because his opponent isn't a hat."

We hit Clarksdale and found Captain Pete Tam's house on a street of split-levels and ranches from the 1960s. Here were more Santas, reindeer, and piles of blow-up gifts, plus strings of lights in anything that resembled a fir tree. Not at Pete Tam's, though. His house didn't even have a wreath. I guess when you've had a murder in the family, Christmas cheer is in bad taste.

Like some of his neighbors' houses, Pete Tam's was showing its age. New vinyl siding had replaced old in irregular white patches on its flanks. Half the roof was dark gray asphalt tile; the other half, along a jagged seam, was brown.

"Sale on roofing at Lowe's?" Bill asked. But the front lawn, though generously sprinkled with crabgrass, was neatly mowed, and a double line of dwarf shrubs escorted the flagstone walk to the door.

We parked and got out on the sidewalkless street. I could hear tree branches creaking, and the rustle of a stream at the bottom of the sloping backyards. The air smelled of fallen leaves and dampness.

Captain Pete Tam's porch was a concrete pad with a rocking chair. The first thing that happened when I pressed the doorbell was nothing. Then a neighbor's dog, behind a slat fence, began to bark.

The door opened. A smallish, wiry Asian man, maybe five foot six—but at that, still taller than I am—stood in the doorway. Under his sailor's cap, his eyes twinkled and a wide smile shoved aside the creases at his mouth. According to my mother, Captain Pete Tam was fourteen years older than she was, which made him seventy-five. Could've fooled me. If you'd told me he was her age, I would've believed it;

if you'd said he was younger, I would've felt disloyal, but probably would've believed that, too.

"You must be Cousin Lydia! Why didn't you ring the bell?" He pushed the cap back on his forehead. "Well, well, if you don't look just like your daddy."

"I am. I did. I do?"

"You did? It's defunct again? You sure do. Captain Pete Tam. Pleasure's mine!" He stuck out his hand.

I shook it. "Lydia Chin. Bill Smith, my partner."

"Pleased to meet you, Captain." Bill, of course, at six foot three, towered over both of us.

"Same here. Yeah, HB, thanks!" Captain Pete called, and the next-door dog stopped barking.

"Captain Pete," I said, "you knew my father?"

"Met him that time he came down. Stayed here with me, you know. I laid on a big banquet, right out there in the yard—oh that was a good time! Corn bread and ribs, moonshine till the cows came home. Took a liking to your dad, I did. Wasn't surprised when he decided not to move down here, though." He stepped aside and swept a hand back. "Come on in."

The door opened directly into a living/dining room, with a kitchen off to the left and a hall that led to bedrooms on the right. Sprays of gladiolas, chrysanthemum bouquets, and rows of condolence cards crowded the dining room table, surrounding a photo of a serious, pudgy-faced man. A black ribbon wrapped its silver frame.

First things first. "Captain Pete," I said, as he shut the door, "my mother asked me to extend her sympathy. She wants the funeral details so she can send flowers."

Pete Tam's face grew a bit more solemn. "Well, that's right nice of her. Especially considering her and me never did see eye to eye.

But the funeral, that's waiting on some of this trouble to get cleared up."

"The coroner hasn't released the body?"

"Oh, no, he did. Leland's over to Grace Funeral Home. I just don't want to put him in the ground until Jefferson can be there."

"Even if Jefferson's in custody, they'd let him come to his father's funeral, wouldn't they?"

"Most likely, and if it has to be that way, we'll do it. Happened last month, some lifer from down on Parchman got brought up here to his mama's funeral in chains. But I was more hoping this would be gone by then."

I looked at Bill. Considering that Jefferson was in jail on a homicide charge, to make this gone in time for the funeral would require some fast stepping. If making it gone could be done at all.

"But come on, you two, set yourselves down." Captain Pete waved at a brown sofa and a pair of plaid armchairs, one showing a good deal more wear than the other, companionably facing a wooden coffee table. "I'll get the tea. Hard trip?"

"No, no," I said. "Smooth flight, easy drive. Can I help?"

"Got everything ready, just be a minute." He headed for the kitchen.

"Walk in and there's tea," I whispered to Bill. "That's how you know you're in a Chinese home. What? What's that grin for?"

Bill nodded to the kitchen doorway, through which Captain Pete was returning with a black lacquer tray. It held three tall glasses of ice, a plate of cookies, and a sweating pitcher. Oh—iced tea. Well, it was the South. Even if, as Bill had pointed out, it was December.

Unsurprisingly, after he'd poured the tea, Captain Pete dropped into the more tattered of the armchairs. My father's easy chair had been shabby like that. He'd declared it "worn in" and would never let my mother even discuss reupholstering it. After he died, of course, there was no question of that. The chair is in the same position and condition still, and it's the one my mother offers to particularly honored visitors.

I reached for a glass. Just before I sipped, I noticed Bill's grin hadn't changed. At the first taste, I knew why. Bill took a chug and covered for me. "God, I haven't had sweet tea like this since I was a kid," he said. "This is great."

Sweet. There must have been a pound of sugar in that pitcher. Tea might have been what was making the water brown, but if it was I couldn't taste it.

"Hah! Not a Yankee, then, Mr. Smith?"

"Bill. No, army brat from Louisville. When I joined up, it was the navy. Traveled a lot of the world but no one makes sweet tea like they do down here."

"That's the truth. Navy, that right? Me, too. Based where?"

"Diego Garcia."

Captain Pete beamed. "Naples. With the Sixth Fleet."

I left them to the bounding waves of memory while I pondered what would make an heir to one of the world's oldest and most subtle culinary traditions give this liquid sugar-shock house room. Finally, I put down my glass and interrupted their male bonding session.

"The navy—is that why they call you Captain?" I asked my new-found relative.

"Here, Cousin Lydia, you must be hungry." Pete Tam waved the plate of cookies in my direction.

"Oh, I'm good, thanks."

Bill reached for a pink-frosted square. It's always astounded me—how much sugar he can consume—but if this had been his childhood, I was starting to understand.

Pete put the plate down. "No, 'Captain' came later. In the navy I was just a squid, swabbing decks. Got out of the service, spent some time on the river. The Mississippi, that would be," he explained to me, turning to Bill for fellow-Southerner confirmation. "Back then they still had the gambling boats. None of this hooey about casinos on islands. They're not, you know. Islands. Just sandbars in the shallows, on a good day. That's when I got to be the Captain, on those boats." He raised the pitcher. "You folks need a topper? Bill, here you go. Lydia?"

"No, thanks," I said hastily.

"Born and raised in Clarksdale," Pete went on. "But always been too restless to stay. Keep coming back, though. You're Delta born and bred, place kind of gets a hold of you. Well. Y'all ready to go see Jefferson?"

"Wait," I said. "Before we meet him. You don't think he . . . did this, right? Killed his father? So tell us what you think happened."

Pete spread his hands. "Must've been some punk, probably a meth head, Lord knows we got enough of them around here. Tried to rob the place, Leland fought back, got himself stabbed for his trouble."

"And Jefferson?"

"Happenstance. Came in, found him. Tried to see was he still alive, ended up covered in blood."

"His prints were on the knife, weren't they?"

"It's a counter knife from the store! They cut up lunch meat with that thing."

"Jefferson had made a sandwich recently? Or they don't wash it much?"

Pete Tam scowled. "Leland's not—wasn't much of a housekeeper. Is that a crime?"

In Chinatown, where city inspectors popped in often and irregularly, it well might be. But maybe this was one of those things that was different in Mississippi.

"Was anything stolen?" I asked.

Captain Pete shook his head. "Cash register wasn't even open," he admitted to his glass of tea. "I guess seeing what they did scared them off."

I glanced at Bill, who looked as unconvinced as I felt.

"Y'all didn't come down here already having in mind that Jefferson's guilty, did you?" Pete looked up. "Because if that's how it is—"

"No, of course not," I said. "We're just looking for the lay of the land." That seemed to me a fairly Southern way to put it, but it got no reaction. "The more we know, the more help we can be."

Pete flattened his lips and nodded.

"All right, then," I said. "Let's go meet Jefferson."

Bill threw back the rest of his tea and stood. "Our car or yours?"

"Yours," Captain Pete answered. "I'm paying the gas either way, right? Seeing as I'm the client. So let's put the mileage on the Avis."

The rental was from Enterprise, but his point was valid. Although I wondered how much mileage we were talking about to the Coahoma County Jail, which was in Clarksdale just like we were. His point was also surprising; I wasn't expecting to even get my expenses covered on this one.

I did what I had to do. "Don't be silly, Captain Pete. I don't take money from family."

He wagged his finger. "Don't you be silly, little lady. I'm a gambler but I'm nowise a freeloader. Your mama may think they're one and the same, but they're not. I respect the work people do even though most folks don't respect mine."

"Work?" It took me a minute. "You're a professional gambler?"

"You bet." He grinned; I guessed that was an old joke. "Like I said, after the service, I took to the river."

"I thought you meant you worked on the riverboats."

"Well, I sure did, but not the way you're thinking of. From the day I quit the navy there was only one kind of deck I was interested in anymore. When the gambling boats thinned out, I went off to Reno, then Atlantic City, Vegas . . ." He smiled, a gleam in his eyes. "Been around, oh, I have. Macao, for a month once. Nassau, Niagara Falls. Those Indian casinos in Connecticut, but I didn't like the weather. Came back to the river when they built the casinos. Still play them all, from St. Louis to Natchez. Never worked a straight job, ever. Nine-to-five, day shift, night shift—none of that for Captain Pete."

We stepped out onto the porch, and he locked the door behind us. "Came across lots of folk like your mama, though. She didn't want to know me." He looked me in the eye. "On account, I guess, of your granddaddy."

"You know about that?"

"Your daddy told me. It's why you didn't move here. He thought being stuck down here in a gambling family, not a lot of other Chinese folks around, that would be hard on her."

Thus was answered the question of why I never knew about the Mississippi cousins.

I'd just clunked the Malibu's door shut when a Coahoma County Sheriff's cruiser screeched around the corner and rocked to a stop in front of us. We weren't exactly parked in, but their intentions were clear.

"Oh, my good Lord." In the back, Captain Pete blew out an exasperated breath. "Can't that boy just drive up and park?"

"What boy?" I said.

"Gotta be Bert Lucknell." He powered his window down. "We got regular po-lice here in Clarksdale," he said, emphasizing the *po*, which I'd only heard in movies, "for giving out traffic tickets and looking to see if your window's broken on both sides. The big stuff gets handed off to the sheriff, Montel Bradley. You got bad luck, deputy who shows up is Bert Lucknell."

Two big men, one black and one white, both wearing mirrored sunglasses, lumbered out of the cruiser. The black one, in uniform, walked over by Bill's door with his hand hanging loosely near his holster. The white one wore khakis, with the lumpy bulge of a gun under his sport jacket. He leaned in Pete's window.

"Afternoon, Pete. Speak to you for a minute?"

He turned his Ray-Bans to me, to Bill. He nodded, said, "How you folks doing?" and turned back to Captain Pete as though that hadn't been a question. "We're looking for Jefferson."

Captain Pete pushed his hat back. "Don't Montel give y'all a morning briefing, like on TV? You've got Jefferson down at the jail, two days now. Where you been, Bert?"

"Well, I been right here, doing my job. And you said that wrong, Pete. Had. We had him down at the jail. The boy went and broke himself out this morning."

6

The Coahoma County deputies didn't have a search warrant, but Captain Pete didn't have Jefferson Tam, so he let them into the house. They went through it in a perfunctory way, peeking into closets and under beds while Bill and I took our seats again and Pete made more sweet tea.

It wasn't long before the search was complete and the deputies returned to the living room. The black man, whose name badge read *Thomson*, leaned against the doorway. Bert Lucknell's fat-folded, watery blue eyes traveled between the two easy chairs. Under pale, thinning hair, his complexion was pink and ragged. He guided his bulk in for a landing on the worn chair. Everywhere, cops are the same.

"Obliged," Lucknell said, sipping from the glass Captain Pete handed him. Pete said nothing about his chair being occupied, but he didn't take the other one; he perched on the sofa arm next to me. Deputy Thomson, despite an invitation from Pete to sit, stayed in the kitchen doorway behind us, drinking his tea. A way to observe without being observed. Everywhere, cops are the same.

Bert Lucknell asked, "So, now, is the boy down by the river, Pete? He run and hide in the brush when he saw us coming?" Lucknell thumbed to the picture window framing the backyard and the creek.

"So he could get his ass bit off by alligators?" Captain Pete snorted. "I wasn't here for a lot of his growing up, but I never heard his mama raised an idiot child. You sure he broke out, not just y'all lost him in the jail there someplace?"

"Gators would be sleeping now, cold weather and all." The blue eyes turned to me and Bill. "Good to meet you folks. I'm Detective Sergeant Bert Lucknell. That there's Deputy Tom Thomson. Y'all friends of Captain Pete's?"

"My cousin Lydia Chin," Captain Pete answered for us. I was happy for him to take the lead because I wasn't sure of the best way to play the situation. "And her partner, Bill Smith."

"Partner." Bert Lucknell nodded and sipped. "That one of them new words for 'boyfriend'? Or meaning, you folks are in business together?"

"They're in business together, and whatever else don't concern you," Captain Pete snapped. "They're private investigators down from New York City."

"Private investigators?" Lucknell smiled. "That for real?"

"I asked them to come see if there's anything they could do for Jefferson. Lydia's kin to him, too. Look here, Bert, what do you mean he broke himself out? What happened?"

"You asked them to come down, now, did you?" Lucknell turned from Pete to Bill. "Private investigators. And what exactly are you hoping to accomplish here in Clarksdale, Mr. Smith?"

"I'll be doing whatever the boss wants me to do." Bill nodded toward me.

"You don't say." Lucknell's smile widened into a grin, and I was reminded of the alligators. "You the boss, little lady?" He didn't wait for my answer. "So, by anything you can do, Pete wouldn't mean you folks came down to grab the boy up and take him on out of here, would he?"

"You mean, did we break him out of jail?" I asked in disbelief. "Are you serious? We don't even know where your jail is. We just got to Clarksdale an hour ago. Check the car rental papers."

"Oh, now, don't go on. No one's accusing y'all of anything. But if you're looking for things to investigate, it'd be my duty to say that's a waste of time. We investigated that murder six ways from Sunday." He laid an emphasis on *investigated* as though it were a foreign word it tickled him to use. "Jefferson killed his daddy. We found Jefferson in the store, Leland's body not cold yet, Jefferson's prints on the knife, and him without a tale to tell."

"Now why on earth would he do that?" Pete demanded. "You got a motive, Bert?"

"Well, luckily I ain't the prosecutor, so I don't need one. But everybody knows they didn't get on. Got so bad to where Jefferson left town."

"Jefferson went to Oxford, where computer geeks like him can find gainful employment. Not a family around here doesn't have kids who left the Delta to look for work."

"That's as may be, Pete. Seems every time he came home, though, they had a dustup. You ask me, it's most probably drugs, like all them young kids. Or maybe Jefferson's got a gambling problem and Leland cut him off, said he wasn't gonna keep giving him money like he gave his daddy."

"I thought Leland *was* Jefferson's daddy," I said.

"Leland's own daddy, I mean by that. Jonas Tam, Pete here's brother. Everyone knows Leland spent the best years of his life saving his daddy's ass. Maybe he didn't want to be stuck saving his son's ass, too. Begging your pardon, little lady."

Lucknell trained his toxic smile on me. I gazed back steadily—I'm a New Yorker, I have a lifetime's worth of experience on the subway—and eventually he broke off and slugged back the rest of his tea.

Putting down the glass, Lucknell slapped his hands on his knees. "Thanks for the refreshment, Pete. Come on, Tom. We got to find

Jefferson, and I guess these fine folks don't know where he is." He stood. "Of course, if he does happen to pop into your sights, I'll hear about it right quick, I know I will. Be a big mistake if I don't, that's for sure. Oh, and there's even a reward, so y'all could make yourselves a chunk of change.

"Nice meeting you folks. Have a good trip back to New York City."

Captain Pete jumped up. "Bert, you sit yourself back down! You can't just walk outta here like this. Tell me what happened."

Lucknell smiled benignly down at Captain Pete. "What happened? Well, it's a funny thing. Seems Jefferson got himself carried off by two uniformed fellas in a County Prisoner Transport van. They said he had a court date. Waved around the paperwork and everything. They headed up First Street, made the left onto Yazoo like they was going behind the court building where they take the prisoners in. Now, they got those vans coming and going from the courthouse all the time; no one on Yazoo specially remembers that one. But it must've been that it never did stop. Couple hours later, Sheriff Bradley had someone call over there, ask when he was getting his prisoner back. They had no notion what he was talking about." Lucknell's smile swept around like a searchlight. "Pretty slick, huh? You can think whatever you want, Pete. He's your flesh and blood and you can't be faulted for trying to hold a high opinion of him. But this sure don't sound like something you'd anyhow expect from an innocent man."

7

Pete shut the door behind the cops. "Well," he said. "Bert Lucknell's never gonna strain himself carrying his brains around. Nor his portion of the milk of human kindness, neither. But still, this is a worrisome thing."

"It sure is," I said. "Captain Pete, is there—"

"No, no, no." Pete shook his head. "A chance Jefferson's guilty? Of killing his own daddy? No way."

"How are you so sure?"

He patted his belly. "My gut's looked out for me my whole life. Right now, it's shouting loud and clear that this here, you bet on Jefferson and it's a lock."

"Then why escape? And with such a well-organized plan? Sounds like what he did took a lot of thought. And a little money."

"I have no idea."

"Well," Bill said levelly, eyes on Pete, "his not being guilty of this homicide doesn't mean he's not guilty of something else."

Pete seemed to deflate. He walked to his plaid chair and sank into it. "What's the 'else' you got in mind?"

Bill looked to me. I said, "Pete, we don't know Jefferson, or much about him, so we can't say. But someone went to a lot of trouble for him. Who would do that?"

"No one I know. The kid's my flesh and blood, like Bert said, but like *I* said, I missed a lot of his growing up. I didn't even know Leland was dead and Jefferson was grabbed for it until his lawyer called me yesterday."

"You didn't? How could it not have been all over Clarksdale?"

"No doubt it was. I was up in Tunica. Poker tournament at the Golden Spike."

"Who's Jefferson's lawyer, that called you?" Bill asked.

"Callie Leblanc. From the Coahoma County Public Defender's Office. Real nice lady, and a good lawyer, or so I've been told, but mighty busy. What the public defenders do here, they call it 'meet 'em and plead 'em.' Works out good if they actually did it, which most of them probably did. But for Jefferson, I was thinking to hire a lawyer out of Oxford, or maybe Jackson." Pete turned to me. "But I wanted to talk to you first."

"Me?" I was taken aback. "I don't know anyone—" I stopped. Bouncy Pete Tam was sagging in the chair, a look in his eyes I'd seen before, though not from him: a mixture of worry and guilt. The Chinese I-failed-my-family look.

"Pete," I asked gently, "are there things you know that you haven't told us?"

He shook his head. "Don't know a blessed thing. It's just Bert's onto something when he says Jefferson and Leland didn't get on. And I'm feeling bad about that, because I'm maybe more a part of it than I got any business to be."

"All right," I said. "We're listening."

He sighed. "Thing is, me and Leland didn't get on all that good ourselves. Leland has—had a stick up his nether parts about gambling."

"Unusual, in a Chinese person," I said.

"Well, there's your mama."

"Point taken."

"And like in her case, where it's about her daddy, in Leland's case, it's about Leland's daddy, my brother Jonas. The store did fine when we were kids, but once Pop—Harry Tam—was gone and Jonas took over, fast as his missus saved their money, Jonas found it and gamed it away."

"Jonas wasn't the oldest, was he? Why didn't your other brother take over? Paul, right?"

"Paul was five years older than Jonas, twelve older than me. Never had an interest in the store. Took himself to law school, married a white lady, had a practice up and running in Jackson by the time Daddy passed. Paul's Reynold Tam's daddy." I must have looked blank, because he added, "The congressman running for governor."

"Oh!" I said. "We saw signs on the way down. He really is a relative?"

"My nephew, same as Leland."

"Why didn't my mother tell me I had a cousin running for governor? Does she know?"

"I told her when he first announced, but that was a while back. Most probably she forgot."

This told me two things. One, because my mother never forgets anything, I didn't have a scoop to drop. Two, my mother kept in touch with the Mississippi-gambler cousins, though she'd never mentioned them to her children.

Neither of those things, nor the politician cousin himself, was the issue of the moment, though. A troubled look in Pete's eyes made me say, "I want to hear all about this congressman. But not right now, I think. Let's go back—you were talking about Jonas taking over the store."

Pete nodded. "Jonas didn't mind that it was him, not Paul. He never had ambitions to leave Clarksdale, and he liked his customers and all. But he never could shake that gambling monkey. Leland started running that store when he was seventeen. He hadn't've done that, Jonas would've lost it, sure as shooting. Put his two sisters through college, Leland did, and barely finished high school himself, though, ask me, he was the smartest of the bunch. By the time your daddy came down, Leland was a full-time shopkeeper, going on twenty years. But your daddy could see what was happening. Jonas would swear up and down he was through, Leland would pay off his debts. Next thing you know, Jonas is back up in Tunica, or over to Hot Springs. Leopard can't change his spots. Your daddy didn't want your mama to have to live with that."

I pictured my father considering the idea of moving here, the soft summer nights, the trees and grasses, a family business . . . and then thinking of my mother's father. And so I grew up in New York.

"And that's what was between Leland and you? That you're a gambler, too?"

"Not exactly. I don't have that fever Jonas had. That's the difference between a professional gambler and a problem one. I win, I say thank you, walk away. Like this place—bought it years ago after a good weekend in Atlantic City. Jonas, when he'd win, he'd buy theater tickets for everyone at the table, then stake himself to the high rollers' room. Now, I'm not denying I get a rush when Lady Luck smiles and the cards fall my way, but I'd bet"—he grinned—"you get the same rush, when a case comes together."

I couldn't help but return his smile.

"What I thought," he said. "Anybody's business, they get a charge when it goes well. Now, I did start at the tables because I wanted to do like my big brother. Jonas was the sort of fellow could charm the stripes off a skunk. Pop was like that, too, but between you, me, and the fence post, Leland must've been standing behind the door when they handed out personality."

I realized I had no picture of Leland Tam at all. "What was he like, Pete?"

"Plain stodgy. Well, I don't like to speak ill of the dead, so maybe I should just say dependable." Pete tilted his head. "He's—he was a shopkeeper, after all."

"Any enemies? Did he have trouble with anyone?"

"Not that I knew. Him and Lucie pretty much kept to themselves, Leland even more since Lucie passed. Ran the store, went to church."

"When's the last time you saw him?" Bill asked.

"Thanksgiving. Store was open in the morning, in case anyone needed anything last minute. That was his way. Then he and Jefferson came here for dinner."

"How did they seem? Leland and Jefferson?"

"Like they had a truce. It was nice. We had turkey and watched the game. Games, really. Three NFL plus the Egg Bowl—Ole Miss versus Mississippi State. Jefferson does that online gambling. He had a few dollars on each game, so we kept going back and forth."

I said, "I thought online gambling was illegal."

"It is if it's games of chance. Craps, roulette, and them. Poker and sports, those right there are games of skill. You got to put thought into them. So they're legal."

I wasn't sure how much sense that made, but I let it go. "Did you have money on the games, too?"

"Not me. I play poker, against fellas I can see. I'm feeling crazy, I'll throw some dice, spin the wheel for the thrill. Long as the house and the other fellas aren't crooked, I know my odds and I'm good. I'm at a tavern, maybe I'll put a few bucks on a game just to keep things interesting. But these online sports books—DraftKings, FanDuel—that's a whole other thing. They put you up against folks you don't know, can't see, got no idea what they're up to. What I hear, some of those whales got computer programs to pick their lineups, field hundreds of 'em a day."

"Whales?"

"Big fish. Besides, where's the fun in being home, hunched over a computer? Where's the lights, the drinks, the girls? At the casino, you win big, you find some female companionship, go see a show. Lose"— he winked—"you find some female companionship, go see a show. Online gambling, where you're all alone *and* your odds are bad? No sir, not for me."

"But Jefferson does it?"

"Well, being a geek and all, I expect it comes naturally to him."

"Did Leland object?"

"To Jefferson's gaming? No. Whatever Bert Lucknell says, that wasn't the problem between them."

"What was?"

Pete sighed. "Well, see, home and family, that's what it was all about for Leland. He sacrificed every day for that. His sisters, his mama and daddy, Lucie, Jefferson."

"Jefferson's an only child?"

"Turned out Lucie couldn't have but the one. Leland and her, they pinned a lot of hopes on Jefferson. Cancer carried Lucie off a few years back. Jefferson went a year to Delta State, dropped out when Lucie died. Moved himself to Oxford, got work. Leland grumbled about him going up there. Why live an hour away when you could stay right here at home?"

"My mother said the same thing about each of my brothers when they moved out of the apartment. So Thanksgiving was the last time you saw Leland?"

Pete nodded. "Went up to Tunica right after. Didn't . . ." His voice caught. "But I talked to him last week."

"About what?"

"He called me. Said something strange happened, wanted to talk about it. Wanted to know could I come over. But I was up in Tunica, and I was kinda busy at the table right then. I asked could it keep for a few days and he said he thought it could. So that was that. I expected I'd see him when the tournament was over."

"Did he say what it was?"

"No. He might've sounded more worried than usual, but the next pot was coming up and I wanted to be dealt in, so I just told him I'd call him when I got back."

"'More worried than usual'? Leland doesn't sound like a happy man."

"Well, his point of view, everybody skedaddled and left him holding the bag. I'd help out in the store time to time, send him money, too, but still, I'm in Macao, Niagara Falls, he's in his apron in a sorry-ass neighborhood in sorry-ass Clarksdale." Pete stopped himself. "Apologies, Cousin Lydia."

"I'm a New Yorker, Pete," I said, ignoring Bill's smile.

Captain Pete grinned. "Apologies for the apologies, then. Anyways, you see what Leland saw: everyone someplace else but him. His sisters in California, his daddy at the gambling tables, me pretty much the same, and Paul married to a rich white woman in Jackson, never came around."

"Will the sisters come for the funeral? And Paul, and Reynold? They're my relatives; I'd like to meet them."

"Sorry, Cousin Lydia. Paul and his missus, plus both Leland's sisters, they all passed some years back. Reynold, I doubt he'll come."

"Oh, I'm sorry to hear that. But why won't Reynold come? Did he not get along with Leland?"

"Hardly knew him. Reynold takes after his daddy. Doesn't come down here much. And just now, he's mighty busy. Primary's in early March. He wins that, he's in."

"But surely he could take the time for a family funeral?"

"Nothing to do with time. This is Mississippi."

I must have looked blank, because he went on.

"Liberal wing of the party's taking a chance nominating a half-Chinese fellow for governor. In fact, some people say they did it because the thought was, no one could beat the other guy anyway. That's Stirling Mallory, from an old plantation family. That boy wants to club the whole state over the head and drag it back to the Stone Age. Reynold, he wants to push us the other direction, into the twentieth century, seeing as the rest of the country's well into the twenty-first. Funny thing is, he seems to have a chance. Once his people caught on to that, they didn't want to jeopardize it."

Now I got it. "By emphasizing his Chinese family, you mean?"

"His people probably think it's better not to get the voters skittish."

"But it can't be that he hides. If he's half-Chinese."

"His mama was a white lady, and he mostly takes after her. It's okay with me. If he can shine a little light on this state, I'll do without family togetherness."

I didn't know how to react, or how I wanted to. Bill stepped in. With a glance at me, he said, "Captain Pete, tell us what the problem was between you and Leland, if it wasn't gambling."

Pete grinned. "Sorry. You have to pardon us Southerners. We start telling tales, we can go far afield. So: there's everyone else everywhere else, like I said, and here's Leland, spent his life looking after family, and what does he have? Old photos, scrapbooks, and the store. He wanted me to help bring Jefferson around to taking the store over so it wouldn't have to close when Leland passed, because of all the history there, but all I ever told the kid was, follow your gut. That's what made Leland mad. That's what was between Jefferson and Leland, and between me and Leland, too. I kept thinking, sooner or later, Leland would back off, quit blaming me for something that wasn't even really wrong. Now . . ."

The "now" was obvious, and as sad as could be. I left it alone, and Bill also sat silent. Captain Pete sighed. "See, Cousin Lydia, I always did what my gut told me and I'm nohow sorry about that. But what I am sorry about, I've been a disappointment to my family. Don't expect you know much about that, but it's not a good feeling, I'm here to tell you."

I looked at Bill, then back to Pete. "I'm not as much of a stranger to that feeling as you might think, Pete. All right, let's get to work. We don't want to disappoint Jefferson."

8

When I said "get to work," Pete perked up. It occurred to him that if the sheriff's men had come looking for Jefferson, the Clarksdale PD might also.

"We don't want to have to set around here all day trying to convince a gaggle of uniformed fools—bless their hearts—that Jefferson's not under my bed. So, you big-city detectives, let's hit the road. What do we do now?"

"Well, I'd love to be able to find Jefferson before the police do," I said. "You have no light to shed? Nothing you didn't tell the deputies?"

Pete shook his head.

"How about people he's close to?" Bill asked. "Friends in town? Does he have a girlfriend?"

"If he does, I don't know about it, but generally speaking, I'm not in on the details of his love life. If there is someone, I'd suppose she'd be up in Oxford. Same about his friends—mostly up there, I bet."

"Do you know who he works for?"

"Works freelance. Computer geek stuff, whoever needs him. The Chinese tech wiz, what a cliché, huh? I think he's a little embarrassed about it, tell you the truth."

"Well, he's not the only one in the family."

"Really? You do that stuff, too?"

"Me? Oh, no, no." I gave Bill points for not laughing out loud. "One of the cousins on my mother's side, Linus Wong. He has a computer security company. Their slogan is 'Protecting People Like You from People Like Us.'"

"Hah! But I'll tell you, Cousin Lydia, that computer's done well by Jefferson. He's been able to write his own ticket, work his own hours, make decent money. Not a fortune," he added quickly. "No—what do you call that?—bling. Just a good, steady living."

"So you're saying whatever he exactly does, it's legit work, not anything lucrative because it's illegal."

"I got no reason to think otherwise," Pete replied, with less conviction than I might have hoped.

"Okay," I said, changing the subject to keep Pete from sagging again. "I guess the next thing would be to talk to Jefferson's lawyer. Normally before that I'd want to check out the crime scene, but I can't see Detective Lucknell lifting the yellow tape for us."

"Hah! Don't need him to. I have the keys."

"It's still a crime scene."

"Been processed and released already, as of last night. In case I wanted to open today."

"You?"

"Like I said, I did my duty by the store. I used to spell Leland sometimes, like say if he wanted to go to California, see his sisters and their kids. A couple of weeks running the place was a nice vacation for me." He sighed. "Haven't had the heart to go over there yet, but probably it's a good idea, before every lowlife in the county finds out Leland's gone. Leland kept the store tighter than Fort Knox, but these no-goods, they could figure a way in."

"But Pete, they released the crime scene, really? It's just over forty-eight hours since the murder."

"Right. Like Bert Lucknell said, they *investigated* six ways from Sunday."

As we locked up and got into the Malibu, I found myself muttering about blind squirrels.

I turned to face Pete as Bill drove. "I think I'd like to see the house, too."

"What house would that be?"

"Where Leland lived."

"Easy-peasy. Leland lived behind the store. We all did. Mama and Daddy raised Paul, Jonas, and me there. Jonas brought up Leland and his sisters there, and Leland and Lucie raised Jefferson there, too."

That's the Chinese village tradition: shop in the front, family in the back. Kids doing homework on the store counters, playing tag in the aisles, stocking the shelves before dinner. Your whole life, right there. If that was how Jefferson had grown up and what he'd seen coming, I could understand the itchy feet.

Pete's cell phone rang. "You got Pete Tam." He listened, had a brief conversation in a tone of surprise, said, "All right, then," and clicked off. "Well." He pocketed the phone. "I guess it's true, if you live long enough, you could see everything. That was the office of the candidate."

"Reynold Tam?"

"Wasn't the man himself, of course. His chief aide. Reynold wants to pay a condolence call later today."

"I thought he didn't come down here."

"He doesn't. Must be, oh, fifteen years since I even saw him, and that was over in Jackson. I happened to be in town, heard he was having a rally. Well, Reynold was right welcoming, but afterwards his people whisked him away to the next place he had to be. He said he'd call, we'd get together, but he never did. Truth is I didn't call him, either. I knew what was going on."

Knew, and went along with it. I was beginning to get a sense of

what both Bill and Pete meant when they said, *This is Mississippi.*
"But now he's coming here?"

Pete shrugged again. Bill said, "Well, when you lose family, it's the
right thing to do."

"But if his people are so concerned about his image, wouldn't you
think they might be worried about this kind of—well, scandal?"

"Maybe he ran them off," Pete said. "Maybe he said, never you
mind, I'm going. Or on the other side, could be some image consultant
told him you don't lose your cousin to murder and not pay a call."

"Even when the accused is also your cousin?"

"Especially then," Bill said. "You start by showing solidarity. Everyone's had family troubles, so everyone can relate. If it turns out the
kid did it, you move on to what a troubled youth he always was and
what a tragedy this is for the family, but it won't stop you from doing
your duty, bringing to the people of this great state the leadership they
deserve—"

"Hey, you're pretty good at that," Pete said. "Might be you ought
to run."

"Talk to my people."

We drove past houses similar to Pete's, ranch or two-story structures
square in the middle of their lots. Trees weren't numerous, and they
were bare, although every now and then we rolled under one whose
thick trunk and spreading branches suggested it had somehow avoided
the ax when the subdivisions came along. Along with wreaths, more
Santas, and the occasional crèche, Tam and Mallory signs appeared on
lawns in what looked like even numbers.

I'm no expert on the architectural aesthetics of Southern towns,
but it was obvious when Pete told Bill to pull over that we'd gone
from middle-class, though down-at-heel, Clarksdale to what used
to be called the wrong side of the tracks. In fact, during our drive,

we'd slid under the tracks, which crossed overhead on a concrete bridge.

We parked at a storefront that had seen better days, and lots of them. Green paint cracked off fractured stucco. Heavy-gauge mesh covered the windows; the steel door had been riveted and reinforced. A faded red sign read H. TAM AND SONS GROCERY. Crime scene tape drooped across the doorway.

"H. Tam, that's Hong-Bo," said Captain Pete. "Harry, folks called him. Me, Jonas, and Paul's daddy."

Tam Hong-Bo, born Chin Song-Zhao, I thought. *My great-grandfather's brother.*

Three black men sat in the weak sun in front of the store, two on a bench and the third on the stoop. The other storefronts in the area all seemed boarded up or broken down, except for a Sudsarama and a liquor store in the middle of the next block. Across the street, a mannequin's head lay forlornly in the window of a long-abandoned dress shop. Next to the shop, the wind creaked a faded sign reading DOWN HOME CLUB. Thick grime on the windows led me to believe the club was left over from the same era as the mannequin. I was surprised, then, when the dented door swung open.

Two middle-aged black men spilled onto the sidewalk, one thick and muscular, the other wiry and tall. The thick one spat words like nails. "I told you, I ain't having none of that shit in my place, Tremaine. You welcome to drink here, but that's all, and you not gonna be welcome to do that much longer, you keep this up."

Gold teeth glinted as the tall one smiled. "Just trying to keep your customers happy, Pelton. Be a shame they start drinking somewheres else."

"They want what you selling, they can drink in hell, for all I care. You been warned, Tremaine, and you ain't gonna be warned again. I see you in here with anything besides a beer in your hand, it better be your dick, or you gonna be lying out on the street before you can say 'shotgun.'"

With that, the thick man turned and slammed back into the Down Home Club.

The other man stood smiling after him. He shook his head, strode to a pickup truck parked a few doors down, climbed in the cab, and roared away. Neither man acknowledged us at all.

"Whew," I said as the truck's taillights swerved around the corner. "What was that?"

"That," Pete said, "was Pelton Dawes. Down Home Club's his. The fellow just left was Tremaine McAdoo, and that's enough said about him." Pete turned back to H. Tam and Sons and addressed the three men now standing on the porch. "So, you reprobates. I see you're still wearing out the furniture. My furniture now, so you'd best watch yourselves."

They variously shrugged, grinned, and nodded. "Hey, there, Captain Pete," said the grinning one, a bald, jowly guy. "You gonna open?"

"Nah. Leastways, not today, Sam."

"Ah, come on. Where I'm gonna get my malt at, store stays closed?"

The broad-shouldered man scowled. "Sam, shut it. That how your mama raised you?" Stiffly, he faced Captain Pete. "Pete, all of us, we're very sorry for your loss." At his pointed glare, the other two also mumbled condolences.

"Thank you, Henry. And you two worthless derelicts, I appreciate your sympathy, too. Gentlemen—if you don't mind that little falsehood—this here's my cousin, Lydia Chin, and this's Bill Smith." He gestured to the broad-shouldered man. "Henry Watson."

Bill and I shook hands with Henry Watson while Pete pointed his thumb at the bald man. "This here's Sam Shoemaker, who never made a pair of shoes in his life nor hardly wore any." The bald man's smile came back and he stuck out his hand. "And Bobby Lee Smith," Pete finished. "Hey, Bobby Lee, maybe you and Bill are related."

Bobby Lee Smith was smaller, darker, and older than the others, in his sixties maybe, with mahogany skin and close-cut white hair. He surveyed Bill up and down. "Yeah, he look like my big brother. The rich one, always give me nice presents."

Bill nodded. "Wouldn't be surprised if you were my long-lost little brother. The grifter."

Solemnly, the Smiths shook hands.

"When's the funeral, Pete?" Henry Watson asked. "I'd like to pay my respects."

"Not sure yet. I'm hoping to get this trouble about Jefferson cleared up first."

"I hear that. Be too bad if the kid couldn't come to his daddy's funeral for being in jail. Just so's you know, Pete, ain't none of us think Jefferson's a killer."

"Amen," said Bobby Lee Smith.

"Thanks for that," Pete said. "But didn't you hear the news? Jail's not so much the problem. Jefferson broke himself out this morning."

Three pairs of eyes widened. Sam Shoemaker grinned. "Out from under Montel's nose? Bet that put pepper in that boy's soup."

"Haven't spoken to Montel, but Bert Lucknell's not so happy about it."

"Bert Lucknell." Bobby Lee Smith spat on the splintered sidewalk. "Every breath that boy takes is a waste of air."

"No argument." Pete turned to me and Bill. "Sorry to say it, but when Montel Bradley made Bert a detective, he proved how little talent we got to choose from here in Coahoma County."

"Let me ask you gentlemen something," I said.

"Gentlemen!" Sam Shoemaker exclaimed. "Step aside, you two, this lady can see class when it's standing in front of her." He moved to face me foursquare.

"Not if she's looking at you, she can't," Henry grumbled.

"You know Jefferson?" They all gave me *yeah*s and nods. "Does his jailbreak change your minds about him being guilty?"

Henry and Sam exchanged glances. "No offense, ma'am," Henry said, "but that ain't how it works in Mississippi. Most prob'ly it makes him look more guilty to Montel and them, but they was holding that view anyhow. All I can say's, what they call justice around here is even harder on a innocent man than a guilty one." He eyed me. "Ain't you kin to him, though?"

"He's my cousin, but I've never met him," I said. "I'm just trying to get a picture."

"Henry, move out the way," Pete said. He stepped forward and jiggled a key in the lock. "Y'all want to come in, I'll see if the cooler's still on. Maybe it's got malts in there." He creaked the door open. "Lydia and Bill, this here's—hey!" Pete stopped in the doorway. "Oh, my good Lord. Oh, oh, oh, *crap*! What the hell—?"

I peered inside over Pete's shoulder; over mine, Bill did the same. Henry, Sam, and Bobby Lee crowded behind us.

Sam said, "Holy cats."

We all stepped inside.

Light struggling through grime-choked windows gave up a few inches in, but even before Pete picked his way behind the counter and flicked on the fluorescents, the situation was clear.

Henry whistled and said, "Look like the Devil had a fit in here."

He was right. What had been a run-down grocery store was now an unholy mess.

Pete started to come out from behind the counter, but Bill put up a hand. "Give it a minute."

Everyone stopped. Bill moved his gaze slowly around the room. I did the same, something I learned from him: stand and take stock, before you impose yourself on a place.

Rows of shoulder-high shelves started a few feet from the counter and ran toward the back. Without much merchandise, though: most of that lay in jumbled wreckage on the floor. Jelly jars and cans of yams, bottles of cooking oil and bright red hot sauce, chip bags and flour sacks huddled together, some intact, some leaking their contents in a crumbly, gummy mess. Faded photographs of sampans and mountains, pagodas and temples, had been ripped from their spiderwebbed glass frames and sat on the rubble like leaves on trash piles. An unpleasant, thick smell clogged the air. I picked out vinegar (broken pickle jars) and coffee (from the shattered pot off the fallen self-serve station). I listened; nothing but the buzz of the lights and the breathing of the men around me.

And Henry asking, "What're they doing?"

"Detective things." Pete waved Henry quiet. "They're detectives."

"*Say what?*" Henry took a step back.

Bill turned quickly. "Not cops. Private. Lydia and I are investigators from New York, come down to help her cousin."

Henry's glare didn't fade right away, but Sam's smile lit up the gloom. "Now don't tell me. That why you was asking about Jefferson looking guilty? Pete, you got a sweet girl cousin that's a private eye?"

"I got a lot of things you fools don't know nothing about, that's for damn sure," Captain Pete retorted. "Tell me, what the hell use are you altogether, settin' outside this place all day and this goes on in here?"

"This much use, maybe," said Bobby Lee. "Can say for sure, this here didn't happen anytime today."

Pete shook his head angrily, but Bill asked, "You sure? You guys have been here all day?"

"Ain't got no place else to be. Leland, he never did mind us settin' out there, nor inside neither when the weather was bad. Have him some stools, right next the counter there. Man made a fine Kool-Aid pickle." Bobby Lee gestured at a jar that had somehow hit the floor intact. Inside it, aged cucumbers floated in a sea of neon blue.

"Look to me like this was some of them gangbangers," Henry said. "Must've come last night, hoping the register ain't been emptied." The ancient machine sat in tarnished metal splendor on the front counter.

I would have answered him, but Bobby Lee surprised me. "You got that wrong, Henry. Them kids would've carried off all these chips and Slim Jims. And what they gonna make a mess like this for? Only two things I can see would account for this. One, someone got a real hate on for Leland, or for Chinese folks in general." He pointed to the photos torn from their frames. "Or other, someone was looking for something up in here."

9

We stood—Bill, me, and Captain Pete, with Henry Watson, Sam Shoe-maker, and Bobby Lee Smith—amid the debris inside H. Tam and Sons. Pete started to sag, as he had in the house. I put a hand on his shoulder.

"Whoever killed Leland," he said, "if it was a robbery, if they fought, couldn't that . . ." He trailed off, seeming to know the answer.

"Not all the shelves, Pete," I said. "Not up the walls to where the pictures were."

Bill turned back to the mess. "If it wasn't today, it must have been last night."

Pete nodded, looking dazed.

I considered. Both of Bobby Lee's theories sounded plausible to me, though the second made a lot more sense.

"Tell me," I asked him, to eliminate the first, "is it likely someone here hated Leland, or Chinese people in general, enough to do all this?"

"Well, ma'am," said Bobby Lee, "there's always somebody hatin' on everybody."

"Yeah," said Sam. "Like old Miz McAdoo, rest in peace, lived out to Oldman's Brake? That her son Tremaine out on the sidewalk just now, with Pelton. Always cussing out Chinese, Miz McAdoo. Just last month, right before she die, I be telling her, Miz McAdoo, you sound like some of them white folks talking about black. She say, 'No, it's different.' Don't everybody always think their hate is different?" He shook his head.

Henry leaned on the counter. "And see how bitter repay bitter. Two boys she raised, Trevor's down on Parchman—guards brought him to his momma's funeral in chains—and Tremaine, wasn't never no good in him at all and now there's less. That boy's lower than the belly on a beat-down rattlesnake."

I got the feeling some of this talk was to give Captain Pete time to absorb what had happened. That was fine with me. I'd heard of Parchman Farm, more formally known as the Mississippi State Penitentiary. So much for Trevor McAdoo. But I wasn't sure how low the belly was on a beat-down rattlesnake, so I asked.

"Ain't no one never got tangled up with Tremaine and come out the better for it," Henry said. "I suppose he don't think no more of Chinese than his momma did, but I wouldn't take it personal. Tremaine don't think nothing of hardly nobody, including his own brother. He don't even care for his mama's sister Lunetta. She come back down from Chicago to spend her last days with family, now she sitting alone in a nursing home. That what hate do, you raised that way."

I thought about that. "Could Tremaine McAdoo have killed Leland? If Tremaine had a long-standing hate, maybe it just boiled over?"

"Wouldn't say no, Tremaine being who he be. But that hate, like I say, it ain't personal," Henry said. "And it been going on for all Tremaine's life, so why now?"

"Okay," I said. "But is there someone else around here who hated Chinese people?"

"Well, ma'am," said Bobby Lee, "even if Miz McAdoo, neither her boys, they didn't never set foot in here, still, Leland have his share of trouble with no-accounts. But those type of people, they lazy, for the large part. What we looking at here is a pretty thorough job. You do this to a man's business when he's living, you be telling him something. Pay up your protection money, or get outta town 'cause we don't like your kind, whatever you got to say. But after a man's gone, it ain't even clear who you're talking to."

"You sound like you've seen this kind of thing before," I said.

Bobby Lee shrugged. "Seen all kinds of things. Worked railroad security on the Amtrak, thirty-two years." He smiled, pointed at Bill. "Following my big brother's footsteps."

The Smiths fist-bumped.

"Plus, there's another thing," said Sam. "Miz McAdoo and them aside, even them wannabe gangbangers around here mostly got love for Chinese. Chinese grocers carried a whole lotta sharecroppers through the Depression, and through bad crops in years after, too. These ignorant children don't hardly got no idea what the Depression might have been, but most of them was raised thinking Chinese was good people."

"Chinese grocers," I said, remembering my father's letter. "This is something I only just heard of. Are there a lot of them? This store isn't unusual?"

The three black men looked at me like I was from Mars, and Captain Pete seemed to revive. He turned around, frowning. "You serious? You Yankee Chinese don't know this?"

"Know what?"

"Used to be there was Chinese grocers all over the Delta. Every city, every two-bit town, from Tunica to Vicksburg."

I looked at Bill. He shrugged, shook his head. "Pete," I said, "I never—"

"Pah." He waved me quiet. "I'll give you a history lesson some other time." I was glad to see the color back in his cheeks, even if it was my ignorance that had brought it. He straightened his shoulders. "Right now, I gotta go check about the house." With a "Damn!" he strode forward, crunching chip bags as he went. At the back of the store, the door in the rear wall was standing open.

I walked through after him into a combined living/dining/kitchen area the width of the store. It was another mess. On the right, above the sink, air blew in through an open window, its mesh cut away. Formica cabinets gaped wide. Dishes, whole and broken, blanketed the linoleum floor. Knives and forks glittered menacingly, the drawers they'd come from hanging open. Over on the left, beyond the dining table, the faded upholstery of the sofa and chair had been filleted. Does anyone, I wondered as I stared around the wreckage, ever really hide anything in a sofa cushion?

As in the store, the walls here were bare. Photos and pictures littered the floor, as did the frames that had once held them. The same tornado of destruction had hit the two back bedrooms. Mattresses had been dragged from the beds and bookshelves emptied. Toothbrushes and vitamin bottles were strewn all over the bathroom tiles.

"Oh, my merciful Lord," Pete muttered as he surveyed the damage.

Bill and the others had crunched on through the store to join us in the back but had stayed silent, out of respect, it seemed to me, for the rubble of Leland Tam's life.

And Pete's. He pointed to one of the doors opening off the back wall. "That was Ma and Ba's room," he said, his voice unsteady. "And that there was me and Jonas's."

"And Paul's?" I asked, as much to distract him as anything else. "Did he share the room with you, too?"

Pete shook his head. "Him and Jonas shared, until I came along. After that, Paul didn't want to bunk in with no crying baby. Daddy built a little wall over there, crowded everything else up." He nodded to what was now the living room. "Paul had him a bed, little bookshelf, door he could close. Damn, would you look at this?"

Pete's voice went from unsteady to quavering. So much for distraction. I put my arm around his shoulder.

"Pete," Bill said, "it seems pretty clear now this was someone looking for something. Do you have any idea who, or what they might have been looking for?"

"Can't imagine. Leland didn't have anything. He was a grocer, for God's sake." Pete looked around. "All this mess, just to find something? They had to break his dishes?"

"No," I said. "They probably did some of this to cover up that they were looking, so it would look like vandalism."

"I can't imagine. I just really can't."

I wasn't sure what Pete couldn't imagine: what it was Leland might have had that someone wanted this badly, or the reality of all this gratuitous destruction.

"Well," I said, "I think we'd better call the sheriff."

Pete looked at me. "Bert and them? I got to?"

"The place might have been robbed, Pete. You don't know what's gone. And all the stock in the store—if insurance is going to cover this you'll need to file a report."

"Also," Bill said, "it might help Jefferson if you report this."

Pete turned to Bill. "For real? How?"

"Well, what happened here could mean there's more to Leland's death. And if this happened last night, it wasn't Jefferson. He was in jail."

"Now that makes sense. All right, I'll call. Can't stand to look at this mess anymore, anyhow."

Pete spun around and made his way to the front of the store. The others went with him. I pulled out my phone and took photos before I joined the rest of them on the porch out in the waning day.

10

It seemed like a good time for me and Bill to head for the office of Callie Leblanc. We had a case to work on, and no one could see any upside to our being at H. Tam and Sons when the law arrived.

"Most likely they'll just send some deputy to take a report," said Pete. "Or either it'll be Bert Lucknell, and he'll think up all kinds of questions, not a one of them useful. Then he'll arrest us for disturbing his lunch. You two should be off asking questions your own selves. I'll stay here, be a decoy."

"We'll stop with you, you want us to, Pete," said Henry, and though both Sam and Bobby Lee shifted uncomfortably, neither objected.

"Nah," said Pete. "Kind of you, but I gotta start going through Leland's papers, see can I find his in-surance." He emphasized the *in*; the *r* was completely silent. "Also, see if I can't get this place cleaned up some."

"But after the cops come, right?" I said. "So you don't disturb any evidence."

Pete shrugged. Bobby Lee said, "Evidence? Bert Lucknell wouldn't recognize no evidence if it jumped right up and bit him."

The Public Defender's Office was in downtown Clarksdale, which meant it took all of three minutes to drive there from the store. We were prepared to meet Callie Leblanc at the courthouse or wherever she could be found, but when I called, we were told she was in and could give us a few minutes if we came right over.

The attorneys' workplaces I knew, in Chinatown and elsewhere, were all in office buildings, a few, or many, flights up. Here in Clarksdale, the office of the Coahoma County Public Defender occupied a wide storefront on one of the town's main streets. That could be accounted for by the lack of multistory office buildings, and also by the relative wealth of empty storefronts. Clarksdale was by no means a ghost town. The street was neat and clean, with Christmas stars strung across it and flowerpots hanging from the lampposts. Posters advertised blues musicians, Christmas carol sings, Sunday afternoon football, and upcoming playoff parties in the bars, with the occasional Tam or Mallory sign sprinkled in. Still, any enterprise looking to establish itself would not lack for real estate choices.

The Public Defender's Office was buzzing when we pushed through the glass door. The receptionist barely looked up from her keyboard when I introduced us. She pointed over her shoulder, past young people on phones and at desktop computers that even I could see were a few generations old. At the back of the space were six cubicles, all piled high with paperwork. My mother's original idea, that Jefferson Tam didn't trust his white lawyer, might still be right in concept, but it was wrong in detail. In one of the cubicles—the one with the window, even if only onto the alley—sat a thin woman with smooth walnut skin and short cropped hair just starting to gray. She looked up when I knocked on the partition.

"Hi," I said. "Ms. Leblanc?"

She didn't smile, rise, or offer her hand. "You're Jefferson Tam's cousin from New York. The investigator."

"Yes. How did you know?" I hadn't told the receptionist anything but my name when I'd made the appointment.

"News travels fast." Her drawl was identifiably Southern, but clipped and shortened, as if in her world, time were a valuable commodity not to be wasted in any way. "Do you know where to find him?"

"Find Jefferson?" I was taken aback. "No. I've never even met him. We were hoping to learn something more about him from you."

She didn't reply, but looked pointedly at Bill, so I said, "Bill Smith. My partner. Ms. Leblanc, I'd appreciate anything you can tell me about Jefferson."

"I know very little. I've only met him once myself."

Her office had a single visitor chair, its stained fabric starting to separate from the plastic frame. She didn't offer it, but I sat anyway.

"I really don't think I can help you," she said coldly.

"I'm a little perplexed. Aren't we on the same side? Don't we both want to help Jefferson?"

"I don't know what you want to do. My job is to build his legal case, which was looking bad enough before he ran. Now he's a fugitive and you say you don't know where he is. Until he turns up, there's nothing I can do for him. Meanwhile, I have three dozen active cases." She tapped her pen on the papers before her. "I'd like to see if I can get some of them home for Christmas."

"There's nothing you can tell me about Jefferson that would help?"

"Help what?"

"Find him."

"Is that why you came to Clarksdale?"

"Not to find him. I didn't know he'd broken out. But I'm his cousin. I came to help."

She threw down her pen. "Look, Ms. Chin—"

"Ms. Leblanc, ma'am." Bill stepped forward. "We do apologize for taking up your time. Captain Pete Tam told us you're a busy lady, and anyways we can see that." At the mention of Captain Pete,

Callie Leblanc's frown relaxed a bit. "My partner's just real worried about her cousin," Bill went on, and as opposed to Callie Leblanc's, his Southern drawl, usually imperceptible, was wide and luxurious. "Being on the run's a serious thing, and we're thinking it'll go better for Jefferson if kin finds him before the law does."

Callie Leblanc regarded him. "You local, Mr. Smith?"

"No, ma'am. I'm from Louisville. Been in New York for a number of years, though," he added, as if ruefully admitting a flaw.

"Well, then, maybe you remember how things work in the South. You're right, Jefferson Tam would be better off if the first person to find him wasn't someone with a weapon. Or if he hadn't escaped custody to begin with. Or if he'd told me something I could use other than, 'I didn't do it.' But he didn't, so I know no more about him than the circumstances of his arrest."

"We'd be obliged if you'd tell us about that, then."

I spied her foot jiggling with impatience. She spied me spying it, and it stopped. "Jefferson called 911. By the time the police got to the store, Leland was dead."

"Jefferson called them?"

"Which means nothing, as I assume you know."

She was right, of course. I said, "He had blood on his clothes and his prints were on the knife, is that right?"

"He says the blood's from trying to stop Leland's bleeding and the prints are from the last time he used the knife."

So he did tell you something, I thought, but I only asked, "Which was when?"

"He doesn't remember."

"How did he come to be in the store at exactly that moment?"

"He claims he'd gotten to town earlier in the day. He says Leland had called the day before, wanting to talk about something, but before they got to whatever it was, Leland started laying into Jefferson about how he was conducting his life. Jefferson got mad, left to cool off, and then he came back and found Leland bleeding on the floor."

"Did Leland say anything before he died?"

"According to Jefferson, something about a picture. Jefferson thought maybe Leland got a picture of the killer on his phone. But the police didn't find a phone."

"The killer might have taken it."

Callie Leblanc shrugged.

"Do you know what it was Leland wanted to talk to Jefferson about?"

"No."

"The fact that Jefferson admitted to an argument makes him seem a little less guilty, to me," said Bill.

"Without a better story from him," Callie Leblanc said, "it's a hard case to build. 'I didn't do it' only goes so far. And without *him*, it's looking worse every minute." She blew out an exasperated breath. "I wish he hadn't run. The wound was in Leland's leg. It severed the femoral artery. He bled to death, but it's the kind of thing that happens in a scuffle, not an intentional homicide. I likely could have pled it down to manslaughter two. A few years and out. But this . . ."

She shook her head. Then she looked me in the eye. "Justice isn't very flexible in Mississippi and neither is my budget. I can't spend time on a client I might never see again."

I returned her look, thinking, *Lydia, be water, not stone.* After a few moments, Callie Leblanc picked up her pen again. "The paralegal out in the bull pen, in the blue shirt," she said, looking down at her papers. "Tolson Reeves. He's the one who told me Jefferson Tam's cousin was in town. They went to school together. He hasn't had his lunch break yet."

I could take a hint. "Ms. Leblanc," I said as I stood, "one more thing. Will you—will the Public Defender's Office—hire us?"

"Will I—?" Now she did look up, and paused. "So anything you find is covered by lawyer-client privilege, is that what you want?"

"It would pertain if we were working for Jefferson's lawyer. But not if we're working for Pete Tam."

"I'm not sure it would anyway, unless you're licensed in Mississippi."

I shook my head and waited.

She stood. "On the other hand, I'm not sure it wouldn't. I have no time to research the question, and I can't see how it could hurt. Understaffed the way we are, volunteers are always appreciated. Come with me." She strode past us volunteers and out into the bull pen.

"Tolson," Callie Leblanc said to a large young man with shining dark skin and a shaved head, "this is Lydia Chin, Jefferson Tam's cousin."

Tolson Reeves stood to shake hands, but he didn't smile and his eyes seemed guarded. The other paralegals and secretaries paused in their bustling to check us out.

"She and her partner will be doing some investigative work for us," Callie Leblanc continued, "so please draw up a contract. They'd like to speak to you, too, since you know Jefferson. I don't want the disruption in here so—"

"So can we buy you lunch?" I stuck in.

Tolson Reeves eyed me uneasily, and he didn't seem any happier with Bill. His boss had clearly issued an order, though. He nodded. At least he'd get lunch out of it.

"You can do the contract when you get back," Callie Leblanc said, clearly meaning, *Hurry up and get out of here so everyone can get back to work*. Her gaze swept the bull pen, and people took their eyes quickly off us and picked up their phones and their papers. She turned to me. "I'm warning you. If you step an inch over the line, I'll tear that contract up and personally call the law. The last thing I'll tolerate is you people compromising whatever case I might still have, once Jefferson's found."

"Yes, ma'am," I said.

"Concerning your retainer, I assume a dollar's enough?"

It was a dollar more than I'd expected to make on this case, so I said again, "Yes, ma'am."

11

At Yazoo Pass, a café two empty storefronts and three occupied ones down from the Public Defender's Office, Tolson Reeves, Bill, and I collected lunch and caffeine and slid into a booth. Christmas carol Muzak filled the air.

"It's probably just my Yankee prejudice," I said brightly, hoping to come across as friendly and disarming, "but this isn't the type of place I expected to find in Clarksdale, Mississippi. I mean, dried cranberries in the salad bar, cappuccinos, and a guy by the window writing the Great American Novel?"

Tolson Reeves sipped his coffee, which, like Bill's, was a straight-up cup of dark brew, the fancy concoctions on the blackboard notwithstanding. "Well, I couldn't rightly say anything about Yankee prejudice," he drawled, his tone implying that he actually had a good deal to say on the subject but didn't see much point in saying it to us. "But the espresso machine doesn't get much play. The guy by the window's with Teach for America, most likely working on a lesson plan for kids who come to school hungry and can't follow a thing he says in his Yankee accent. And half the people in here are blues-trail foreign tourists who have a certain comfort level with cranberries in a salad bar."

So much for friendly. He was right about the tourists, though. Animated German was being spoken by the couple in the next booth, and four camera-draped young Japanese men with interesting haircuts were working through a pile of fried chicken.

Okay, to business. "You grew up in Clarksdale?"

"Yes, ma'am."

They sure could do a frosty *ma'am* in Mississippi. "And you went to school with Jefferson?"

"High school. Concord Academy."

"Ms. Leblanc said you were friends." She hadn't, but I thought it might cut through some hostile jockeying if I put the idea out.

Reeves didn't deny it. "We were tight back in the day, because of the situation we found ourselves in."

"What situation?"

"Concord Academy." I must have looked blank, because he asked, "Do you know anything about the Mississippi school system? The academies?"

I didn't, but Bill did. "When the Supreme Court ordered public schools desegregated," he said, his eyes on Reeves but speaking to me, "Mississippi white people's way around it was to start private 'academies.'"

"This was legal?" I asked.

"This was Mississippi," said Reeves. "Anyone could apply, and the tuition was low, but it was obvious who'd get in and who wouldn't. And hard to prove why."

"But the academy you and Jefferson went to was a different kind?"

"No, ma'am. A few years before we were set to start high school, black families started filing challenges to the system. The academies didn't want a court fight in case the whole house of cards crashed down. Better to each let in half a dozen or so of the 'right class' of colored folk. They'd look innocent, and how much pollution could we really cause, so few of us? My father's a doctor and my mother's a pharmacist, so there I was, the right class. And Jefferson, of course he's colored folk of a different color."

I sipped my tea, getting used to this information and the way it was delivered. I'd never in my life heard anyone say "colored folk" out loud, not even with the cold irony tingeing the voice of Tolson Reeves.

"So you and Jefferson stuck together because you were . . . outsiders?"

Reeves's eyes held a sardonic glint. It amused him that I was having trouble saying it. "There were only six of us *colored folk* that first year. Me, him, and four black girls. You wanted to know someone had your back."

"There was trouble?" Bill asked.

Reeves shrugged. "I was a big guy. I could handle it."

"And Jefferson?"

"Could be I saved him from a beatdown once or twice in those first weeks."

"Well, as his cousin, I appreciate that," I said. "Did things change after those first weeks? Or that was how it was, the whole time?"

"No, ma'am, it wasn't. Soon as the school year started, they had football tryouts. I made the team."

"Not an easy thing for a freshman," Bill said. "Anywhere."

Reeves nodded. "Any team has holes, in defense or offense. I was a two-way player in Pop Warner and I'd studied the Concord team. Been to their games, read their clippings. They had holes both ways. I went out for the positions where the holes were."

"Shrewd," I said.

"This is Mississippi." He sipped his coffee. "I knew what it would be like at Concord, and I knew what my best chance was. Pop Warner on my side of town, we had a tougher style of play than the white kids did." He smiled.

"So you were a star," said Bill.

"I wasn't bad."

"And once they saw that, they backed off, and backed off Jefferson because he was a friend of yours?"

"Pretty much."

"Just like that?" I asked. "Football trumps racism?"

Tolson Reeves allowed himself another tight smile. "Ma'am, in Mississippi, the only thing football doesn't trump is deer season."

He picked up his sandwich, and I tried my salad. The kale was fresh and the goat cheese was delicious. I wondered if they were local.

"Are you and Jefferson still close?"

He looked me in the eye. "If what you're fishing for is, do I know where to find him, no, ma'am, I don't."

"No, we don't mean that," said Bill smoothly, though I sort of had. "It's just, if we had a better picture of him, we might know what direction to look in."

Reeves shifted his gaze to Bill and didn't answer.

"Listen," I said, "I don't know what's going on here, but Jefferson Tam's been accused of *murder*. He's your friend, and that may not matter to you, but he's my cousin. I want to find him, or at least to know as much as possible so that when the law finds him, I'll be ready. Can you help?"

Reeves looked out the window. A pedestrian or two on either side of the street, a single car rolling through in each direction on the light change; not a lot of action, but maybe that was from my NYC point of view. This could be a big day in Clarksdale.

"Right before Thanksgiving," Reeves said, "Jefferson blew back into town and we went for a beer."

"So you are still friends."

He didn't answer that. "The next day, Jefferson dropped into the office and asked could he borrow my car. His was in the shop and he had some business to take care of. I said sure and gave him the keys."

"And what happened?" I prompted, when he paused. "He had an accident?"

"No, ma'am, he returned the car a few hours later, not a scratch on it, a six-pack on the passenger seat as a thank-you."

"Then—"

"Montel Bradley, the sheriff? He's my mother's cousin. He called me that night. I was up in Oxford. I'm doing my law school at night at Ole Miss. He wanted to know what the hell I was doing in Burcell that afternoon. I told him I wasn't there, and he said don't even, a deputy spotted my car parked on Cottonwood. I said I'd loaned the car to a friend and he said, uh-huh, sure, then I'd better tell my *friend* he needed to stay away from that place and he wasn't going to tell me again. So I just said thanks, sorry, appreciate him looking out for me. But you can see what happened. That was Jefferson down there."

"Okay," I said. "I follow, except for the part about 'Burcell.' Where's that, and why shouldn't you go there?"

"Pretty little town." Reeves sipped coffee. "Prosperous. Sleepy-looking. Eight or so miles from here. White town, so less likely I'd be down there anyway, unless I was going on through to Oldman's Brake. But if I was, I would've kept moving. My car just sitting there, that's bad news and that's what Uncle Montel was warning me against, me going for a legal career and all. It angered me that Jefferson didn't think of it." Reeves put his coffee down. "See, ma'am, in Burcell, everyone in that pretty little town, one way and another, is in the business of cooking meth."

12

The knowledge Tolson Reeves had just dropped was not the sort of thing I'd been hoping to hear.

"Everyone?" I asked. "There's no other reason Jefferson might have had for going to Burcell? He has a friend there, or something?"

"There's one guy there we went to school with. Johnny Ferguson. Nasty piece of work. Jefferson and I both tried to keep clear of him. Though if Johnny went up in your face, you had to man up and deal with it, because he wasn't going to stop. I'll tell you this—if Jefferson went to Burcell to see Johnny, it's sure as hell not because they're friends."

"What about Oldman's Brake?" Bill asked. "You said you might have been going on through to there. Couldn't Jefferson have been, too, and he stopped for something in Burcell?"

Tolson shook his head. "First off, who lives in Oldman's Brake is a bunch of black families. No law against Jefferson going, but I never heard he knew anyone there. And stopped for what? There's nothing in Burcell but cookers and tweakers."

"Cookers, in context, I get it," I said. "What's a tweaker?"

Reeves had just bit into his sandwich, so Bill said, "Drugs have different effects. Heroin knocks you out, grass spaces you out. Meth makes you hyperfocused, hyperalert. What you do in that state is called 'tweaking.' It's great for detail work. Like model airplane building. Or identity theft."

"Lovely. And really, there's nothing else in Burcell? No gas station, no grocery store?"

Reeves shook his head. "Only thing open's a bar, for your meth-buying convenience. That's for the retail trade, but retail's just a side business in Burcell. Most of what they cook gets hauled off to Memphis. These backcountry good ol' boys, they don't have a talent for distribution. That's handled by professionals."

"And the sheriff knows this? Why hasn't he stopped them?"

"Where do you want me to start? For one, they fit out labs in trailers or else broken-down shacks. Hard to spot. And it's not like the citizens would just sit on their porches and let deputies comb the back forty. They'd be out with deer rifles, demanding search warrants. They know their rights, you better believe it. Two, this is one of the poorest counties in the poorest state in the Union. I wouldn't want to say law enforcement is turning a blind eye, but to get picked up for doing something that brings income into Coahoma County, you'd have to be about as big and stupid as it's possible to be. And three, every now and then, they do decide a raid's a good idea, but by the time they go swooping in, everything's cleaned up and gone."

Bill asked, "You think the Burcell labs have someone in law enforcement protecting them?"

Tolson shrugged. "Or just, someone with a brother or cousin or poppa in law enforcement was drinking out at Po' Monkey's with someone with a brother or cousin or poppa in Burcell, and after a pint of moonshine, who knows what got said?"

I asked, "Did you talk to Jefferson about his going there? Did you ask him why?"

"I called and told him how pissed off I was—begging your pardon, ma'am—and no way he'd catch me doing him any more favors. I said I hadn't told Uncle Montel it was him, but if something came of it, I'd have to, so if I was Jefferson, I'd make sure from now on to be squeaky-clean."

"What did he say?"

"What you'd expect. It wasn't like that, he couldn't tell me about it, but it was nothing to worry about. I told him when the sheriff starts calling me, that's something to worry about. I said I didn't want to know what was going on, but maybe it was a good time for him to get out of town. Then I hung up."

"Did you speak to him again before he was arrested for Leland's murder?"

"No, ma'am, nor since, either. Damn fool should have taken my advice."

13

Tolson Reeves was through with us, so we thanked him and headed back to H. Tam and Sons. When we got there, Pete was sitting on the porch. The door wore a shiny new lock. "Too depressing in there," he declared. "Plus, it smells. I'll come clean it up tomorrow. Can't take it right now."

"Is anything missing?"

"If it is, I don't know what, except what cash was in the till."

"Empty?" Bill asked.

"Down to the pennies. Though truth is, it's just as likely a representative of the law cleaned it out while they tromped around 'investigating.'" Captain Pete clearly knew all about air quotes. "Actually," he added, "I'd prefer if it was that. It would mean when these no-accounts came to trash Leland's store, least they didn't get away with money. Hell with them."

It was clear from the way he thrust out his jaw how upset he was and how hard he was trying not show it. I gave him a squeeze. "We'll help you clean up tomorrow, Pete."

"You just go about finding Jefferson and proving he didn't kill Leland. That's the best help you can give."

"What did the police say about this?"

"'Store's been vandalized, Pete.'"

"Seriously?"

"You got to admire the fine way they got with the obvious, don't you? Good news was, it was the Clarksdale PD, not the sheriff, so it wasn't Bert Lucknell. Guess a little wanton destruction's not important enough for a big detective."

"Where's your backup group?"

"Henry and them? Gone home. Before, Henry drove over to the Ace Hardware, got those kinds of locks with sirens in them. When Leland was living behind the store, he didn't need those, but now . . . "

Yes, I thought, *now*.

We drove back to Pete's place, where HB next door barked up a storm until Pete thanked him. Pete set about making iced tea, and I laid out a platter of cookies from an impressive selection in the cabinets. "I have a sweet tooth, I guess," Pete admitted. I made a mental note to tell my mother to send him a tin of her egg tarts. Bill walked down toward the creek for a smoke.

I brought my cookie platter into the living room in time to see a car pull up to the curb. Nothing showy, just a quietly stylish black sedan. HB started up again. Bill came in through the kitchen door as Pete was opening the front one.

The buzz-cut, broad-shouldered driver stood to the left on the tiny porch, leaving a lanky, softly smiling man front and center. This had to be Congressman and gubernatorial candidate Reynold Tam. My cousin.

Pete had been right about his looks: under his tortoiseshell glasses, and with his bronze skin and the curl in his salt-and-pepper hair, it was hard to tell his half-Chineseness right off the bat. Though the bronze might have been not from the sun of the American South, but from the genes of a southern Chinese. We Guangdong peasants are too dark to fit the moon-skinned northern Chinese standard of beauty.

"Uncle Pete," said Reynold Tam. "It's been too long." He held out a bouquet of white irises. "I was so sorry to hear about Leland."

Captain Pete's *thank you* carried no hint of recrimination, no sense of whose fault that too long might have been. He took the flowers, stood back, and looked Reynold Tam up and down. "Well," he said, with that cheek-creasing grin. "Tams sure do age well, don't we?"

The Tam he was addressing, according to what Pete had told us, had just turned sixty, his father, Pete's brother Paul, being Pete's elder by twelve years. Reynold Tam did look good, straight-shouldered, in a gray suit, white shirt, blue tie. He smiled at us all with the kind of openness and interest in other people that makes a person attractive, and marks the best bartenders, hairdressers, and politicians.

"This," said Pete with a bit of a flourish, "is our cousin Lydia Chin. From New York. And her partner, Bill Smith. They're private investigators."

"Private investigators? My goodness." Reynold Tam's smile lit his eyes as he took my outstretched hand. "Cousin Lydia. What a lovely surprise! You'll have to tell me how we're related. Mr. Smith, a pleasure. I'd like you folks to meet Frank Roberson. He's my chief aide, and also happens to be my son-in-law." Reynold Tam winked.

Roberson, who looked to be in his early thirties, also wore a suit and tie. "Pleased to meet you." Both men had that Mississippi drawl, though Roberson's was more pronounced. "I just wish the circumstances were more pleasant."

"Mr. Tam's son-in-law?" I said as we shook hands. "Then you're my cousin, too. By marriage, anyway."

"Cousin Lydia, you have to call me Reynold," said my cousin Reynold. "And yes, my Megan was smart enough to marry Frank, so he's family, too."

"Now look what a position you put me in." Frank Roberson grinned. "If I agree Megan's a bright lady, I sound all swellheaded. If I honestly say marrying me wasn't so smart, I'm insulting my wife."

"Sounds like a no-win, so I suggest you just come in and sit down," Pete said.

They came in, but Frank Roberson and Reynold Tam both remained standing until I sat. When they seated themselves, neither made a move toward the worn armchair. I gave them good-manners points.

Pete laid the bouquet on the kitchen counter and brought in iced tea and glasses on a tray. "Cousin Lydia, if you'd look after these gentlemen while I locate a vase, I'd be obliged."

I poured out as my mother taught me: guests first, in descending order of age; family the same, meaning Pete, then Bill; and lastly me. I was hoping that by the time I got to myself the pitcher would be empty, but no such luck.

Pete came back into the room and set the flowers on the coffee table in their located vase. He sat and raised his glass. "Well. To the Tams, and reunions."

We lifted our glasses. Reynold sipped and said, "Uncle Pete, you look just like the last time I saw you."

"Considering when that was, I think all that means is, I was an old man young. But you're doing well, I know that. Hearing your name everywhere. People say you've got a real shot."

"Surely hope you're right. Just have to get past my primary."

"That going to be a problem?"

"My opponent hopes so." Reynold smiled at Roberson, who gave a genial shrug. He said nothing, but the slight lift in his eyebrows was reassuring: *bring it on.*

"But we're not here to talk about politics," Reynold said.

In his smile, and in the smile Pete gave him in return, I saw something that made me put down my tea—not that that was a sacrifice— and say to Bill and Frank Roberson, "Let's take a walk down to the creek, check out the local flora and fauna."

"Fauna includes rattlesnakes." Pete grinned, but though it was obvious what I was doing, neither he nor Reynold objected.

"It's winter," I said to Bill and Frank Roberson as the door closed behind us. "Aren't the rattlesnakes hibernating with the alligators?"

"Yes, ma'am, I'm sure they are," said Roberson. His tone of voice matched the smile Bill was trying to hide. Well, what did they want from me? The only alligators we had in New York were the ones in the sewers.

We strolled through the backyard toward the stream. "Thanks for indulging me," I said to the men. "I think the Tams needed a moment alone."

"I completely agree," said Roberson, serious now. "Reynold was very upset when he heard what happened. It brought home to him how he's never really known his Delta kin."

The ground began to get soggy. We stopped and I said, "I know Reynold's father never paid much attention to his relatives here, once he moved away. But Pete also implied you—Reynold's staff, I mean, not just you—want to play down his Chinese side."

After a moment, Roberson said, "That bothers you."

"I'm sorry, but yes, it does. Especially since you're married to his daughter."

I expected a shrug and a *This is Mississippi*, but instead Roberson stuck his hands in his pockets and gazed out over the sluggish brown water. "I was a senior at Ole Miss when Reynold made his first run. I was fixing to go north when I graduated." He nodded toward the river. "This is home. My people go back five generations here. But to get Mississippians to change—I swear, it's like pushing a rope. Folks here take pride, sometimes, in their backwardness. I was impatient. I was pretty sure I knew what was possible in Mississippi and what wasn't, the way you're sure of things when you're twenty. When this progressive, half-Chinese attorney announced for Congress, I laughed."

"You didn't like him?"

"The reverse. I didn't know him, only what I read, but his positions seemed like they lined up with mine. That was enough to mean he'd probably lose, never mind about his race, except in Mississippi, you never do never mind about race. But I was in poli-sci, so I applied to do a practicum with his primary campaign. No way we were going to win, but I didn't care. I just wanted a little experience in the field before I headed north.

"I should have thought it through, but I hadn't. I was blindsided when my dad was furious. 'You're working for that Chinaman? What does a Chinaman know about what's good for Mississippi?'"

"But Reynold was born in Jackson."

Roberson gave a small laugh. "Yes, and my dad has nothing against Orientals. He'd tell you that, and that's the word he'd use. He just thinks people should stick to their own. It should have occurred to me, how he'd react to me being on Reynold's team."

I didn't know what to say. I looked at Bill.

"I was raised with people like that, too," Bill said. "In Kentucky. I'm surprised Mr. Tam's gotten as far as he has."

"I was, too, believe me," said Roberson. "We won the primary, and I continued through the general, and we won that, too. By then I'd graduated. Reynold asked me to stay on, offered me a staff job. I took it because I wanted to see how far we could go. If a man like Reynold Tam had a chance, I thought, maybe I wouldn't have to leave Mississippi. Maybe I could stay where my family is, where my roots are. I was hoping my parents would be pleased. After all, I wasn't going north."

"They weren't?"

"My mother, yes. She was willing to overlook my reasons as long as I stayed close to family. But Dad, he'd been counting on Reynold losing the general so I could put that foolishness behind me. When we won, he took it personally. Like I'd engineered it just to prove I was smarter than he was. Then I started dating Megan. You can imagine how that went over." Roberson watched water drift between the reedy banks. "We have two little girls now. To look at, they're as white as I am. But my dad's a one-drop guy. My kids are Chinese, as far as he's concerned. Mom comes up to Jackson to visit, on a Saturday or whatever. Takes the kids to the zoo. But we spend holidays with my in-laws. Reynold, Alicia, Megan's brother, Donald—I count my blessings every day for the way they've welcomed me."

"But really, your father? He doesn't come see his own grandchildren, because they're, what, one-eighth Chinese?"

"In Mississippi, during Jim Crow, you were white or you weren't. That's what 'one drop' meant. The law's changed, but a lot of people haven't. Dad's not so unusual around here."

I thought about my mother. Nothing—hell, high water, or the whole heavenly host—would keep her from my brothers' children. Even, I was rock-solid sure, if their mothers hadn't been Chinese.

"I'm sorry," I said. "I guess I assumed that kind of thinking was a thing of the past."

Frank Roberson, my cousin by marriage, smiled. "It is. And here in Mississippi, we love the past. We especially love the kind of past that never was. Reynold can do great things as governor of this state. But he's got to get elected first."

14

HB sent up a greeting yip when we came up to the kitchen door. When I entered the living room, Reynold stood. "Well. See any snakes or gators?"

"Not a reptile," I replied.

We all sat. Pete offered more sweet tea and cookies, and Reynold turned to me. "Cousin Lydia, Pete and I have been reminiscing about Leland and our relations, but I have to apologize for my ignorance of family history. It must be worse than I thought, for me to have missed a branch of the family tree that produced such a fine sprig as yourself. Would you tell me about our shared kin?"

"I'd be happy to." I skipped over the fact that our ignorance, until yesterday, had been mutual. "Your grandfather who came to Mississippi was my great-grandfather's brother." I gave him a moment to work that through. "My great-grandfather stayed in China, though. My branch of the family didn't come over until my parents."

"My grandfather," said Reynold. "Hong-Bo Tam, the original H. Tam. I never knew him, unfortunately."

"He's the original H. Tam, but did you know he was a paper son? That you're really Chins, not Tams?"

Reynold looked at Pete in surprise. "I surely didn't," he said. "Uncle Pete?"

"Well, of course. Really, Paul didn't teach you anything?"

Frank Roberson looked from Reynold to me. "I'm sorry—what's a paper son?"

So I told them about paper sons, and about Chin Song-Zhao and how he changed his name. At the end of my recital, the sweet tea was all gone, no thanks to me. Pete started to push himself up to go get more, but Bill volunteered. Apparently the fridge was to tea as the cabinets were to cookies.

"Well," said Reynold. "Well. I'd heard about paper sons, but I had no idea I was descended from one." He turned a concerned look on his son-in-law. "Frank, I almost hate to mention it, but you don't think—?"

"Nope," said Roberson. "I don't."

"But Frank, sounds like my granddaddy was an illegal alien," Reynold persisted. "It's the kind of thing'll make Mallory's mouth water."

"Stirling Mallory appeals to the crowd that liked it better when everybody knew their place," said Pete. "Do I have to translate that for you Yankees?"

"No, Pete," I said, and Bill, coming in with a fresh sweating pitcher, shook his head.

Reynold sighed. "Now, Uncle Pete, lots of folks are hurting. They want answers, they need help. Stirling's got a way of telling them he's got those answers. I just happen to think he's wrong."

"Wrong? The boy's a Neanderthal with a set of white sheets hanging in his hall closet."

Roberson grinned. "I guess speaking your mind runs in the Tam family."

Pete poured the tea, eyeing my still-full glass with suspicion. "Well, but look at the good Reynold's done already. Repairing those small-town bridges, and that stopgap school bill—those were you, weren't they? Oh, Reynold, don't look so surprised. We maybe haven't seen each other in a dog's age, but I do live in this state." Pete settled back in his chair.

"Delighted that you follow my career, Uncle Pete, and that you approve of my initiatives." Reynold turned to Roberson. "So, we have nothing to worry about?"

"The paper son thing? I think we'll be fine," Roberson said. "For one thing, if *you* didn't know it, how would Mallory find out?" He looked, eyebrows raised, at Pete, at me, at Bill.

"Well, I sure as hell won't tell him," Pete said.

"Family lore," I said. "None of anyone's business."

"And me," said Bill, "I just work here."

"There you go, Reynold," Roberson said. "Not a problem."

"Unless it does come out."

"And if it does, we'll handle it. Would you please let me do the worrying?"

"Okay."

"Thank you."

They both smiled; it must've been a refrain between them.

Roberson turned to Pete. "But I won't lie, this story makes me curious about these folks. Mr. Tam—"

"Pete."

"Pete. Any chance you'd be willing to bring out the family photos?"

"Don't have many. I travel light. Leland had most of the family records and such," said Pete. "Kept it all neat, organized." A cloud passed over his face; he must have been thinking about the current state of the store and house.

"You do have some, though?" Reynold asked. "I'd like to see them, too, if you don't mind, Uncle Pete. I have just about nothing, myself."

"Well, sure." Pete reached into a drawer in the coffee table. He cleared a space and opened a thin scrapbook.

On the first page, a sepia studio portrait: three scrubbed Chinese boys in bow ties and short pants, between two solemn Chinese adults.

The man, slick-haired and stocky, stood on the boys' left; a permed woman in a straight skirt flanked them on the right. Pete pointed to the boys, largest to smallest. "Paul. Jonas. Me." The boys were distinctive, each from the others. Paul, just coming into adolescence, tall and gangly, with a wave in his hair, had a hand on the shoulder of his rounder brother Jonas, as though to restrain him. Pete, maybe two years old when the photo was taken, stood facing the camera with his chest thrust out, already wearing the same wide grin he'd greeted us with this morning.

"And Ma and Ba," Pete said. "Ba, that would be Hong-Bo," he added, in case Reynold or Frank Roberson needed the reminder. "The original H. Tam."

He turned the pages slowly. More shots of the kids, leaning on bikes or playing on dusty streets. Photos of them older, with school books, with baseball bats. The eldest, now a young man, tanned and smiling, leaning his bony elbow out of the window of a pudgy automobile. "Your daddy, Paul," Pete told Reynold. "His first car. He was so proud. We all were, proud of him." Pete laughed. "Me and Jonas, we practically swelled up with it, because after Paul got that car, it got to be his job to take us down to Cleveland, to school. We used to ride in Daddy's old rattly truck. Then suddenly, there we were, sitting in the back seat like we had us a chauffeur. Paul thought it was funny, too."

"You went to school down in Cleveland?" Reynold asked. "Not here?"

"Oh, sure. Those days, Chinese couldn't go to the white schools. We were somewhere between black and white, you see. Now, anyone could see that the colored schools, they weren't teaching those kids anything more than they needed to know to sign their names to a contract and total up how many bales of cotton they brought in. So Daddy and a bunch of the other shopkeepers, and the Baptist Church, they set up the Chinese school down in Cleveland. Chinese kids from all over the Delta went down there. Paul was one of the first students."

Reynold Tam shook his head. "So much I don't know."

"Well," Pete said, "never too late to learn." He turned the scrapbook page and we all leaned over to look. The next photo was of H. Tam and Sons from across the street, paint sharp, no mesh on the windows, the other storefronts all occupied: a dress shop, a hardware store, a Laundromat, a café. After those, a few shots inside the shop, inside the house. On the last page, the adults, both graying, smiled from the dining room table I'd last seen covered with broken dishes in the back of Leland's store.

As Pete closed the scrapbook, I was hit with a thought: All these people were my relatives. We had roots in the same muddy village in Guangdong, where my great-grandparents' houses might still be standing, the ancestral tablets still in somebody's home. I decided that one day, I was going to go see them.

"That's it?" I said when Pete slid the scrapbook back in the drawer.

"Sorry, Cousin Lydia. Like I said, Leland had most everything. Whatever I find, I'll let you know. Reynold, you don't have any old photos, things like that?"

"I do have that one at the front there, Grandpa and Grandma Tam, my daddy, you and Uncle Jonas. Up on the mantelpiece. But that's all."

The talk then turned to Leland, his love of family and the sacrifices he made for it; to Pete's life, growing up in the Delta with his brothers; and to Reynold's own family: his father Paul, his mother Mary, his wife, children, grandchildren. He brought out from his wallet a crowded photo of a serenely smiling blond woman surrounded by curly-haired kids and their handsome parents, among them Frank Roberson. "My wife Alicia, Megan and Frank and their children, and our son Donald, his wife, and their three."

We all admired them. Reynold's mother had been white, his wife was white, and his children had married white spouses; in these littlest cousins, the Chineseness had been diluted to invisibility. Still, they were adorable, and they were my family.

Reynold tucked his wallet away. "Uncle Pete, I want to say again how sorry I am I never got to know my Delta kin better."

"Hardly your fault," said Pete generously. "Big brother Paul was never interested in us po' folk down here. He didn't raise you with family feeling, where were you supposed to get it from?"

"Kind of you. Still, I feel badly. Anything Jefferson needs for his defense, you let me know."

Pete's eyebrows knit. "You're not worried he's guilty?"

"No man's guilty till it's proved."

"I'm thinking more how it'll appear to your constituents."

"It'll appear that the congressman supports his family through thick and thin," Roberson said. "Mississippians put stock in family. A man can't disavow his kin. Voters will be proud."

A good way to spin it, I thought, *since you can't hide it*.

Reynold smiled, seeming satisfied that his son-in-law was satisfied. "We'd have come down yesterday," he said to Pete, "but truthfully, I couldn't get away. The obligations of public life."

"You came yesterday, you'd have missed Cousin Lydia," Pete pointed out. "And Bill. They just got here."

"Well then"—Reynold smiled—"that worked out for the best. Cousin Lydia, Bill, what brings all y'all to the South?"

"Pete asked us to come see if we could be of any help to Jefferson," I said. "I'm just sorry this is the first time I've ever been here."

"If nothing else good comes out of this, I guess we can still say the Tams reconnected with each other and with our Northern kin." Reynold smiled. "Do you think you can? Help the boy out, I mean."

"I don't know. Especially now."

"Especially now? How do you mean?"

I looked at Pete, who said, "You gents don't know?"

"Don't know what?"

"Oh, Lord." Pete sighed. "I'm sorry to say it, and I don't know what it's all about—hoping it's not what it seems—but the bald fact is, the boy did a runner."

"Did a— He escaped? From jail?"

"Yes he did."

Reynold's eyes widened, and Roberson frowned.

"I admit it doesn't look good," said Pete. "But personally, I'd like to withhold judgment until I have a chance to speak to him on the subject."

Roberson slipped a cell phone from his jacket pocket and said, "Excuse me." He went out on the front porch.

"I'm sorry," said Reynold. "But it's his job. I'm sure he's doing damage control—" Outside, Roberson's voice rose on the porch, then abruptly died down again. "Starting with reaming out our PR people for not being on top of this. Pete, when did it happen?"

"This morning, though those fools down to the sheriff's office didn't notice until a few hours later." Pete painted for Reynold the picture of Jefferson's escape as it had been given to us.

"That's troublesome," Reynold said, rubbing his forehead. "Him having help like that. Makes you wonder."

"That it does," Pete agreed, and none of us voiced what it was we were wondering.

The front door opened, and Roberson returned. "I'm sorry," he said, phone still in hand. His smile had returned, though his eyes were troubled. I liked him for not trying to hide that. "Reynold, I think we'd best be heading back. You have that dinner with those Family First people tonight."

"Right. Have to be on my best behavior. No, no, Frank, don't get your shorts in a twist, you know I take their concerns seriously." Roberson's phone rang, interrupting his nascent protest. With a look at Reynold, he excused himself again and went back outside. Reynold grinned and shook his head. "My lucky day, when Frank signed onto my team. He's the one with a genius for looking ahead. Me, I went into politics to help out. Kind of old-fashioned, I know, but the congressman before me, he wasn't as straightforward in his dealings as he might have been."

"That was Fitzhugh, wasn't it?" Pete asked. To me and Bill, he said, "Boy was so crooked he could've hid behind a corkscrew."

Reynold smiled. "I thought my neighbors deserved better. So I got elected and I was happy, until I started to wonder if there wasn't more we could do for this state. Having Frank with me made all the difference. I had to give him my daughter, but it was worth it." His smile expanded.

Through the door, we could hear Frank Roberson throwing metaphorical dishes against the wall.

"Running against Stirling Mallory, it's a challenge, though," Reynold went on. "That's why we're courting these Family First folks, groups you'd expect to come down on Mallory's side of the seesaw." Eyeing the door, Reynold said, "But Frank's stock in trade is he knows everyone, knows everything about 'em. He's a laid-back fellow, but you can maybe hear how you don't want to cross him. This business about Jefferson escaping, it shouldn't have had to be sprung on us like that. And Granddaddy being a paper son, Frank says it's not a problem and maybe it's not, but it'll be eating him as much because he didn't know it, as for what it is."

Roberson came in again, his color a little high. Reynold stood.

"Uncle Pete," he said, "thanks for seeing me, and for being so understanding about my failings as a relative. Cousin Lydia, now we've met, I look forward to hearing more about the New York Chins. Don't be a stranger. Mr. Smith, a pleasure meeting you. If there's anything I can do to help Jefferson—today's news notwithstanding"—he glanced at Roberson—"you'll let me know. I do hope to see all y'all again soon."

All us-all echoed the sentiment. Everyone exchanged business cards, the better to stay in touch. Pete and I hugged Reynold, and, since he was family, Frank Roberson, too. We crowded onto the little porch to watch them drive off. From the next-door fence, HB sent up a few farewell barks, and then fell silent.

15

"Cousin Reynold seems like a nice guy," I said as Pete closed the door. "For a politician."

"Now, now. I imagine his boy Frank is saying the same of us. 'Your cousin Pete, he seems like a nice guy, for a gambler. And that pretty little Lydia and her friend, they seem nice, too. For Yankees.'"

"I'm sure you're right." I paused. "Pete, do you really think this business, Leland and Jefferson, won't affect Reynold's chances?"

"No idea. Hope it doesn't, though. Reynold's opposition, this Mallory, you may have already figured out he's not my type of gent."

"Is he crooked? Or just seriously conservative?"

"'Seriously conservative'? This politician thing must be catching. No, Mallory's honest—at least, politician-honest, from what I hear. But in love with the past. In Mississippi, we got a lot of folks looking over their shoulders to some magical time when life was simpler. They mean for their kind, of course. Probably you've got folks like that up north, too, but here, it's a cottage industry. The people who think that way, bless their hearts, but they're not my people. Not likely to be any Chinese person's people, especially a grocer's kin. Still, from what I read in the papers, Reynold's playing this one more conservative than he has in the past."

"It's close, then?"

"Seems that way. Reynold's the known quantity, but Mallory's offering something a lot of folks seem to want."

"So it might be a problem."

"Might could. But what Roberson said, I think he's right. Not a lot of families in Mississippi without a skeleton in the closet. Long as Reynold didn't kill Leland himself, people will likely forgive him for being related to Jefferson. No matter what the end of it all is."

"Pete, about the grocers," said Bill, who'd been ferrying glasses and plates into the kitchen. "You promised us a history lesson. Can you tell us about the Chinese grocers, and explain what you mean by 'especially a grocer's kin'?"

Behind Pete's back, I gave Bill a thank-you thumbs-up. He winked and threw a kiss. I'd have rolled my eyes, but that was too predictable, so I threw a kiss back. Pete saw that one.

"If I'm in y'all's way . . ."

"Oh, sit down, Pete," I said while Bill laughed. "We want to hear the story."

"Well, all right. And in return, you'll tell me what kind of detection you accomplished today. But first, why don't you bring your bags in and get settled?"

I glanced at Bill. "Get settled? We were planning to find a motel or something."

"You'll do nothing of the kind. You came all the way from New York, least I can do is offer you hospitality. Lydia, you'll stay in the spare bedroom. Bill, I got a convertible couch in the basement. Don't worry it's a basement, we're high enough above the creek so unless it gets to be like '27, you'll be cozy down there."

"Twenty-seven?" I said.

"Seriously? What do they teach you people up north?" Pete threw up his hands. "The Great Flood of 1927! Mighty Mississippi rose ten, twelve feet, more in places. Wiped out whole towns, from Tennessee to the Gulf. Near to thirty thousand acres underwater. That's like as though all of New England up there was drowned. Hundreds of thousands of folks lost homes, farms, businesses, and I don't mean just had to run away and then came back when the water went down. No, sir. That river took all kinds of things with it, houses, barns, livestock, good Mississippi topsoil. And plus, those towns that got washed away, they lost all their records, too. People come back to where their farm used to be, another guy's there with a shotgun saying this land's mine and you can't prove it's not. That flood's why we have the levees like they are today—" He broke off, dismissing us with a hand wave. "Oh, never mind. Yankee ignorance. Go get your things. Rooms are all made up, both of them. Warning you, though, I can't cook."

"They don't cook at the Days Inn, either," I said. "Okay, Pete, we'll take you up on your offer, and I'm sorry for being ignorant. But as far as cooking, don't look at me. If you were hoping for some home-cooked Chinese meals, we'll have to send for my mother. Although Bill can cook."

"Spaghetti and meatballs," Bill said. "Omelets, I make good omelets. And I'll learn to whip up pork dumplings real fast if it means not sending for your mother. I'll get the bags."

In a fit of optimism, I hadn't brought much, and Bill always, as Pete had put it, travels light. I took my overnight bag down the hall while Pete led Bill outside and around to the basement door.

I paused in unpacking to look out the window, at the sloping yard and the brown, sluggish creek. Across the water, the land angled up again, the hillside covered with bare-branched trees. Ranch houses like Pete's peeked from the undergrowth at the top of the bank. Not much like the Mississippi of my mind, all slow, hot days with flower-scented air, cicada-filled nights, big houses with deep verandas, tar-paper shacks in the cotton fields around them. But then, that Mississippi, the product of movies, TV, and high school history classes, was entirely a story of black and white. Yellow had never been mentioned.

Bill emerged from the door below me. I opened the window, stuck my head out, and said, "Howdy."

He looked up. "Yo."

"How is it down there?"

"Cozy. Up there?"

"Right nice."

Apparently not worried about predictability, he rolled his eyes.

I asked, "Did you know about that flood?"

"Of course. I'm from these parts."

"I do believe those are different parts. Well, I'll be along directly. I'm fixing to meet y'all in the living room."

"Don't go native on me," he warned. "Don't do it."

Back in the living room, Pete offered more sweet tea, but even Bill turned him down.

"Right, then." Pete crossed his ankle over his knee. "Tell me, how far back do I have to start? Y'all didn't know about the Great Flood, so how complete is y'all's ignorance?"

"Hard to say," said Bill. "Not easy to know what it is you don't know."

"Bill knew about the Great Flood," I said defensively. "But about Chinese grocers in the South being a thing, I think we're both mystified."

Pete nodded. "Yup, pretty complete. Okay. Well, the grocers. Not so much in the whole South, though yeah, Memphis, Atlanta, Macon, there were some. But mostly, in the Delta."

"Even weirder," I said. "From a Yankee point of view, of course."

Now Pete rolled his eyes. At least I was provoking consistent reactions.

"Story goes like this," Pete said. "You know we built the railroad?"

"With the Irish," I said. "Bill's people."

"Erin go Bragh," said Bill.

Pete waved a hand. "Yeah, yeah, the Irish. When they drove that Golden Spike in 1869 and the railroad was done, the Irish went and got themselves jobs on farms and ranches and that. Blended in, you might say. But it was the end for the Chinese. All these laborers suddenly nobody wanted. They tried to plant crops, pan for gold, but people ran them off. Burned their houses, sometimes whole towns. Every now and then, lynched somebody. I'm talking about the West here, not the South, which is where you Yankees always think of when you hear 'lynch.'"

"Well, wasn't like these guys could get on a ship and go home. They couldn't pay the passage, and plus a lot of them were supporting families back in China on the chicken feed they were paid here. So some went east, to where there were already Chinese people, like to your Chinatown up there in New York. Meanwhile, here in the Delta, planters had started to clear the land for cotton." Pete paused. "Now, you'll notice this was after the Civil War."

Bill and I both nodded.

"This meant those planters, they didn't have slaves to work their fields. They wanted their cotton picked, they had to pay for it. Now, hiring black field hands, paying them money—well, that just went against some folks' grain. So someone had the idea of bringing in Chinese, recruiting from the railroad workers. They proved out west they could do hard labor, and there wasn't the history of bad feelings like there was between black and white."

"Chinese came here to pick cotton?" That, like pretty much everything else about the Delta Chinese, was news to me.

"That's why they came. But the work didn't suit 'em. Not that it suited black folks, but once Jim Crow took hold, they didn't have much choice. But the Chinese did. They didn't like the picking, but

they liked the Delta. Hot and damp, soil was fertile, hunting and
fishing were good—reminded them of home. They looked around, and
this is what they saw: black folks needed the necessities. Grain, sugar,
coffee. But the stores were all owned by white folks. Some wouldn't
sell to them at all. The ones that did, they'd make them wait out in the
street while the shopkeeper went for their goods. Black sharecroppers,
hard for them to scrape up capital to open stores of their own. But
the Chinese, bunch of them put their pennies together, they'd have
enough to finance a store, and then they'd all work there, sleep in the
back. So all over the Delta, Chinese opened groceries in black towns,
or in black neighborhoods in mixed towns. It was understood, once
a Chinese store made a little money, the group would stake the next
guy to a loan."

"*Hui*," I said. "That's how it works in Chinatown, too. Rotating
shared capital. My father's *hui* group financed his restaurant."

"So there you go. Stores got established, people brought over their
brothers, cousins, friends from the village. The new men would work
in the store for a while, learn the ropes, then start a store of their own
in a different neighborhood or a different town. Bought dry goods off
the Jewish peddlers who worked the river, got their grain and seed,
coffee, salt, canned goods, whatever else, from the same suppliers
the white stores used. Some of those suppliers, they didn't want to
deal with black, but they'd deal with Chinese. We were somewhere in
between—not white, for sure, but not black, either."

"'Colored folk of a different color,' Jefferson's friend Tolson Reeves
said."

"That's the way it was," Pete said. "A lot of the places black folk
couldn't go, we couldn't, either—restaurants, hotels—but sometimes,
we could, depending on the owner. Or, could and couldn't. Daddy, he
used to fish out in the sun in the summertime. Couple of years, he got

so dark they wouldn't serve him in this one restaurant he went to in the winter."

"Didn't they recognize him?"

"Well, sure they did. They apologized, but see, if someone who didn't know who he was saw him through the window, they might think they were letting black folks in there."

"Seriously?"

Pete nodded. "Across the river, in Arkansas, you were black or you weren't, so when grocers started bringing their wives over—now that they were merchants, not laborers anymore, law said they could do that—their kids could go to the white schools. Here in Mississippi, you were white or you weren't, so the kids couldn't. Eventually, the grocers and their churches went and set up Chinese schools. See how it was?"

"I do," I said, trying to digest this. "If you don't mind my saying so, it sounds nuts."

"Why would I mind? But if you're looking for the Mississippi mind-set, that's it right there."

"So all this, it's what your friend Sam Shoemaker meant when he said most blacks were raised thinking Chinese were good people," said Bill.

"Well, it was black customers made it possible for the grocers to survive. And Chinese grocers returned the favor, gave credit as a matter of course. Which the white stores wouldn't, not to black, even if they let them shop there. See, sharecroppers didn't get paid but once a year, when the cotton got brought in. At best twice, if there was winter wheat, too. In the weeks just before, cash could be hard to come by. Chinese grocers carried their customers through some hard times. Those debts got paid, too. Not always, but mostly."

"Are a lot of these stores still operating?" I asked. "Like H. Tam and Sons?"

"No." Pete shook his head. "They were, up to the last twenty, thirty years, but Walmart and them killed 'em off. Don't know that anyone's done a count, but I'd suppose there aren't but a dozen Chinese stores left up and down the Delta. Plus, the second and third generation wanted nothing to do with the stores. Parents sacrificed so their kids could go to college, make something of themselves. Well, they did. Professionals now, doctors and lawyers, teachers, bankers. Even if they wanted to stay in the Delta, there's nothing for them here. Like Leland's sisters, moving to California, and Jefferson running off to Oxford." Pete slapped his hands on his knees and stood. "Hey, giving history lessons is thirstier work than I expected. Anyone want a beer?"

Bill accepted, I declined. Pete made a trip to the fridge and came back with two Budweisers. He popped a top, slurped up foam, and said, "So, Cousin Lydia, is it all clear to you now?"

"Yes. And no. I'm thinking about what it must have been like for those first Chinese men—a couple in this town, a few in that one . . . Out west. there were twenty or thirty of them in a railroad gang, but here, it must have been really lonely."

"Must have been something," Pete agreed.

We sat in silence for a while. The setting sun broke through the clouds long enough to lay strips of gold up the trunks of the riverbank trees. As the brightness faded again Pete said, "So, now tell me what all you two did this afternoon. You talked to Callie Leblanc, right? And a friend of Jefferson's?"

"Tolson Reeves," I said. Together, Bill and I filled Pete in on our meeting.

Pete frowned when we were done. "Jefferson went to Burcell? I gotta tell you, I don't like the sound of that."

"We didn't, either," I said. "Is it true there's no other reason he could've had for going there, besides the meth trade?"

"Can't say. Got to be twenty years since I been down to Burcell myself. Don't know what truly goes on there, what's real, what's tall tales. Never had a wish to find out." He drank some beer, pointed a finger at me. "Tell you who might, though. Just beyond Burcell, behind the levee, there's a town goes by the name of Oldman's Brake."

"Reeves mentioned it."

"Can't hardly call it a town, just a pile of houses, but one of the folks who lives out there's a bluesman called Big Bone Stafford. He's playing this week at the Shacks. Him and me, we go up to Tunica together sometimes. Maybe you big-city detectives could talk to him. Likely Big Bone knows more about what's going on in Burcell than I do. We have to get dinner somewhere anyhow, and the Shacks makes a mean catfish taco. What do you say?"

"Blues and catfish tacos, and we can call it work?" Bill asked. "When do we leave?"

16

The Shacks, known formally as the Shack-Up Inn, turned out to be a constellation of sharecroppers' shacks centered around a former cotton gin a few miles outside of town. "Moved here, most of them," Pete said as we parked, "from plantations all over the Delta. Tourists on the Blues Trail love it, staying in a sharecropper's shack. 'Course, when they moved 'em, they put in plumbing, electric, real roofs."

I walked with Pete and Bill across the lot, impressed by all the stars I could see through the nippy night.

The café and music hall occupied the interior of the old cotton gin. I don't know what actually goes on in cotton gins, but apparently they're pretty much the size of small airplane hangars, high-ceilinged, flat-roofed, and built from corrugated steel. Whatever insides this one used to have were gone, replaced by tables, a bar, and a stage. A pair of electric guitars, a drum kit, and two chairs were onstage, waiting. The grill-scented air was promising.

A thin blond waitress in a Santa hat turned to greet us when we walked in. Her canned smile wavered when she saw Pete. "Oh, hey, Captain Pete. Good to see you. Gotta tell you I'm sorry. About Leland, I mean, and . . . you know, Jefferson . . ."

"Kind of you, Reba," Pete said as she led us to a table. "This is my cousin Lydia and her friend Bill, from New York City. Reba here's from just up the road, in Marx."

"New York City! That old Big Apple. Got to get me up there one day." Reba's relief at the change of subject was as palpable as her discomfort had been. "Well, welcome to Mississippi, y'all. What can I get you?"

Bill and Pete asked for beers, and I got a club soda. We all ordered the catfish tacos, Pete because he knew they were good, Bill because they sounded good to him, me because when in Rome. We'd arrived half an hour before Big Bone Stafford was scheduled to go on. That left plenty of time for Reba's discomfort to be repeated in the dozen or so people who came over to offer Pete their condolences, some of them Shacks staff, others diners or drinkers at the bar.

Reba came back balancing plates along her arm and set one down in front of each of us. "Y'all enjoy," she recommended and left.

"Leland certainly seems to have been well-liked," I said.

Pete nodded. "That's why I thought what happened, it had to be punks, not something somebody meant to do. I mean, you can see. Who'd want to kill Leland?"

I heard a wobble in Pete's voice and changed the subject. "Pete, tell me something. I look around, this whole crowd seems to be white, except you and me. Black people don't come here?"

Pete took a breath and collected himself. "They got places they like better. Shack-Up Inn's kind of touristy." Lifting a deep-fried onion ring, he added, "And plus, I imagine they don't get much of a kick out of the sharecroppers' shacks."

The tacos turned out to be delicious: salty, well stuffed, fishy tasting. Bill doctored his with a flood of hot sauce. I'd gotten a side of coleslaw, but that didn't stop me from reaching to sample a sweet potato fry from Bill's plate. "You can have some coleslaw," I offered, which got the response I expected: sarcastic silence.

A gust of cold air accompanied a thin, red-haired white woman and a large, chubby black man through the open door.

"The talent's here," Pete announced. "That's Angel Sewell.

She's Big Bone's drummer. And there's the man himself. Hey, Big Bone!"

Angel Sewell picked up a bottle of beer at the bar and climbed onto the stage, to do whatever drummers do to their drums before a show. Big Bone Stafford, greeting people as he lumbered through the room, turned at Pete's shout. He lifted his beer and made his way toward us.

"Set yourself down," Pete invited, and the big man did, descending into the empty chair at our table.

"Pete, glad to see you. Real sorry about Leland, you know that. Fine man, he was. And Jefferson, him being arrested, that don't make no sense."

"Amen," said Pete. "Big Bone, this here's my cousin Lydia and her partner Bill, down from New York."

"Welcome to Mississippi, y'all. Come to be with Pete? This family thing all y'all Chinese got going, lots of others could take a lesson." Stafford shook his head.

"We got no patent on it, Big Bone. Nice, though." Pete beamed at me. "But much as I appreciate the company, they've got another reason for being here, too. Lydia and Bill, they're private eyes, come to see if there's anything they can do for Jefferson."

"Private eyes?" Pulling on his beer, Big Bone Stafford looked at me and then at Bill. "Can't recall as I ever met a private eye before. But I can see the boy might need help, especially in view of how he went and let himself out of jail."

"You heard?" Pete said.

"News travels, son. Law's been looking high and low."

"Well, I'm hoping Lydia and Bill can maybe find him before the law does. Big Bone, they got a couple of questions for you. If you got time?"

Big Bone Stafford shrugged. "Show don't start till I'm onstage. Barely know Jefferson, though. Don't see what help I can give."

"Thanks," I said. "It's this: Jefferson was in Burcell a few days ago."

"That so?" Big Bone lowered his beer and looked at Pete.

"Seems to be."

I said, "We don't know why. We're told Burcell's a meth-cooking town, but Bill and I haven't been there yet. Pete says you live out that way, in Oldman's Brake. Can you tell us about Burcell? Is there another reason Jefferson could have had for going there?"

"First off," said Big Bone, "I don't like that 'yet.' Y'all ain't been there, don't go there. Yeah, they's a few folks in Burcell not in the meth trade. They'd be three or four old families and they know enough to steer clear of Fisheye Ferguson—including they wouldn't be inviting outsiders in. Some one of them had business with Jefferson, they'd come out, meet him in Clarksdale, or either at the mall. Sad to say, outsider like him, can't think of no other reason he'd go down there, no."

"Fisheye Ferguson?" Bill asked.

Big Bone drank some beer. "Runs the place, with a couple sons and cousins. Knows what goes on in his town, who's there and who's elsewhere. Folks there, they're in the business. Folks from there don't want to be in the business, best be elsewhere. It's my understanding his boy Johnny and a couple others in that generation are studying on diversifying some, but to Fisheye's mind, they got a good thing going, why mess with it?"

"And what about people in your town? You don't go there?"

"Us from Oldman's Brake, we pass through because the road do, but we don't stop there. Fisheye and his kin, they know us, don't bother us none. Don't none of us want to get tangled up with them. Last time someone done that, it was old Miz McAdoo's son Trevor. Didn't work out so good."

"Someone mentioned Trevor today," I said, turning to Pete, who nodded. "And we saw his brother, Tremaine."

"Ain't y'all lucky."

"They work for the Fergusons?"

Stafford shook his head. "No, ma'am. Trevor was fixing to, couple of years back. Wanted to deal retail. Word was, there was disagreements. Some of the younger Fergusons was against it."

"But you said they're thinking about diversifying."

"The business, not who work in it. They looking to see what else they can be doing besides from what they are. Mighta been okay with shifting weight from production to retail if it wasn't for Trevor being black. On the other side, Fisheye, he don't care for diversifying product. His thinking, they understand the meth business, why go into anything else? But it seem he don't mind who he got working for him if he's gonna make money off it. Especially when he's looking at a whole crop of black customers nobody ain't reached yet. See, y'all, meth's a white drug 'round here. Black people got other sins, but so far, not that one. You bring a black man into the meth trade, could be there's money to be made."

"But it didn't work out?"

"Law got wind of what Trevor was doing, come after him. Some say it was a young Ferguson dropped the dime."

"Even though it could lead back to them?"

"Could've, if anyone'd thought to ask." The curl of Big Bone Stafford's lip made clear that he meant "thought to ask" in the same way Pete meant "bless their hearts." "So Trevor, 'cause the boy was born stupid and never did see no reason to change, he tried to shoot his way out. Plugged a deputy in the chest. Man survived, but a black drug dealer shooting a white lawman in Coahoma County—well, Devil'll be ice-skating the day Trevor gets out of Parchman."

"What about Tremaine?"

"Tremaine, he didn't like Trevor messing with the Fergusons to begin with. He have a better idea. Tremaine the type always have a better idea, long as it don't involve him doing no actual work. Tremaine went and set hisself up in what you might call a related business. Now he deal any kind of poison, long as it ain't meth. See if he can't steal some of Fisheye's customers. Fergusons ain't happy, even though Tremaine, he too parboiled lazy to be any kind of real threat. The law ain't happy neither, 'cause now in addition to meth, we got a local selling horse, coke, crack, and all. Used to be, you had to go to Greenville, or either Memphis, to score any of that."

"So what you're saying is Trevor McAdoo was working for the Fergusons once, and his brother Tremaine's working against them now."

"What I'm saying is," Big Bone Stafford said, "don't go down to Burcell. Fisheye Ferguson'll eat y'all alive." He finished his beer. "Besides, y'all got no call to go. If Jefferson Tam was there, what else is it gonna be about? And whatever it was, not a soul in Burcell gonna tell y'all a word of truth about it anyhow."

Bill looked thoughtful. "Okay," he said. "What about this, though—you said Fergusons who don't want to be in the business better be elsewhere. Are there some?"

Big Bone nodded. "Some folks, even Fergusons, got no stomach for the meth trade. Fisheye's daughter, Anna Rae, left last year, went on over to Oxford, to Ole Miss. Fisheye don't see no need for college—ain't no one else in the family ever been near one—but she's a smart little thing, Anna Rae, and he never could say no to that girl. He have a nephew, Ricky, in Atlanta, I believe, and a cousin, don't recall his name nor where he went to. All of 'em was back for Thanksgiving, likely they coming home for Christmas. Fisheye likes his family around on holidays, calls a truce on the deserters. But that's his rule. Anyone not in deep, they can get out, but that means *out*. Too deep, of course they can't."

Big Bone stood. "Look, good luck, y'all. Hope you can do something for Jefferson, though I got to say, this Burcell business, it don't look good. I'm not blowing smoke about Burcell, about Fisheye Ferguson neither. Pete, you gonna make sure they understand that?"

"Yeah, Big Bone, I will. Thanks."

Big Bone nodded. "Enjoy the show." He signaled the bartender for another beer and climbed the stage steps.

17

We sat through the first set in silence. Big Bone Stafford's deep voice boomed, whispered, howled, and purred. Angel Sewell's drums gave us a soft swishing like rain in the cottonwoods, sometimes a steady beat, all the way up to a thundering pound. The music didn't mean much to me—classical, jazz, and blues are Bill's department; I'm more of a pop, punk, and Chinese opera girl, myself—but I enjoyed the look on Bill's face. I could tell he was following subtleties I didn't hear, making connections I couldn't find.

When the musicians took a break, Bill turned his chair back around to the table.

"You like our music, I see," Pete said.

"I sure do." Bill clinked his beer bottle on Pete's.

"And you, Cousin Lydia?"

"I don't know anything about it, but I'm enjoying it."

"Big Bone, he's the best. They got a couple of young guys coming up, they're pretty good, but I don't know that they'll ever be what this generation is. But listen, y'all . . ." Pete trailed off.

"Yes," I said.

"Me, too," Bill agreed.

"Yes, what? You, too, what?"

"You were going to ask if we think Jefferson might be hiding in Burcell," I said. "We do."

"But—"

"Yes to that, too. If someone in Burcell spent all that time and money helping him put this escape together, it must mean he's worth a lot to them. Which doesn't sound good."

"Not good at all," Pete agreed. He looked at Bill. "This the 'guilty of something else' you mentioned back at the house?"

"I don't know," Bill said. "It's just that, in my experience, things are usually a lot more complicated than they look."

Pete didn't answer, and neither did I. After another minute, Bill spoke again. "As I see it, we have three options. One, we drive over to Burcell first thing in the morning and ask Fisheye Ferguson where the hell Jefferson Tam is." He looked at Pete. "Why do they call him Fisheye?"

"Got one of those walleyes, so he can be staring you down over here when he's looking over there. And you don't mind me saying so, that idea's a stinker."

"I think so, too. Two, we could tell the sheriff why we think Jefferson's in Burcell and let him go do the dirty work."

"That," Pete put down his beer, "stinks worse, because it's got more reasons for stinking. Sheriff finds out the Fergusons broke Jefferson out and stashed him in Burcell, he'll go in there guns blazing. And plus, that friend of Jefferson's, Tolson Reeves, what he told you about the law, everyone knows that. Sheriff's department, or maybe it's the Clarksdale PD, someone's got a leaky pipeline. Law goes into Burcell to flush out Jefferson, could be they'll shoot up the place and never even see his tail disappearing through the cotton."

"And of course," said Bill, "there's the possibility he's not there."

"There is," I said. "Still, it's our best lead. Even if he's not, I'd like to know why he was two weeks ago."

"I would, too. So I'd say—"

"—we need to find a deserter. And since Oxford's closer than Atlanta, and daughter's closer than nephew—"

"—first thing in the morning, we go up to Oxford and talk to Anna Rae Ferguson."

Pete stared at us. "This how you big-city detectives work? List all kinds of dumb things you're not going to do, and then come up with the one that's so obvious, if it was a snake it would've bit you?"

"Generally."

"All the time."

"Well, hell. Where do I get my license?"

We stayed for the second set, and then exhaustion hit. At least, it hit me; Bill would've stayed all night. As we left, he thanked Big Bone and dropped a twenty in the mason jar at the front of the stage.

We were crossing the lot when Pete's phone rang. "You got Pete Tam. Yeah, Pelton, hi. What?" He stopped walking. "Son of a— Well, that's great, they did that. Thanks, Pelton. Yeah, I'll be right by, I got the key. Thanks, thanks, tell the guys I appreciate it."

"What's up?" I asked when he clicked off.

"Those siren locks? They work. One of them went off just now. That was Pelton Dawes. Alarm started shrieking, bunch of the guys from the Down Home Club piled out, saw a car peeling down the street. They walked around the store, and everything seemed okay. Pelton wants to know can I come turn the damn thing off now. Says it's loud as hell."

"Someone tried to break in again?" I looked at Bill. "So maybe they didn't find what they were looking for the first time?"

"And they came back because—?"

"Maybe they have new information." I didn't want to say it, but I did. "From Jefferson."

"Now hold on a minute," Pete said. "You don't mind me saying so, you might be doing a bit too much detecting. Store's empty three days now, whole thing's been in the papers, number one in the gossip.

That's like putting up a neon 'rob me' sign. This is most likely just some of those punks."

"Could be, Pete," I said.

"Yeah, I can tell you don't believe it for a minute. But anyhow, whoever it was, they're gone and us standing here isn't getting that alarm turned off."

We drove over to H. Tam and Sons. From a few blocks away, we could hear an electronic screech slicing through the night. When we pulled up, the door to the Down Home Club was open. A shadow stepped out onto the sidewalk.

Pete waved as he got out of the car. "It's okay, Duverne, it's me."

The shadow, now a man standing under the streetlight, waved back. "Damn good thing you here. That thing driving me to drink." He lifted his beer, gave a gap-toothed grin, and headed back into the club.

Bill and I followed Pete around the back. He punched a combination into the screaming lock and peace flowed in like a river.

"I'm going in the store," Pete said. "See if I can't find some unsquashed bags of chips to carry over to the club, thank them for keeping an ear on the place."

"Pete," said Bill, eyeing the club door as we came back around. "They would've been open last night, right? Maybe someone saw something."

Pete looked at Bill. "You mean, the break-in? Never even thought of that. Could be I'm not ready for that license. But you want to go in there, ask questions?"

"It's the logical thing to do," I said.

"Yankee logic. Down Home Club, like I say, they don't take to outsiders." He looked at Bill. "Particularly, they don't take to white outsiders."

I said, "They seem to like you, Pete."

"Yeah, well, they could get over that fast, I bring 'em the wrong guests. Still, you're right." He paused. "I guess I could go in there myself and ask, but we just now found out I'm not much of a detective. And anyway, they saw you already. I go on in and leave you out here, they'll wonder what we're up to." He rubbed his chin. "All right. But Bill, I notice your way of speaking, it gets more and less Southern, depending on . . . well, I'm not sure what. Can you bleach the South all out of it?"

Bill grinned. "Ya askin' me ta give ya Brooklyn? Or eez thet you vant somevere in da Ukraine?"

Pete snorted. "You mean, a choice between *Goodfellas* or Dracula? Just talk like a normal Yankee." He entered H. Tam and Sons and stopped. "You're not neither of you carrying a gun, are you?"

"We're not licensed down here," I said.

"I notice how that doesn't answer the question."

I smiled. "No, it doesn't. But no, I'm not."

"Me, either," said Bill.

"All righty, then."

We did a quick check inside the store to make sure the would-be intruders had not, in fact, gotten in. Hard to tell, but the mess looked the same and the windows were locked and bolted. We managed to find three undamaged, family-sized bags of potato chips and one of pretzels, and a few cans of peanuts. Pete clutched them in his arms, we locked up, and we crossed the street to the Down Home Club.

18

The faces that turned to us when we creaked open the Down Home Club's door did not look welcoming. Pete went first, bearing gifts, then me, then Bill. In the dim light, I took note of the scarred bar on my left, the card tables and mismatched chairs scattered around the room, the haze of smoke and the beery smell. I searched the shadows for Tremaine McAdoo, the only person I knew to expect in this place, but I didn't see him.

A woman's gravelly voice spilled out of speakers hung from the patched and painted ceiling, singing about her no-good man. No actual women were in evidence. The eyes of the bartender and the men at the tables, maybe a dozen altogether, narrowed when they saw Pete; and when they saw me and Bill, mouths hardened and shoulders tightened.

"Pete—" began the man behind the bar.

"Now, now, Pelton, hear me out before you throw me out."

Since I recognized Pelton as the man who'd been hotly arguing with Tremaine McAdoo earlier, I had no doubt he would, in fact, throw us out if moved to do so.

"First off," Pete said, "I got some little thank-yous here for you gents keeping an eye on the store. Not much, but there's not much left hasn't been trampled underfoot. I guess you heard about that?" He spread his bounty on the bar. "Good, because what happened in there, that's why we're here. Seems it wasn't just some no-accounts or meth heads. It had to do with Leland and all, and maybe if we can figure it out, I can get Jefferson out of jail."

"From what I hear, he got himself out already," said Pelton. "And Pete, I don't know who you got there but—"

"I'm getting to that, Pelton. And I was speaking in the long-term, because the boy's no criminal genius and you know Montel's gonna recapture his ass any minute now. This here's my cousin Lydia, from up in New York, and her partner, Bill."

"He look like po-lice," growled someone from the back of the room.

"Not police, never was," said Bill, all traces of Southern accent gone. He spoke without defensiveness, just correcting a mistaken impression. He seemed relaxed, unaware of the waves of hostility breaking around him, although I was sure he felt them as strongly as I did. "Ex-navy. Private investigator now. Lydia, too. Pete asked us to come down, see if we could help."

"See," said Pete quickly, before anyone else could speak, "Jefferson didn't kill Leland, y'all know that." A few murmurs of assent, shrugs, nods. "I'm just a damn card player, don't know a blessed thing about investigating, except for it's not something you can leave to the likes of Bert Lucknell." More murmurs and a snort. "But these folks, investigating's their business. Now, what happened in the store, someone tearing up the place, that was last night. Didn't even strike me that some of y'all might've been here, until Bill brought it up. So we were thinking, maybe y'all noticed something, like tonight?"

"How come y'all think it have to do with Leland's killing?" I recognized Duverne, the shadow from the doorway. He walked to the bar and ripped open a bag of chips. "That it ain't just some punk-ass kids? Plenty of them to go around."

"Amen to that. Lydia, you want to explain?"

I stepped forward. "Sorry to be interrupting your night, gentlemen, but we could use your help. The way we see it, the store was too much of a wreck for anyone just looking for money or something to sell. We think someone was searching for something, and part of that mess was the search and the rest was to cover it up. We think they came back tonight because they didn't find whatever it was, so they tried again."

"Well," said Duverne, "but even if that right, it don't necessarily follow it have to do with Leland being killed."

"That's true," I said. "But it's a strange thing, isn't it, that Leland was killed right before someone tore his store apart? And as far as helping my cousin Jefferson, it's the only thing we've got."

Silence in the room, except for the rustle of the chip bag going from hand to hand. "Well," said Pelton finally, "I didn't see nothing last night. Or hear nothing, neither. Any y'all?"

Headshakes, shrugs.

Hell, I thought. "What about the car you saw tonight? Can anyone describe it?"

Silence. Then: "Some four-door rambling wreck." That came from the guy who'd thought Bill looked like a cop. "Silver rims, though. Confederate flag sticker on the back bumper, right side."

I'd have expected some reaction to that—grunts, muttered curses—but no one said a word. It struck me that the Confederate flag might be a common sight around here. "Color?" I asked.

"Blue."

"Green."

"Black."

A dark car at night. Okay. "How many people in it?"

A pause. "Two, maybe," said Duverne. "But I ain't sure."

"Black? White?"

Now I got my grunts. "Ma'am, maybe you didn't hear the part about the flag."

Heat rose in my face. "Sorry. Just hoping for more details. Didn't mean to offend."

Nothing at all, except the woman on the stereo singing about some other no-good man.

I tried once more. "I don't suppose anyone caught the license plate?"

One "Is she for real?" and some shaken heads.

Well, it had been a good idea.

19

We thanked the men of the Down Home Club, and we left. The cool quiet of the street returned to me the sense that the world could be a wide, reasonably friendly place.

"Wow," said Bill, grinning as we crossed to the car. "That was like when you took me to that family association in Chinatown."

"Except those old Chinese guys liked you even less."

"Still," said Pete, "you can see why these folks might want to hold onto a place they can call their own, and only their own." He shook his head. "But besides the sociology lesson, we really didn't get anything, did we?"

Before I could answer, a shout jolted me.

"Yo! Wait up."

I spun around to see Duverne striding across the street. He looked at me and laughed. "Relax, ma'am. I just got one more thing to say."

"Duverne, what're you thinking, scaring my relations like that?" Pete demanded. "Cousin Lydia's not used to our ways. Probably when someone shouts after you in New York City, they mean to shoot you."

"Yeah." Duverne grinned. "Like this guy"—he pointed at Bill—"is fixing to shoot me."

"I'm not carrying," said Bill.

"Fisticuffs?" Duverne took an old-fashioned boxing stance.

"If you want."

Duverne dropped his arms. "Nah, next time. Look here, Pete. The nervous lady here said something about some strange thing. Brought to mind another strange thing. Got nothing to do with last night or tonight, neither. But I thought maybe y'all might want to know."

Pete glanced at me. "Okay, Duverne, we're listening."

"See, a few weeks ago, maybe three, four, Leland come out the store with the trash just when I be coming up the street here, heading for the club. He ask do I know someone by the name of Lentitia McAdoo. Well, of course that's old Miz McAdoo, so I tell him I do, but she just die a few days before. He kind of scratch his head, y'know how Leland do, and say, oh, she gone? I ask him why and he say, nothing, just he think he have something of hers."

Duverne stopped.

"That's it?" asked Pete.

"Yeah. It strike me kinda strange, he don't even know who she might be, and he got something belong to her. And asking me about it right after she die. And her always ripping on Chinese, what he gonna have that's hers, anyway? Ain't no way she leave something by mistake in the store because ain't no way she come to the store in the first place. Anyhow, maybe it don't mean nothing. But I always like Leland. Like you, too, Pete. Can't say as much for the company you keeping." He grinned at me again. "But everyone around here hope you planning to keep the store going. And Jefferson, well damn, we seen that boy grow up across the street there. He ain't kill Leland, you can take that to the bank."

Duverne threw a fake punch at Bill, who fake ducked it. Chuckling, Duverne walked back into the Down Home Club.

In the car on the way to Pete's, I asked about Lentitia McAdoo. "She's the mother of Trevor and Tremaine, right?" I said. "Did you know her?"

"Barely ever heard her name before today, when Henry and them talked about her. Never met her. Never met Trevor, neither. And the only dealings I ever had with Tremaine were like yesterday, running into him someplace. Don't believe he even knows my name. Can't imagine what Leland thought he had that might be Miz McAdoo's. Maybe whatever it was, I'll find it when I clean up."

"Pete," I said, "this morning when we saw Tremaine, he and Pelton were having a big argument. Sounded like Tremaine was doing something in the club that Pelton didn't like. Dealing drugs, do you think?"

"Could be. That would make Pelton mad as a hornet. He doesn't want trouble in there any more than he wants blues-trail tourists. Just a place for him and his friends to hang out."

We were all silent for a minute. Then Bill said, "I'm going to come right out and ask this, Pete. Could Tremaine have been dealing from Leland's store?"

Pete's voice went up a notch. "You taken leave of your mind? That's full-out crazy."

"It would explain the searches, if Tremaine's stash was there. It might not have been something Leland wanted to do, but Tremaine might have been a hard man to turn down."

"If Tremaine was threatening Leland, he'd have told me."

"Are you sure?"

Pete's only answer was an angry—but, it seemed to me, not entirely confident—silence.

"Pete," I said, turning around from the front seat, "you understand that we have to look at everything? That's how we do our job."

After a moment, peering out the window into the darkness, he said, "Leland would've told me."

No one spoke again on the drive. When we got home, I pulled out my MacBook Air and hooked up my hotspot. I typed in my New York

State PI license number and password so I could get into the limited-access databases. I was looking for Anna Rae Ferguson.

Pete settled into his worn armchair. With the gruff air of a man making a peace offering, he said, "That laptop there, that's the same as Jefferson's. Except his is a touch bigger. That favored among Chinese?"

"It's a good computer, but I don't know about Chinese," I said. "That cousin I was telling you about in New York, he's got a whole garage full of computer equipment." Something struck me. "Pete, where's Jefferson's laptop? Do you suppose he left it up in Oxford, or did he bring it down here with him?"

"Can't imagine he left it. For geeks like him, that's like leaving your toothbrush. I mean, he toted it over here on Thanksgiving so he could check his wagers while we watched the game."

"Why did he need a computer?" I clicked some keys. "He couldn't remember which teams he bet on?"

"Not how it works, those online sports books."

"Not how what works? You don't bet on teams?" I watched my screen.

"Not real ones. You pick players, could be from all different teams, and you've got them for the week, or the day, or the season—whatever you signed on for. That's your 'team.' Looking at each one's stats, that's how you did."

"And you play against other people who also picked random teams?"

"Not random," Bill said from the other armchair. "You study the talent and pick players who complement each other's skills. Or you could pick dark-horse players you believe in. They have long odds. If they perform, you can win big."

I looked up from my database. "Or lose, I assume, if they don't, which is why they'd be dark horses. What if you go with superstars?"

"You're more likely to win, but not big."

The light bulb went on. "That's what you meant before, Pete, about whales fielding hundreds of lineups? If you're betting on enough combinations, sooner or later you'll hit."

"Yup. And if a couple of your lineups hit big enough, it'll offset the losing you do on the others."

"I get it. And what you said, Pete—I agree. It doesn't sound like fun. All math, no actual sports."

"Spoken like a true jock," said Bill.

"I don't deny it." I clicked into another database. "But Jefferson does it?"

"All the time."

"Hmm. So if he brought his laptop to Clarksdale, do you think it could still be in the store? Or in the house?"

Pete shrugged. "Could be a herd of cows in there, under all that mess."

"I'd love to check it out. Let's have a look tomorrow before we go to Oxford."

"Unless the sheriff has it," Bill said. "Callie Leblanc would know that."

"Damn, you're right. Okay, we can ask her in the morning." Something else occurred to me. "Did Leland have one?"

"A computer?" Pete laughed. "You saw his cash register. When things got complicated, he used Daddy's old abacus. Computer." He shook his head. "And while you're there looking for Jefferson's," he said, his eyes avoiding both of us, "might as well take a look for Tremaine's stash. Which isn't there, by the way."

I smiled and went back to my search. In my third database, I hit pay dirt. It turned up an address in Oxford for one, and only one, Anna Rae Ferguson. It showed no landline, but she did have a cell phone, and after a little coaxing, my database coughed up its number.

"You going to call her?" Pete asked.

"When we get there, if we have to. But I'd rather not. Even if she's not in the family business, she'd probably be leery of phone calls from strangers. Let me think." I did, but nothing popped to mind. As was often the case when that happened, I looked to Bill.

"Facebook," he said.

"Good grief. I had no idea you even knew that word."

"It's not generally in my lexicon," he acknowledged. "But it'll be in Anna Rae's. See if it tells us anything."

I clicked over to Facebook, and of course Anna Rae Ferguson had a page. She also had an Instagram. In a matter of minutes, those sources revealed her fondness for football, chocolate, and a yellow dog named Bozo, whom she missed because he was back home with her big brother, Johnny, in a town I noticed she left unnamed. We saw photos of intramural Ultimate Frisbee games, a line of young women grinning at the camera, excited selfies at a Dixie Chicks concert, and then, there it was: Anna Rae Ferguson behind a coffeehouse counter, smiling as she displayed a heart drawn in the foam of a cappuccino.

I enlarged the photo until I could read the logo on the mug. "Café Café," I said. "Cute." A Google search gave us the café's Oxford address and, as a bonus, the business hours. "Closed now. But they open at six."

"Great." Bill yawned. "You can call them then."

I continued scrolling through Anna Rae's page. "No visible boyfriend." I peered at the photos of smiling college students, always in groups of three or more, the same dozen or so people rotating in and out in different combinations, all of them cheerful, athletic, and white.

"Could be she doesn't have one," Bill said.

I looked up. "Or she has one she doesn't post about."

"Interesting idea." Bill nodded slowly. "You're thinking she's seeing Jefferson?"

"What?" Pete had seemed half-asleep in his chair, but now he perked right up. "Jefferson dating a Ferguson? You two must've been drinking crazy juice over there at the Shacks."

"It might explain why he was in Burcell a few weeks ago," I said. "He told Tolson Reeves it wasn't about drugs, but he couldn't tell him what it was."

"Just hold on here. Boy goes courting to Burcell in broad daylight, what exactly is he keeping a secret, then?"

"Okay, you have a point."

"And her, too," Pete pushed on. "What's keeping Anna Rae from posting it on that Facebook there, if Jefferson feels like he can just breeze in and out of her hometown? Who's she hiding it from? No, that's one of those ridiculous Yankee ideas, probably because y'all are tired. Dating a Ferguson."

I wasn't willing to give up the idea just yet, but we all certainly were tired. We said good night and I went to my room, but before I could sleep, I had one more job to do. I called my mother.

I was hoping she'd be asleep and I could just leave a voicemail, but no such luck. My mother's sleep schedule is a thing of infinite nuance. You're as likely to find her in bed at 8:00 P.M. as you are to find her sewing and watching 3:00 A.M. Cantonese cable TV.

"Hi, Ma, it's me."

"The phone has told me that, Ling Wan-ju. Have you solved the case?"

"No. It's more complicated than it looked."

"How is it complicated? Have you talked to Jefferson Tam? Has he told you what happened?"

"We didn't have a chance. Ma, Jefferson Tam escaped from jail."

"Escaped from jail? He ran away? Where did he go?"

"Nobody knows."

"Someone must know, Ling Wan-ju. Maybe your cousin, Captain Pete Tam, will know. Have you asked him?"

"We're staying with him. I'm in the spare bedroom, Bill's in the basement," I added, because there was no doubt she was about to ask. "Captain Pete's been very hospitable. Though the tea down here is awful. It's a strange place, Ma. I think you and Pa were right not to move here."

"Of course we were." Clearly, my validation of that decision wasn't needed. "Ling Wan-ju, you must find Jefferson Tam. When people escape from jail, it makes them look guilty. It's not good for your cousin to look guilty."

"Ma," I said gently, "it's possible he is guilty."

"No," my mother said, and she couldn't have been more definite. "You must solve this case. Then he will come home."

I stifled a sigh. "Okay, Ma. We're looking for him. But listen, I want to ask you something else. Why didn't you ever tell me we had a politician cousin down here? Reynold Tam, the congressman who's running for governor now?"

I could almost see my mother's look of befuddlement. "Why would you ever have needed to know that?"

"Because he's family?"

"Oh, Ling Wan-ju! We have a very large family, with many things about it that you don't know."

Yes, I thought, *like the fact that your father was a gambler.*

"If I filled your head with every detail about our family, you would never have room for anything else. Will knowing that Reynold Tam is a politician who wants to be governor help you solve your case?"

"No, but—"

"Please concentrate on the work you have gone to the Delta of Mississippi to do. Call me tomorrow when you have accomplished something. Give my best regards to Captain Pete Tam."

With that, she was gone. I let out a sigh, brushed my teeth, and went to bed. I was disappointed not to hear cicadas outside my window, but probably they'd have kept me up anyway.

20

First thing in the morning—all right, it was seven, not six—I made hot black tea without a granule of sugar in it, phoned the Café Café in Oxford, and asked for Anna Rae Ferguson. A peppy, over-caffeinated young woman told me Anna Rae worked the ten to two shift, called me "baby doll," and advised me to have a blessed day. I recommended the same to her, and hung up.

"Detect anything?" asked Pete, coming into the kitchen in khakis and a pink polo shirt. He opened a canister and began spooning grounds into a Mr. Coffee.

"Detected an appointment with Anna Rae Ferguson."

"She know about it?"

"No."

Pete nodded and measured water. Just as coffee aroma began to permeate the air, HB next door set up a wild barking. That turned out to be Bill, coming in through the kitchen. Pete stuck his head out and thanked the dog. I handed Bill a mug of coffee as he crossed the threshold.

"I look that bad?"

"No," I said. He didn't, either; his hair was wet from a shower, and he was freshly shaved. "It's just, I know you won't be able to make breakfast before you have your coffee."

"I'm cooking?"

"I hear you make good omelets."

While Pete showed Bill around the kitchen, I called Callie Leblanc.

She was in early, as I suspected she would be, and not entirely thrilled to hear from me, as I suspected she wouldn't be.

"You have something?" Hearing her clipped words, I could almost see her in her office, shoulder pushing her phone to her ear while she made notes in a file with one hand and tapped her keyboard with the other.

"Just a question. Does the sheriff have Jefferson's laptop?"

A pause, papers rustling. "No. Is it important?"

"I don't know. You're sure?"

Breath hissed. "This office makes it a point to document the items clients are arrested with. And whatever evidence comes in later. Jefferson didn't have a laptop in his possession. Since his arrest, deputies have searched the store, his apartment in Oxford, and his car. They've found nothing else that's been entered in evidence."

Which meant, I realized, no drugs. *Be grateful for small favors.*

"All right. Thanks."

"Why are you asking about the laptop?"

"Nothing specific. But he has one, and you never—"

"If you find it, you'll call me."

This was not a question, so I just said, "Yes," and then repeated, "Thanks," because I had a feeling Callie Leblanc didn't get thanked enough.

After breakfast, we drove to H. Tam and Sons. A sun stronger than yesterday's brought colors and sharp shadows to the buildings and bare trees. The Clarksdale streets were wide, planted, and pleasant, but the cheerful morning sunshine made the empty storefronts and lack of bustle all the more obvious.

"Pete, what happened here? You can see this was a prosperous place. Why the decline?"

Pete tapped the window glass. "King Cotton. Used to be you needed labor, by which I mean actual folks, to plant your cotton, pick it, and bale it. All that's mechanized now, starting forty, fifty years ago. No living to be made as a field hand anymore, so lots of folks left. That means no one to shop in the stores, so they close. Rich planters, they're still here, running their million-dollar machinery up and down the rows. And people like me, who get our living elsewhere. But you're trying to make a few dollars in Clarksdale—hell, anywhere in the Delta these days—it's mighty hard." He sighed. "You know, in some ways, this mechanized farming, it's like that online gambling. What I mean is, what's the point? I know, I know, the point is to make money. But what's it for, you're living by yourself in an empty world?"

"That's pretty poetic there, Pete," said Bill.

"Yeah, sorry. Poetry's a hazard of the gambling trade."

We pulled around the corner. "Look here," I said. "There's Henry an' them."

Pete laughed. Bill shook his head. "I'm warning you, it won't end well."

Henry stood as we parked and got out. "Heard there was some excitement here last night," he said.

"A man can't have secrets in this town, can he?"

"You know that's right. Things okay inside?"

"If by okay you mean same mess as yesterday but not worse, yeah, I suppose so. Whoever they were, they didn't get in. Pelton and them ran 'em off. Couldn't tell us anything about them, though."

Henry's eyebrows went up. "You ask them? At the club?"

"Reception was a little chilly, but they did their best."

"These two go over there, too?"

"They're the detectives."

Henry shook his head. "You full of surprises, Pete. Well, we here to help you clean up."

Pete looked at the three men. "You and Bobby Lee, maybe. Sam's here for his malt."

"I clean up better with a malt," said Sam Shoemaker, grinning his wide grin, rubbing a hand over his shiny head.

"Ain't nothing you don't do better with a malt," grumbled Henry. "Though I can't say as I ever seen you cleaned up."

Pete disarmed the siren lock on the front door. Bill and I followed him in, and the others followed us, Sam propping the door open so fresh air could begin to herd out the ghosts of spilled coffee and stomped Cheetos. Pete flicked on the lights, crossed to a humming cooler, and threw a can of Colt 45 to Sam. "Anyone else?"

"Too early for me," said Henry. Bobby Lee also shook his head. Henry leveled the coffee station and plugged it in. He grunted in satisfaction when the red light came on, and stepped back, searching the debris. Lifting an unbroken pot, he said, "Gonna make some coffee, you got no objection, Pete."

"Why would I object? Knock yourself out. Running water at the sandwich counter. Y'all other layabouts, there's garbage bags, brooms, what have you, over in that closet there. Bill, Lydia, you want to come in the back with me, see if we can find that computer?"

"What computer would that be?" Bobby Lee asked.

"Jefferson's," I said. "A laptop."

"You think it's here?" Sam asked.

"Wouldn't be looking for it if we didn't," Pete said. "Sheriff doesn't have it, so chances are Jefferson left it behind."

Henry washed and filled the coffeepot while Sam grabbed work gloves from the closet. To the sound of rustling and clinking from the store, Bill, Pete, and I searched the back rooms where Leland had lived.

Pete had clearly made a point yesterday of picking up the papers that had carpeted the floor. After a fruitless laptop hunt through the living room—Bill had the kitchen and bathroom, Pete the bedrooms in the back—I took a break and lifted a faded advertising photo of the Great Wall.

"Pete?" I said in the direction of the bedroom door. "Have you ever been to China?"

"Me? Nah." Pete straightened up from where he'd been bending at a dresser drawer. "None of us. Even Daddy, once he was here, he never went back. Sent for Paul and Mama when Paul was about three."

"Paul was born in China? I didn't know that."

"Not surprising you didn't, seeing as how until the day before yesterday you didn't know us Delta kin existed. Yeah, Mama was pregnant when Daddy left China. Couple years later, Daddy'd been working in a store down in Merigold, had himself a stake, was fixing to open a place of his own. Sent for Mama and Paul. Then came the Great Flood."

"Nineteen twenty-seven," I said.

"I'd be impressed, I didn't know who told you that yesterday." Pete snorted, sounding just like my mother. "Towns wiped out, thousands of people in emergency-type tent camps. Malaria, typhus, nothing to eat but canned beans. Daddy didn't want none of that, so he went up to Memphis soon as he could. Worked at some friend of a friend's laundry. Mama and Paul stayed in San Francisco for a few months, then met him up in Memphis. By that time, the water was down. Some towns were just rubble, Merigold included, but Clarksdale was rebuilding. So they came here." Pete looked around. "Kinda looks like the flood came back, ninety years later."

His shoulders slumped, and again, as much to distract him from what we were seeing as anything else, I asked, "Did your daddy tell that story a lot, Pete?"

"Used to tell it all the time. Wanted us to remember how the flood interrupted his family reunion, put off his shopkeeping plans. And how even at that he was luckier than most, because so many people lost family, lost everything." Pete looked at me. "Didn't your folks do that? Tell their story, how they came over, so you wouldn't lose it?"

"Yes. Except I know now that they left out the part about my grandfather the gambler."

"Well, yeah. Some things, you don't necessarily want folks to know. Look here, we aren't finding this computer, are we?"

"Doesn't look like we are," Bill said, joining us from the kitchen. "Maybe we should leave it be, get on over to Oxford."

"'Leave it be'?" I repeated. "'Get on over'? Never in all the years I've known you have I heard phrases like that coming out of your mouth."

"I'm reverting to my roots."

"I think a wise man once said, it won't end well. Oh, wait, not a wise man, a wiseguy."

"Mighty funny, little lady."

Three could play at any game: I rolled my eyes.

As we walked back into the store, Henry was hauling a garbage bag out to the sidewalk. Sam was sweeping, and Bobby Lee, standing in a now-clear aisle, lifted cans and bags of undamaged goods onto the shelves.

"Wow," I said. "It looks great in here."

"Wouldn't go that far," said Pete. "Looks a lot better, though, I'll give you that. I guess y'all aren't as useless as I thought."

"Yeah, we are," said Bobby Lee. "For the most part. Find that computer?"

"No. Don't suppose any of y'all did?"

"That happened, you'd've heard the news."

"Maybe he left it up in Oxford," Henry said.

"Don't think so. He always brought it with him when he came."

"Also," said Bill, "deputies searched Jefferson's apartment in Oxford and didn't find it."

"Local deputies, or Oxford men?"

"Local boys went up there," said Pete.

"Well, then, what they found or didn't find, it don't mean much, do it?" Bobby Lee rubbed his chin. "Still." He walked to the counter. "Pete, I got your permission?"

"To do what?"

"Mess with your register."

"Nothing in it. Be my guest."

Once behind the ornate old register, though, Bobby Lee didn't press any of the keys. Instead, he squatted down and peered up under it, at the bottom of the counter it sat on. "Yee haw." Reaching in, he jiggled something. He pulled out a sheet of quarter-inch plywood and laid it on the floor. Grunting, he stretched to reach farther, and when he straightened up, he handed Pete a silver MacBook Pro.

"Well, butter my butt and call me a biscuit! Bobby Lee Smith, how'd you know where the damn thing was?"

"Didn't." Bobby Lee's grin was wide. "But the shelf, that's what I was counting on."

"Why?" I asked.

Bobby Lee, still smiling, reached to catch a celebratory malt Sam Shoemaker threw him from the cooler. "When I was a kid, I worked after school in a dry-goods store in Greenville. Old Jew named Kreloff, his place. Mighty nice fella. Always give me snacks, Dr Pepper when I wanted. Bought me schoolbooks one year when times was bad. He have a shelf like that, kinda hollowed out from the counter under the register. Like a false bottom in a suitcase, you know?" He pointed to the plywood sheet. "Old man Kreloff keep his passport there, his important papers. His thinking, anyone break in, they gonna open the register. Maybe if they get into the house in back, they gonna go through the desk drawers. But no one's gonna think about under the register. Under the counter *next* the register, sure, because there's shopkeepers keep a sawed-off or a pistol there. But under the register itself, nah. Some of them other Jew shopkeepers, they seen old man Kreloff's shelf and they done the same. So it occur to me, Pete, maybe your daddy, he mighta knowed some of them, shopkeeper to shop-keeper like. He coulda got the idea from them. Might be he built that shelf his own self."

"Bobby Lee, I got to start holding you in higher regard. I grew up here, sometimes run the store for weeks on end, and I never knew the first thing about that shelf."

"I wonder whether that was where Jefferson usually left his laptop?" I said. "To be safe."

"Or," Bill said, "if he hid it when he saw trouble coming."

"Wouldn't've had to be he saw trouble," Henry said. "Jefferson gets his living with that thing. Your tools, you keep an eye on them. Couple of months ago, that friend of yours, Pete, wasn't it something like this someone went off with?"

"Who? Oh, you mean Lucky Culligan?" Pete turned to me and Bill. "A gambler who calls himself 'Lucky,' how about that? Man's just begging to be knocked off his perch."

"Who's he?" I asked.

"Fellow I know. His second ex-wife, or maybe it's his third, lives around here, so he comes down sometimes. Nice enough, but always has some new bright idea. Not one of 'em worth a bar of soap after a week's wash. Yeah, he was down middle of September. Had this new laptop, was gonna make a fortune with it, but for crying out loud,

Jefferson had to show him how to use it. Jefferson liked doing that, too."

Pete looked wistful, as though Jefferson's enjoyment in teaching was something he wished he'd attended to before. "Anyways, just when Jefferson got him up and running on the thing, someone ran off with it. Well, nobody in Clarksdale didn't know by then the thing was the key to Lucky's fortune. Never could keep his mouth shut, Lucky." Pete shook his head. "Lucky was real upset, too, you're right, Henry. So maybe Jefferson, he had that in mind when he went and hid this." Pete looked from me to Bill, and then at the silver rectangle in his hand. "Here, Lydia, you take this thing. I don't even know how to open it."

Belatedly, I thought about prints. "Put it on the counter, Pete," I said, and pulled a pair of latex gloves from my shoulder bag.

Watching me, Sam Shoemaker said, "Well, lah-di-dah!"

I winked at him.

Pete set the laptop on the counter, and I lifted its lid. When I turned it on, the familiar Apple chord rang out, but as I assumed he would, Jefferson had it password protected. I tried a few obvious things—his birthday, which Pete gave me; *Clarksdale*—with little expectation of success. And of success, I had none.

But I had an idea.

The number I needed was on my speed dial. Two rings, and then, "Cuz! Hi! Wassup, homegirl?" A hollow echo told me I was on speakerphone.

"Hi, Linus."

"Hey, Lydia!" came another, more distant shout. Linus's girlfriend and only employee, Trella, must be on the other side of the Queens garage that served as the home of Wong Security. "Want some coffee? I just made a fresh pot."

"Can you live stream it here?"

"No, but we just got a new drone and Linus is dying to test it."

"Yeah!" said Linus. "It's totally bleeding-edge. Bet we could deliver coffee to Chinatown in twenty minutes and not spill a drop."

"It would be still wasted. I'm in Mississippi."

A pause. "Is that a new club?"

"No, it's an old state."

"Oh, wow. Mississippi, the South? For reals? What for?"

"A case. My mother sent me. And Bill, too. We're both here."

"You're on drugs. Auntie Yong-Yun wouldn't send you to the next room with Bill."

"And yet, she did. We have cousins here, Linus. At least, I do. You only sort of do. They're on my father's side."

"Now I know you're on drugs."

"The only drugs they have down here are meth, which may be part of the case, and iced tea with enough sugar to cause hallucinations."

"Bring me some!" called Trella. She had a serious sweet tooth. Maybe I should introduce her to Pete.

"But," I said, "what I do have is a laptop I can't get into."

"Oh, wow, the Bat Signal! Okay, Mighty Mouse is on the way!" I could hear Linus grin as he mixed his rodent metaphors. "What kind?"

"MacBook Air."

I gave him the year and model and he gave me some things to try, but none of them worked.

"It's owned by a serious geek, Linus. The cousin in question, Jefferson Tam."

"That'll make it more fun. But I think we may need to do it up close and personal."

"I'll send it to you."

"Do they have the Pony Express down there?"

"We'll find a way. Let me know when you get it. But Linus, use gloves, okay? In case there are prints. And once you've got everything on another drive, send this to be dusted." Neither he nor Trella commented on my absolute faith in their hacking abilities. No disclaimer, no "We'll try." Everyone should have such cousins.

I gave him the name of the private forensics lab we use. "Tell them it's for Bill Smith."

"The name carries weight?"

"The name carries bourbon. Bill sends them a case at Christmas."

When I thumbed the phone off, Bill asked, "He thinks he can do it?"

"I'm not sure he thinks we're in Mississippi, or even that there is such a place as Mississippi, but the computer, yes, he thinks he can do it."

At that point, we left Pete, the store, and the clean-up crew, took Jefferson's computer with us, and got on over to Oxford.

21

Oxford came much closer than Clarksdale to fulfilling my Southern-town fantasies. No cicadas, no magnolia, no bougainvillea; after all, it was still winter. But brick houses with porches sat on tree-lined streets. A central square with two-story, arcaded, winking-light-strung shops surrounded a grassy island. On the island, a cupola-crowned court-house was fronted by an angel-crowned Christmas tree.

We circled the square twice before we found a parking place. I fed the meter, and we headed first to FedEx, where we shipped Jefferson's computer to Wong Security same-day, for evening delivery. As we walked to Café Café, I texted Linus not to go out clubbing.

Café Café's yellow sign hung under the arcade, presiding over out-door tables occupied by fleece-clad students, December be damned. I found a booth inside while Bill went to the counter to get green tea for me and coffee and a pecan roll for himself. A slim, smiling young woman, blond hair under a yellow Café Café bandanna, took his order and his money: none other than Anna Rae Ferguson herself.

We sipped and nibbled while we watched her. She deftly made change, took an order, and assured someone his latte was on the way, all with athletic grace and a cheery good humor that seemed genuine to me.

I tore my eyes from Anna Rae Ferguson and looked around. "You know, this is the first place since the airport where black people and white people are just hanging around together."

"College coffeehouse," Bill said. "Cutting-edge in sociological developments."

"Am I hearing a touch of cynicism?"

"From me?" He finished his coffee. "There seems to be a lull in the action. Should we?"

"We should."

I got up and wove my way through the tables of students studying calculus, studying Facebook, studying each other. Bill got up, too, leaving our jackets to hold the fort. I asked Anna Rae for a tea and a coffee, and after she relayed the order, I paid her and asked if she was Anna Rae Ferguson.

One of the things about being a short, young Asian woman is that you're not instantly threatening. This isn't so hot in bodyguard work, but it's useful if you're sneaking up on a subject.

"I sure am," Anna Rae replied, tilting her head, still smiling. Probably she was trying to figure out which class she knew me from and what notes I wanted to borrow.

"I'm Lydia Chin," I said, handing her my card. "I'm an investigator from New York. Not police, and this isn't about your family, Anna Rae."

Her smile went to the place smiles often go when people read my card. "What about my family?"

"Nothing. Really. It's about *my* family, and I need your help."

"I'm working."

"It's okay."

Anna Rae glanced over at a young man Bill and I had pinpointed earlier as the manager. It hadn't been so hard: his name tag read, *Freddie, Manager*. From his post pulling cappuccinos, Freddie smiled and nodded at Anna Rae. He waved Bill's card in the air and shooed her along, then handed Bill the coffee and tea I'd ordered, plus a pumpkin spice latte for Anna Rae.

That the card was one of the ones Bill has that identify him as a reporter, and that it had come with a twenty folded behind it, might account for some measure of Freddie's cooperation.

I spoke low to Anna Rae. "He thinks we're doing a newspaper article on nontraditional college sports. Like Ultimate Frisbee."

"I— Who's we?"

"My partner and I," I said as Bill slid into our booth with the drinks. "Please. I need your help. And talking to us will be easier than explaining to Freddie why you're not."

Anna Rae looked again to the manager, who shooed her a second time. A young black woman with curls bouncing out from her yellow bandanna came over from the baked goods counter. "Go ahead, girl. I got you."

"Thanks, Darlaine." Anna Rae managed another smile, but it, too, was gone by the time she'd followed me across the café and into our booth.

I sat next to Bill so Anna Rae wouldn't feel hemmed in. That gesture didn't seem to improve her mood. She spoke low. "What kind of stupid game is this? Who are y'all? Leave me alone."

"Anna Rae, we don't mean to scare you," I began.

"I'm not scared."

Could've fooled me. Anna Rae folded her arms across her chest and gave us what I assumed was her hardest stare.

I said, "Jefferson Tam is my cousin."

That derailed the glare for a moment. "Jefferson? What about him?"

"Do you know him?"

"Sure, I do. He grew up near me. He went to high school with my brother." Still eyeing me with suspicion, she reached for her pumpkin spice latte. "What about him?" she repeated.

"You know he's been arrested?"

"For killing his daddy. Did he do it?"

"I don't think so."

"Good."

"Is he a friend of yours?"

She shrugged. "Guess you could say that. I see him around town sometimes. He lives up here now, you know. We get a drink, now and then go to a game. And killing your daddy . . ." She shook her head.

"Do you know he escaped from jail yesterday?"

Her eyes widened. Then she snickered. "Road Runner beats Wile E. Coyote again. Sorry, y'all, I guess it's not funny. Just, the Sheriff's Department down there in Coahoma County . . ." She shook her head again, still smiling.

"We met a couple of deputies yesterday."

"Not Sheriff Bradley's fault," Anna Rae said, putting her mug down. "Got to give credit where it's due, he tries. But he's just a couple of years in the job, and some of what he inherited, they couldn't find their private parts with both hands and a map." She looked from me to Bill. "But I still don't understand why y'all are here."

Since her eyes rested on Bill, he took it. "Jefferson Tam's escape was well organized, from the outside." He told her how it went, and when he was finished, added, "A few weeks ago, Jefferson was in Burcell."

"He was? When?"

"Just after Thanksgiving."

She was silent for a few moments, I guess maybe expecting more. Bill said nothing else, so she looked to me. I didn't speak, either.

"Hold on a minute here. Y'all are thinking someone in Burcell helped Jefferson to escape? That's just craziness!"

"Is it?" I said.

"Who'd do that? Why?"

"Maybe Johnny? Maybe because Jefferson's gotten to be part of your family's business?"

"*Jefferson?*" She sat back sharply. "I don't know what you mean."

I leaned toward her. "Anna Rae, you family cooks meth in Burcell for distribution in Memphis. We really don't care about that if Jefferson's not involved, but this escape makes it look like he is."

I watched her eyes as she went through her options: pretend surprised insult; hotly deny; silently stand up and leave. At the end she did none of those. Dropping her voice, she said, "Are y'all nuts? Whatever my family does, and I'm not saying it's one thing or another, but it's family business. Jefferson's no part of that, no way."

"Then why was he in Burcell?"

"I have no idea. Maybe he and Johnny had a bet to settle."

"What kind of bet?"

"Who knows? They could have laid money on the game or something."

"What game?"

She stared at me. "Football. The Egg Bowl."

"Ah," I said, full of Pete's knowledge. "Ole Miss versus Mississippi State. They'd have bet on that?"

"There's nobody in Mississippi doesn't have an opinion one way or the other, so why not put a few dollars on it?"

"All right," I said. "We'll look into that. Anna Rae, are you dating Jefferson Tam?"

Her eyes widened, and she burst out laughing. "Seriously, y'all crack me up. Tell me all y'all came to Oxford just to ask me that."

"Are you?"

"Of course not! Me and Jefferson? It's a good one, though." She placed her palms on the table. "I need to get back to work. I hope y'all find Jefferson and I hope he didn't kill his daddy. If I can help any more be sure to let me know." Smiling, she stood and walked away.

Bill and I watched her go. "What do we think?" I said.

"Either she's a really good actor, in which case American history's a waste of a major, or she's telling the truth."

"Meaning, she knows Jefferson, but she's not dating him. I actually believe that, not so much because she told us, but she just doesn't seem as upset as you'd be if your boyfriend had been arrested for murder. But what about Jefferson going to Burcell to pay off a bet?"

"Or collect on one."

"Good point. Either way, it makes Johnny more of a friend of Jefferson's than we knew. Which makes it seem even more likely that he's working with the Fergusons, no matter what Anna Rae says."

"She may not know. She's one of the—what did Big Bone Stafford call them?—one of the deserters."

"True. And let me ask you something else. We think she's telling the truth. All of it?"

"No," he said, looking at her back behind the counter, smiling, taking orders. "No, I think she's hiding something."

"Any idea what?"

"No."

"Me, either. But you know who I'd like to have a word with now?"

"Johnny Ferguson himself?"

"None other."

22

We didn't head directly back to Clarksdale, however. I fed the meter again—I had the feeling Oxford's square was like a New York street, where once you've found a parking place you give it up for no man—and we walked west, toward the Ole Miss campus. Out in this direction, the brick houses gave way to smaller wooden ones, a touch more shambling and bicycle adorned. This was a student neighborhood, and though Jefferson Tam was not a student, his address turned out to be a green clapboard house flying the flag of the Ole Miss Rebels.

"Rebels?"

"Football," Bill told me. "Also basketball, volleyball, baseball, track and field. Probably darts and Ping-Pong. Women's teams, too, by the way."

"Don't they have black athletes?"

"Sure, they do."

"What do they think of being Rebels? Oh, wait, I know. It's complicated. And plus, this is Mississippi."

He nodded somberly. "If that ain't the truth, then grits ain't groceries."

I laughed.

"You like that one?"

"And plus, I like how you said it with a straight face."

We climbed the porch steps under the Rebels flag. The mailboxes told us Jefferson's apartment was number four. "That just shows how far Jefferson's gotten from his roots. Four's an unlucky number. No

Chinese person in his right mind would live in apartment four." I was reaching for the house doorbell when Bill stopped my hand.

"Why draw attention?"

"How are we going to get in?"

"Why, little lady. This ain't the big bad city." He turned the knob. The door was unlocked.

The apartment door at the top of the stairs with the big wooden four on it was not unlocked, but with me keeping an eye out for the other denizens—who didn't appear—Bill had it open in under sixty seconds. We went in, closed it, and stood looking around.

The walls held posters for Skrillex and Deadmau5, and one for the Japanese cyberpunk anime *Akira*. That didn't surprise me. What did was one from a museum show of Chinese paintings, of the Three Friends of Winter: pine, plum, and bamboo. Loyalty, perseverance, and resilience. A flat-screen TV hung on one wall, and controllers for Wii, Xbox and various other video game systems sat on the coffee table. Large speakers flanked industrial metal shelves full of CDs, DVDs, Blu-rays, and the occasional book. A kitchenette took up one wall, and dirty dishes took up the sink.

The air smelled of socks (visible) and un-emptied garbage (not visible, but I could guess). Through a doorway, I glimpsed a linoleum-floored bathroom and a dim room with a storm of an unmade bed. Shades hung on all the windows, but no curtains.

The place was a mess. It was hard to tell single-young-male-computer-geek sloppiness from cops-just-tossed-the-place disarray, though the dishes and the socks were, I thought, a clue.

Bill already had his latex gloves on, from the door-opening process. I snapped mine on and we went to work.

Forty-five minutes later, we'd unearthed nothing. We worked as methodically as possible in the clutter. We weren't looking for anything in particular, and that's what we found. By the time we decided to call it quits I knew what kind of toothpaste my cousin Jefferson used, and that he didn't put the cap back on it; I knew nothing was hiding under his mattress, in the back of his closet, or in the jumble of unconnected socks in his dresser drawer. He didn't keep a journal, or a gun. If the deputies had found those things, they'd have been on Callie Leblanc's inventory list. I didn't know how thorough the deputies had been, but I knew how thorough we were, and finally I peeled off my gloves and suggested we get back to the square before the meter ran out.

The denizens were still not in evidence as we trundled down the stairs. As soon as we stepped out under the Rebels flag, though, I felt eyes on me. On the next-door porch sat a middle-aged woman with a tight blond perm and a thin, sour face. She was staring straight at me, so I smiled and waved as I started down the porch steps.

"Are y'all looking for that Oriental boy?" she called. "He's not coming back. Got himself arrested." She sat back smugly.

"He did?" I said, as though this were news to me. I gave Bill a tiny stay-back hand gesture and turned along the sidewalk to the neighbor's house. Bill stopped at the bottom of Jefferson's stairs to light a cigarette. "What for?" I asked the sour lady.

She sipped from a purple porcelain cup, holding the matching saucer in her other hand. A wreath of artificial lilies and violets decorated her door. At her feet, a small dog with a lavender bow stood up and growled. "Hush, Pixie," the lady said, in a tone that, to the contrary, implied she'd growl at me herself if I came much closer. She looked over at Bill, who had his phone out and was pretending to text, which I don't think he has any idea how to really do. The dog settled down, and the lady leaned forward and dropped her voice to a conspiratorial whisper. "They say he killed his daddy," she told me, and narrowed her eyes in satisfaction. "I declare, I don't know what these young people are capable of." From the way she looked at me, I got the sense that *young* wasn't Jefferson's only flaw. I was about to thank her for the update and turn to leave when she sniffed and said, "I always knew that boy was no good."

I paused. "Really? Why?"

She eyed Bill, then shifted her gaze back to me. "It's my belief people should stick to their own. I have no argument with Orientals, or with colored, either, but too much mixing just isn't natural."

"Just give me a minute, Mr. Smith," I called over to Bill, and he waved a thumbs-up. Back to the lady, "My real estate agent. He'll wait. Could you tell me what you mean? Does that young man not keep to his own?"

She seemed to relax on the news that Bill and I weren't involved in a mixed-race romance; and just like the gossips I grew up surrounded by in Chinatown, she didn't for a second stop to consider why, if I was just a random apartment hunter, I'd ask her to tell me more about someone I presumably didn't know.

"His name is Jefferson Tam, or some such." Waving her hand exactly like my mother's friends, she pretended not to care about the information she'd just superciliously imparted. "Not that he did me the courtesy of coming over to introduce himself, neighbor to neighbor. None of them do, those students. They think the neighborhood is one big hotel, where they can come and go and let other people clean up their messes. I swear the number of times I've had to clean their garbage off my lawn—"

"I know what you mean about students," I said in my most sympathetic voice. "They can be so inconsiderate. I'm a secretary, myself. I just got a new job here. I hear Oxford's a wonderful place to live."

At this, the lady softened a touch, giving me a small, condescending smile.

"But students . . . " I shook my head. "Are this Jefferson Tam's friends worse than most students?"

Now came a sneer of distaste. The lady took a sip and put her purple porcelain down. I just stood there, smiling kindly. Finally, she said, "No. I can't fairly say they are." She spoke in an aggrieved tone, as though it were unreasonable of Jefferson and his friends not to demonstrate the debauchery of which she knew they were capable. "But still, it's wrong."

"What is?"

"Bringing those people here. Why, as far as I can see, the boy doesn't even know any other Orientals."

"Then who does he bring here?"

She leaned forward again. "That big bald colored boy," she said. "And the skinny, smiley blond girl. Sometimes all three of them, here at the same time! It's just so wrong."

23

I was tempted to take the arm of my real estate agent as we walked away, because I knew that would make the neighbor lady gnash her teeth. But I maintained a prim silence and a proper distance until Bill and I had sauntered another block and turned the corner. Then I relaxed into my normal New York stride and told Bill what she'd said. I had to make air quotes around "colored boy," but I got the words out.

"Big and bald?" Bill said. "She didn't happen to tell you his name?"

"Did she have to?"

"We may be jumping to conclusions."

"So let's jump. Tolson Reeves told us he sees Jefferson when Jefferson comes to Clarksdale. He never mentioned anything about up here."

"We didn't ask."

"We asked if they were still close. He sidestepped, but if this is him, it's obvious they are."

"Or at least close enough for Reeves to visit Jefferson's apartment."

"If my apartment looked like that, I'd only let my close friends in. The question is, why hide it? If this guy is Tolson Reeves, I want to know why the big secret, and if it isn't, I want to know who it is."

"And the blond girl?"

"Skinny? Smiley?"

"Anna Rae did tell us she knew Jefferson."

"And went to games with him. Not to his apartment. In the company of Tolson Reeves."

"It may not be either of them."

"Uh-huh. And grits may not be groceries. Let's go ask her."

We were stymied on that plan, however. When we returned to the square and entered Café Café, we found Anna Rae Ferguson gone.

I called her cell phone, got voice mail, left a message in a neutral voice saying I had another question and could she give me a call back, and hung up without a lot of hope. I looked around.

"If Anna Rae's shift is over, it must be past two," I said.

"Yup."

"And we haven't had lunch yet, have we?"

"Nope."

"Good. I have an idea. What can I get you?"

He checked the blackboard. Panini, wraps, salads: the universal food language of college coffee houses.

"Ham-and-cheese panini."

I should have known; it was the thickest, gooiest, unhealthiest thing on the menu.

No customers were at the counter, but Darlaine, who'd taken over for Anna Rae earlier, was behind it. "Hi!" she said when I walked up. "Y'all looking for Anna Rae? Her shift's done, she left already."

"That's okay, we'll catch up with her later. But we're hungry, so we thought we'd have lunch. Besides, I want to ask you something, too."

"Me?"

I gave her our lunch orders. She passed them through a cutout to the fellow at the grill, then turned back.

"You don't play Ultimate Frisbee, too, do you?" I asked.

Darlaine grinned. "Tried it once. Got hit square in the mouth. Gave that game up so fast! Don't know what Anna Rae sees in it."

"I've been hit in the mouth myself. Pretty unpleasant." I didn't mention that the occasional scuffles I got into in the course of business had nothing to do with Frisbees. "Anyway, that's not really what I wanted to ask you about." I'd led with that to determine if Anna Rae had said anything to Darlaine about the real subject of our conversation. It sounded like she hadn't, so I went on. "It turns out I have a distant cousin here in Oxford, but I don't know where to find him. I bet everybody comes into this place sooner or later, right? Do you know him?" I took out my phone and showed her Jefferson's photo.

She wrinkled her forehead. "I can't really be sure, because—" She stopped herself and threw me a quick, awkward glance. She'd so obviously been about to say, "y'all look alike," that I almost finished the sentence for her, but instead I just cocked my head and looked hopeful. Clearly relieved, she said, "Yeah. I think I did see him, a couple of times. Matter of fact, last time was a few weeks ago, when Anna Rae's brother was here."

"Anna Rae? Wait, my cousin knows Anna Rae's brother? Or you just mean they were here at the same time?"

"No, they came in together. Not the first time, either. I mean, if he's the guy I'm thinking of." She tapped the photo.

"Wow," I said. "What are the chances? Anna Rae's brother."

Darlaine nodded. "Johnny. Anna Rae misses her big old dog, so Johnny brings it up here, time to time. Anna Rae's people don't live but an hour from here, down in the Delta, but she doesn't go home much."

No, only during truces. "And my cousin came here with Johnny and the dog?"

"Yes, ma'am." She pointed to the sidewalk tables. "They sat out there. Because of the dog. Can't bring it in here, law says so. Also—" She looked around; I followed her eyes and located the manager straightening the magazine rack. He couldn't have heard us over Tom Petty from the speakers, but Darlaine lowered her voice anyway. "Also, because they were gambling."

I dropped my voice, too. "Playing cards or something?"

Darlaine shook her head. "Online. DraftKings or FanDuel one. On your cousin's laptop. They did it in here before, but Freddie said they couldn't. Probably if he knew they were doing it outside he'd make them stop, too. Freddie doesn't hold with gambling."

From behind Darlaine, a bell clinked. She turned, picked up Bill's panini and my salad, and put them on a tray. I got coffee and ginger tea to go with them. "You don't have any idea where I could find my cousin, do you?" I asked.

"No, sorry. But I bet Anna Rae does. You'll be talking to her again, won't you?"

"Oh, yes," I said, picking up the tray. "We sure will."

24

"So Jefferson Tam sits out in the sunshine and gambles online with Johnny Ferguson." I'd recounted Darlaine's story to Bill as we ate. "Both of them on one laptop. Sure sounds like a buddy movie to me."

"Doesn't prove they're in the drug business together."

"Isn't that supposed to be my line? You say it looks like my cousin's a drug dealer and I jump to his defense."

"Sorry. It looks like your cousin's a drug dealer."

"You may be right," I said glumly. "My mother isn't going to like this."

We finished our lunch in silence.

"Any other business we have here in Oxford?" Bill asked.

"Not that I can think of. I'm a little less charmed by the place than I was before."

"In that case, let's leave."

We considered holding an auction for our parking place—it even still had eighteen minutes on the meter—but in the end we just drove off, leaving it to whoever had the best parking karma.

We motored down the highway, listening to hill-country blues on the radio. Bill explained the difference between that and the Delta blues Big Bone Stafford had played last night—fewer chord changes, more percussion, a kind of hypnotic effect—but though I enjoyed it, I couldn't have distinguished between them.

At one point, a highway patrol car came up behind us. Bill was driving five miles under the speed limit. Unusual for him, but *this is Mississippi*. The cops pulled out and passed us soon enough.

We were almost back in Clarksdale, having rolled through the once obviously lovely, now picturesque in a ruin-porn kind of way, town of Marks, when another law enforcement vehicle slid into our rearview mirror. This time it was a Coahoma County sheriff's cruiser, light bar flashing.

Bill pulled over beside a plowed and empty field. The cruiser stopped behind us and, surprise, Bert Lucknell and Tom Thomson climbed out.

Bill lowered his window. Lucknell sauntered over, bent down, and said, "Afternoon, folks. Find him?"

I leaned over. "Find who?"

"Jefferson Tam, ma'am." Lucknell spoke with the patient air of a smart man humoring a woman who thought, mistakenly, that she was also smart.

"No, sir," I said, paralleling his *ma'am*. "But I can't deny we'd be happy if we had."

"I imagine you would. If I found him, I'd be happy, too. I got to admit that what doesn't make me happy, ma'am, is civilians interfering with a law enforcement investigation."

"I completely understand, sir. And I assure you, we won't do that."

"Well, I'm pleased to hear it. Can I ask where y'all are coming from?" With each question, Lucknell looked at Bill, but Bill said nothing, leaving it to me.

"Driving around," I said. "To see some of your great state."

"Anyplace in particular catch your fancy?"

"No."

"Y'all wouldn't have been over in Oxford, chasing down that cousin of yours?"

"We did go to Oxford. I'd been told it was beautiful. And we stopped by Jefferson's apartment. I wanted to get a sense of this cousin I've never met."

"A sense. Did you get much of *a sense*?"

"Yes, sir. He plays Xbox and he really should take out the trash."

Lucknell nodded. With no change in his tone, he said, "I'd be deeply obliged if from now on y'all would plan to stay as far away from this investigation as a person could think how to do. In fact, if y'all headed back to New York City tonight, that might be best. Go ahead and say goodbye to Captain Pete, and I'll send over a police escort for the trip to the airport, how about that? In case there's traffic, or any other kind of a difficulty."

"That's kind of you, sir. But Pete asked us to stay on for a while. My mother really wants the family to get to know each other. Sir."

Lucknell's steady gaze didn't waver. "Ma'am," he said, "please don't piss down my leg and tell me it's raining. Call it 'getting to know the family,' or whatever else, but y'all were rooting around in my case. I do want to say that right now the only thing stopping me from running y'all in is your other cousin, the one who wants to be governor. I don't care for him, myself, and crossing him wouldn't lose me any sleep. But Sheriff Bradley, he wants to keep people happy, meaning Democrat Party people, because the sheriff's got an election of his own coming up this fall. So it's been suggested I make allowances for the fact that maybe y'all don't know how we do things around here."

I thought the wisest response to this was silence. Bert Lucknell took a long pause, too, and then said, "But I got an itchy feeling I might be running out of allowances. Y'all have a nice day." He turned, lumbered back to the cruiser, and waited for Silent Tom Thomson to climb in.

Once Lucknell's car was out of sight down the road, Bill started ours again.

"Wow," I said. "We've just been threatened by a Southern sheriff."

"Deputy."

"Why doesn't that make me feel better? Can he really arrest us for going to Jefferson's apartment?"

"He can arrest us for looking at him cross-eyed. He wouldn't be able to hold us, but I have an itchy feeling the time between the arrest and the release might be long and leisurely."

"And do you also have an itchy feeling they were lying in wait for us?"

"That, too."

"Two questions, then. One, Coahoma County can afford to have its deputies just lounging around until their prey turns up? Okay, that's not a real question. The real one is, how did he know where we'd turn up? And the corollary—did he figure we'd been in Oxford because that's where this road goes, or did he figure we'd be on this road because it's how you get back to Clarksdale from Oxford? In other words, because he already knew we'd been there?"

"I'd say the latter."

"And you'd say that the highway patrol car that didn't pull us over told him we were coming."

"I would."

"So he's been keeping track of us, and asking his brothers in law enforcement across the state to do the same. And now he's warning us off. The question, then, is why?"

"And the corollary—since he presumably knows there's nothing to find in Jefferson's apartment in Oxford, because his brothers in law enforcement already found nothing, what was he really warning us not to do?"

"That's not actually a corollary, you just wanted to use my fancy word. But the answer would probably have to do with what else we did in Oxford."

Bill glanced over at me. "Anna Rae Ferguson."

"So. We are, once again, being warned away from the Fergusons. Did she call Lucknell, do you think, or did she call some other Ferguson, who called him?"

"Does it matter? It means Lucknell and the Fergusons are a little too close to make me happy."

"I don't imagine your happiness is one of their priorities."

"As long as it's one of yours."

Route 278 came to an abrupt end, depositing us on Martin Luther King Jr. Boulevard. I took out my phone to call Pete. Before I'd pressed a single number, it rang in my hand.

"Callie Leblanc," I told Bill, and then answered the call.

"Ms. Chin," the public defender's clipped voice said, "can you come to my office? There's something I want to discuss."

"Now?"

"If possible." And, the implication was, if impossible, try a little harder.

"We're just coming into town. We'll be right over."

I told Bill we'd been summoned.

"That's handy. We can talk to Tolson Reeves while we're there."

"Exactly what I was thinking."

I called Pete.

"Well," he said. "The detectives. How'd it go?"

"Not sure. We were on our way to pick you up, but Callie Leblanc wants to see us. Can you hang out at the store a little longer?"

"Seeing as I grew up here, I suppose I can. What does she want?"

"No idea. We'll talk to her, and then we'll be along directly."

Bill shook his head sadly at my phraseology. We hit downtown Clarksdale and parked two doors up from the storefront office of the Coahoma County public defender.

25

The receptionist spoke over her headset to Callie Leblanc and then pointed us to a windowless conference room carved out of a corner in the back. I scanned the bull pen as we crossed it, but Tolson Reeves was not in evidence.

Bill and I sat at a battle-scarred laminate table. Through the open door I saw Callie Leblanc and a young, freckled black woman heading over. They joined us, the young woman closing the door behind them.

"This is Sarah Byrne, one of our attorneys," said Callie Leblanc. "Lydia Chin—Jefferson Tam's cousin—and Bill Smith." We all shook hands, and the two public defenders sat across from us.

"We have a weekly meeting," Callie Leblanc said, "to discuss the progress of cases. Other than that, we work independently, so I didn't know Sarah's information until now. Sarah?"

The young woman sat forward. "I have a client at Parchman Farm—the state penitentiary. Trevor McAdoo." Sarah Byrne had clearly studied at the Leblanc School of Wasting No Words.

"We've heard of him," I said. "He shot a deputy in the course of a drug arrest."

Callie Leblanc tilted her head. "You're well-informed."

"Thank you," I said, though I wasn't sure she meant it as a compliment.

Sarah Byrne continued, "Trevor's doing twenty to life, which is the best I could get him. A few days ago—Monday—he called me to come down. I went, and he had an odd request. He wants to speak to Reynold Tam."

"He does? To Reynold? Why?"

Callie Leblanc said, "I'm correct that Congressman Tam is Jefferson Tam's uncle?"

"Cousin," I said. "Actually, first cousin once removed. Though that's a distinction Chinese people don't really make."

"Mississippians don't, either," she said with faint amusement, the first trace of any emotion besides annoyance that I'd seen in her.

I asked, "What did he want to see him about?"

Sarah Byrne said, "I don't know. He wouldn't tell me, and he won't put it in writing because anything he writes to go outside will be read by prison authorities, even if it's being carried by his attorney. He said, 'Just tell Tam he'll be happy if he comes and sorry if he doesn't.' I warned him against threatening a congressman. He smiled and called for the guard. That was all—the meeting was over."

"What did you do?"

"I conveyed the request to the congressman's office, but I didn't expect Mr. Tam to go and, of course, he didn't. His office said they'd need more information to even consider it. I told Trevor that and he still refused to tell me any more."

"So we don't know what it's about?"

"No," said Callie Leblanc. "But I found it strange that a lifer on Parchman asked to speak to a gubernatorial candidate the day before the candidate's cousin is murdered and another cousin is arrested for it."

"I agree."

"As an office," Callie Leblanc said, "there's nothing we can do. Or should do. We have two separate cases. In one the client's disappeared and in the other the client won't say anything more. I called you because I thought you'd want to have this information. Now we need to get back to work. Thank you for coming." She stood, and Sarah Byrne stood with her.

"Thank you," I said, standing also. "You wouldn't mind if we went to see Trevor McAdoo?"

"He can have whatever visitors he'll see. We don't control that."

"But," Sarah Byrne added, "you can't see him until next week. He's back in solitary."

"Why?" I asked, and Callie Leblanc also turned to the younger woman.

"For one thing, he's a troublemaker who won't keep his head down. For another, he shot a cop. Even with your head down, that can land you in a world of hurt at Parchman."

The two attorneys stood waiting for us to exit their conference room. "Is Tolson Reeves around?" I asked. "We'd like to speak with him again."

"He has a class tonight. He's already gone to Oxford."

Damn. I wondered if he'd see Anna Rae Ferguson and if she'd complain to him about us. Or if he'd complain to her.

The attorneys went back to their desks, and Bill and I crossed through the bull pen, where work showed no signs of slowing down even this late in the afternoon.

"Well," I said once we were back on the street, "you sure were quiet in there."

"Seemed like a women's conclave to me. Didn't want to disrupt the solidarity of sisterhood."

"Noble of you."

"That's me, chivalrous to my core. And plus, psychic."

"How so?"

"I know exactly what you're thinking right now."

"Is that a fact?"

"Uh-huh. Two things. One, this is even more interesting, though unfortunately maybe less strange, than Callie Leblanc knows. Trevor McAdoo's bid at Parchman goes back to a connection to the Fergusons, and Jefferson, whose politician cousin Trevor's asking to see, may also be involved with the Fergusons. Which makes the whole thing smell of blackmail."

"I hate to be thinking that, but yes, you're right. What else am I thinking?"

"That maybe we can't talk to Trevor McAdoo until next week, but there's someone else who might know what he wanted with Reynold Tam."

"Two," I said.

"Two what? I get two points for my psychic genius?"

"Two someones who might know. You only get a half a point." I leaned on the car, took out my phone, and called Frank Roberson.

"Cousin Lydia!" he answered, which told me he'd been as efficient in entering numbers into his phone as I had. "Great to hear from you so soon." Voices murmured in the background, and I wondered if he was at a campaign event.

"Is this a good time? I have a question."

"Setting up for a rally, but go ahead."

"Thanks, I'll be quick. Jefferson Tam's lawyer just told us there's a lifer on Parchman who wants to talk to Reynold."

"Yes, the staffer who took the call passed it to me. I told the attorney we'd need more information before we'd consider it. Actually, between us, I'm not sure what would make us ever consider it, but certainly not a blank-check request."

"You don't think it's strange? Especially with Leland's murder and all?"

"Well, the request came the day before Leland was killed, so it's a little hard to see how they could be connected. And no, this kind of thing isn't so unusual. All kinds of people want to talk to politicians all the time. Part of my job is to keep them away."

"What would a convict want?"

"I imagine he thinks he has information about something—maybe a fellow prisoner—and if he gives it to Reynold, Reynold can help him get some kind of a better deal."

"How?"

"No way, really. A congressman doesn't have that kind of influence at a state prison. But he may not have thought it through. It may be more of a power thing. Dragging a congressman down to Parchman— you can imagine how that makes a guy look to the other convicts."

"Has it happened to Reynold before, this kind of request?"

"Lots of strange people, but not convicts before. I've heard of it from other peoples' staffers, though."

"So you have no idea what this was about?"

"None. I have to tell you, the couple of times I've heard about, it never came to anything. Once, a guy had real information, but there was no reason to involve a congressman. He ended up talking to the prosecutor. If there's anything here at all, it's probably something like that."

"Okay, thanks. If you hear any more about it, would you let me know?"

"I don't expect to, but will do."

"Good luck with your rally. Tell Reynold hi."

I slipped the phone back into my bag and told Bill what Frank Roberson had said.

"You think he's right?" Bill toed out the cigarette he'd been working on.

"Could you please put more skepticism into your voice?"

"I think that's all I have."

"Well, as it happens, I agree with you. It's not that I don't believe in coincidences, but this is a particularly odd one. I'd love to know what it's about."

"Well, then, you're thinking: let's get in the car."

That was exactly what I was thinking, though as to Bill's psychic abilities I remained in doubt. Leaving yet another parking meter with time on it, we headed out to see if we could find the other someone, Tremaine McAdoo, at home in Oldman's Brake.

26

"What's a brake?"

We'd left Clarksdale and were traveling a flat road between stubbly fields. By June, according to Bill, this would all be waist-high cotton, green and white under broad blue skies. Now, though, the occasional bare tree was the only thing mediating between gray clouds and dull brown earth.

"Canebrake," Bill said. "The South has a native grass, called cane. It's kind of like bamboo."

"You're just saying that because I'm Asian."

"It grows up to eight feet high. A thick stand of it is called a brake."

"Because . . . ?"

"It stops you from going through it." Bill turned the car off the asphalt onto a smaller, bumpier track. As we drove, brush and scrub trees began to crowd the road.

"That's a little anticlimactic. Speaking of going through, you realize we're going to go right through Burcell?"

"We're coming up on it now."

"And we did want to speak to Johnny Ferguson."

"I say we try Tremaine McAdoo first and Johnny second."

"Agreed. But as we pass through town, keep an eye out for stray young Chinese men."

The real chances of seeing Jefferson Tam, if he was in fact hiding out in Burcell, were slim to none, and while we rolled slowly through town, no Asians appeared. Very few of anybody appeared, in fact, though those who did—a man on his porch and a woman carrying groceries into her house—turned to watch us pass. The road took us by the bar Tolson Reeves had mentioned. It was called Rupert's, it had an unlit Bud sign in the dusty window, and it may have been open, but if so, you couldn't tell. Burcell was pretty, as Reeves had said, with neatly painted wooden houses, Christmas lights in the windows, flowerpots by the doors. We saw one or two trailers, though even those looked well-kept, and the occasional derelict car up on blocks in a side yard, but you see those in New Jersey, too.

"Small," I said as we left the last house behind, about ninety seconds after we'd driven by the first. "Doesn't even look as though it has any streets besides the main one."

"There'll be houses down some unpaved twists and turns, but yes, I think that's pretty much it."

"Did you notice that some of the yards had Mallory signs, and none of them had Tam signs?"

"I did."

"This is Mississippi?"

"The Mississipiest."

Potholed asphalt gave way to rutted, gravelly dirt. The brush and trees thickened until I felt like the track we were driving was barely tolerated by the woods, subject to being choked off whenever the plant life felt like it. The scent of damp earth rolled in our open windows. Bill deftly avoided a few craters, steered around a wide curve, and I found myself blinking as a clearing released a flood of light from the gray sky. We'd arrived at Oldman's Brake. At least, I hoped that's where we were, because the road had ended.

Bill turned off the car and we sat facing a group of wooden houses. Scattered with what looked like no particular organization, they covered the muddy flat between the end of the road and a dense stand of eight-foot-high grass, no doubt the famous cane. A few cars and pickup trucks rested on the flat beside us.

Muddy, grassless paths between the mostly one-story houses connected them or swerved around them. Some houses had porches. Some were shacks. Some were painted, some had once been painted, and some had never been painted, insulation patching their flanks. Two houses were strung with Christmas lights, and through the window of a third I could see a decorated tree. The cool air smelled of damp and faintly of coffee, and it rustled with the sound of wind in the cane.

"That's the levee." Bill pointed to the slope on our left as we got out of the car. I realized I'd never given much thought to what a levee actually was.

"Basically it's a hill? Man-made?"

"Right. If the river rises it's supposed to keep the land from flooding."

"That big flood in twenty-seven—they didn't have levees then?"

"They didn't hold. These are higher. Still, if the river tops the levee here, Oldman's Brake is in for a bad time."

I thought about what that bad time would look like: people standing on the levee, maybe in the pouring rain, or in the deceitful sunshine because the rain was upstream, watching the water just keep rising. Running down, grabbing family photos, throwing armfuls of clothes into their cars, their pickup trucks, racing away. Or hoping the levee would hold, until it was too late, then climbing out the windows onto their roofs to pray. And what had it been like in 1927, when cars and weather forecasts were fewer, the levees lower, and the flood epic?

I shook my head. We had business here.

I was about to wonder out loud how to go about finding Tremaine McAdoo when the answer—and the source of the coffee aroma—offered itself. A screen door creaked and Big Bone Stafford, mug in hand, appeared on the front porch of one of the painted houses.

"Hey! Pete's detectives! What are y'all doing down here?" He frowned. "Don't tell me y'all was just now in Burcell."

"No, sir," I said. We walked across the lumpy ground to stand before his porch. "We passed through but didn't stop, just like you said."

"Don't recall saying y'all should come down to Oldman's Brake, but I didn't say stay away, neither, I guess. Y'all got more questions? Want some coffee?"

"We'll take a rain check on the coffee, thanks," I said, though Bill will sit and drink anyone's coffee at any time of night or day. "And we do have questions, but they're not for you. We're looking for Tremaine McAdoo."

"Tremaine?" He raised his eyebrows. "Y'all are thinking Tremaine got something to do with Leland and Jefferson?"

"We're not sure. We just want to talk to him."

Big Bone sipped his coffee. "Well, if Jefferson's hanging around Burcell, I don't suppose it's a particularly long step to Tremaine. That's his place over there." He took another sip, then rested his cup on the porch railing and lumbered down. "I best come with y'all. Tremaine ain't the friendliest of gents."

"We've seen him," I reminded Big Bone.

"Well, then."

We walked together toward a house backing onto the cane. No Christmas decorations here. Curtains in the open windows swayed in the breeze. The pale blue paint, though a few years old, had been applied with care. "Watched those boys grow up here," Big Bone said. "Trevor, might've been some good in him once, but big brother Tremaine, that boy was always a difficulty."

"Is this where their mother lived? The lady who died recently?"

"This's it. Sons stopped with her, too, and Lunetta from when she come down from Chicago to when she have her stroke. Now she at a nursing home. Tremaine don't even go see her, from what I can tell. I go from time to time, bring her a box of fudge, sit with her, just so she don't feel all alone in this world."

A door banged as a man carrying a lunch box stepped out of a house. Big Bone Stafford waved to him. The man returned the wave and walked over to us.

"Big Bone."

"Hardison."

The overall-dressed man nodded to me and Bill. "How y'all doing? Friends of Big Bone's?"

"Lydia Chin," said Big Bone. "Cousin of Pete Tam, over to Clarksdale. And Bill Smith. Hardison Lambert."

"Pleasure, sir." Bill shook Lambert's hand. I echoed the sentiment and did the same.

"Y'all friends of Tremaine, too?"

"Actually, we were hoping to have a word with him," I said. "Why do you ask?"

Lambert squinted at Bill. "Guy came yesterday to see Tremaine. Thought it might be you. But you bigger than him."

"A guy came yesterday?" Bill asked.

Lambert nodded. "White feller, ain't seen him down here before. He go on over to Tremaine's place. Us down here"—he nodded to Big Bone—"we keep a eye out. Well, y'all have a good day now." He turned to leave.

"Wait," I said. "If you have a minute."

Lambert turned back.

"This man. Would you recognize him if you saw him again?"

Lambert shook his head. "No, ma'am. He have his hoodie up, and big old sunglasses. Plus, it starting to get dark. No, can't say as I would."

"So," I said, "he might have been Chinese?"

Lambert looked at me and smiled. "I suppose he might've. Never thought of that. Don't get many white folks down here. Don't know as we ever had us a Chinese before. Until you, ma'am," he added courteously. "Alls I can say is, the feller ain't black, and he ain't as big as you." That last was directed at Bill.

Bill asked, "Did you see what he was driving?"

"White four-door, or maybe tan. That time of day, hard to tell. Not local, though. Alabama plates."

"Thanks," I said. "Sorry to delay you."

Lambert nodded and continued to his car.

Big Bone eyed me. "You're not thinking your cousin Jefferson come here to see Tremaine?"

"I hope not. But I'd like to be sure."

"If Tremaine's in the drug business, couldn't it have been a customer?" Bill asked Big Bone.

"Better not be. That's what Hardison meant, we keep a eye out. Tremaine don't conduct business down here. Been asked politely."

Big Bone didn't crack a smile. I was sorry I'd missed that community meeting.

We reached the blue house. Big Bone stopped and called, "Yo! Tremaine! Got some folks here want to talk to you!"

No sound but the wind scraping through the cane.

"Tremaine!"

Big Bone walked up onto the porch and pounded on the door.

"Tremaine!"

Still no response.

"I suppose we have no reason to expect him to be here," I said.

Big Bone thumbed toward the flat. "That his pickup right there." I remembered the truck peeling out from the Down Home Club. Big Bone tried the door knob. It didn't turn.

"Hmmph." Big Bone left the porch, and we followed him around the house, where he pulled on the handle of a rear door. "Tremaine!" The door opened with no argument.

Big Bone took one step inside and stopped, his bulk filling the doorway. "Oh, shit," he breathed, and for the first time in Mississippi, a man didn't apologize to me for swearing.

He backed out. I saw Tremaine McAdoo lying beside an overturned chair on the kitchen floor. A messy red hole in his chest explained the congealing pool of blood under him. His wide eyes looked surprised, as if being shot hadn't been what he'd expected.

Bill said, "Stay back," and took one long careful stride into the kitchen. A fly rose lazily from the blood puddle as Bill checked for a pulse in Tremaine's neck. I knew someone had to do it and I felt guiltily glad it didn't have to be me.

Bill stood. "No. He's cold. You use 911 here?"

Big Bone Stafford nodded, his eyes on Tremaine's motionless form. "How about I call it in, and y'all go back on out of Oldman's Brake like y'all was never here."

"Thank you," I said, watching the fly circle and resettle. "But I think not. People already saw us and we'd only end up in trouble— and getting you in trouble."

He shrugged his huge shoulders. "Been in trouble before."

"It's not our job to get you in any more. Pete would be mad. Though I appreciate the offer. And anyway, it's not like we have anything to hide."

Big Bone turned to me. "Ma'am, around here, folks with nothing to hide hide things all the time. Honesty often ain't the best policy in the state of Mississippi."

"I hear you," I said. "But no."

Bill took out his phone and called it in. I took out my phone, too, and called Pete. I filled him in on what had happened and told him we'd be a while.

27

The three of us walked to the flat, keeping to the grass to avoid pathways the killer might have used. Leaning on our car waiting for the law to arrive, Big Bone Stafford asked again what we'd wanted with Tremaine.

I said, "It was just that we'd heard he didn't get along with Leland Tam."

"That mean y'all are thinking he have something to do with killing him?"

"He might have," Bill said. "But also, it's my experience that when someone doesn't like you, they take an interest in your killing, even if they're not involved. Maybe Tremaine had a theory he would've been willing to share."

I caught Bill's eye. That would be our story, then. It had the great advantage of being true, and it would keep Tremaine's brother, Trevor, and his interest in my cousin Reynold, out of it until we had more of an idea what that actually meant.

"That feller that come yesterday," Big Bone said. "Gonna have to tell the law about him."

"Yes," I said. "I know we are."

We heard the sirens before we saw the sheriff's department car come tearing around the curve, kicking up muck and clumps of grass. The driver rocked to a stop right up by where we stood, and I found myself wondering if a car that heavy, driven with such a lead foot, might ever find itself stuck in the mud.

"Ain't we lucky," Big Bone Stafford muttered under his breath when Bert Lucknell and Tom Thomson clambered out. "Y'all met these gents?"

"Yes, thanks," I said. "Hello, Detective. Deputy."

Lucknell tramped up to stand in front of us, Thomson in his wake. The detective did a slow survey of us all. "So," he said, fixing on me, "coming out here to Oldman's Brake, this is the way you're proposing to get to know your relatives?"

"My cousin Pete suggested we talk to Tremaine McAdoo," I said. "Sir."

"How about that, Tom? Excepting for us, seems this little lady does everything her elders and betters tell her to do. Talk to Tremaine about what?"

"He had a problem with Leland Tam. We wanted to know what it was."

"That so? And what was it?"

"We didn't get to ask. He was dead when we found him."

"Uh-huh." He turned his attention to Stafford, looking him up and down. "Big Bone, you know these people?"

"They come to my show last night. I saw they was here, so I come out to say hello."

"You there when they found Tremaine?" Lucknell managed to make *found* sarcastic.

"Yessir."

"Good. Lead me to him."

"Blue house, that one right there. He lying just inside the kitchen door round to the back."

Lucknell stared at Big Bone. "I'd be obliged for the company. Now, while we go take a look, why don't y'all wait right there in the car. Dangerous out here. Tom, keep a close eye on them. Don't want anything to happen."

Lucknell waited for Big Bone to start in the direction of the McAdoo place. Big Bone scowled, but he headed over. Tom Thomson opened the door of the cruiser for me and Bill. The sirens had drawn people to the doors and porches of Oldman's Brake, and our ignominious entry into the car was watched by a half-dozen pairs of eyes. Tom Thomson swept his gaze across them all. Some met his look and some turned away, but no one came over to see, or called out to ask, what was going on.

Having held the locals at bay, Thomson climbed in the front seat and turned around. He slid back the Plexiglas plate in the divider between officer of the law and disrupter of it.

"Ma'am," he said, and I realized that was the first word I'd heard him speak. "Sir." Thomson's voice was deep and measured. "I just want to make sure all y'all understand what a bad idea it is to be messing with Detective Lucknell. He's a man with his own way of doing things."

"I appreciate that," I said. "But we're not trying to mess with him. Really."

"No, I suppose not." Thomson shook his head. "Just, y'all *happen* to be the ones found Tremaine McAdoo's body, same way you, ma'am, *happen* to be a relation of Leland Tam and Jefferson Tam. And Congressman Reynold Tam."

"I don't just happen to be related to the Tams. It's why we came here, to see if we could help my cousins. But as far as Tremaine McAdoo, you're right. We came to talk to him and found him dead. That's all."

"Meaning, there's no connection between this here, and what happened to Leland Tam."

"Oh, no, it doesn't mean that at all. There might well be a connection. But if there is, it isn't us. And about Detective Lucknell's way of doing things? Once Bill and Mr. Stafford and I realized we were at a crime scene, we tiptoed away to preserve whatever evidence we could. Bert Lucknell just ordered Mr. Stafford to go over there with him and between the two of them, they've now stomped any footprints there might have been right into the mud. What kind of investigation is that?"

Thomson nodded slowly. "Ma'am, it's not my place to be criticizing Bert's methods, and most especially not to civilians. I'm not saying if it was me, I wouldn't maybe do things differently. But it isn't me. I'm a deputy. Bert's the detective and he'll run things the way it seems right to him. And he don't take to interference. From me or from anyone."

"We're grateful for the advice," I said. "Can I ask you something?"

"Well, we're just sitting here."

"This afternoon, when you stopped us on Route 278. You knew we were coming. You were waiting for us. Right?"

"Yes, ma'am."

"How did you know?"

"Highway patrol radioed us."

"Why?"

"I suppose, ma'am, the officer didn't like y'all's driving."

"I see. It wouldn't be because some Ferguson called Bert Lucknell and told him to get on our case?"

Thomson met my gaze. "You saying Detective Lucknell might be cozy with the Fergusons?"

"The thought occurred to us."

Thomson nodded. "See, that right there, that's the kind of thinking I would not advise. I'm not going to say anything to Bert about it. And if I was y'all, I wouldn't mention it, either."

With that, Tom Thomson slid the panel into place and clambered out of the car, leaving me and Bill to exchange looks and then settle back. We had nothing to do, and deemed it wisest to have nothing to say, until Bert Lucknell returned.

28

I had a little bet with myself whether it would be Bill or me left stewing in a police station interview room while the other got the first chance to bask in the light of Bert Lucknell's attention. It turned out to be me who stewed, which was what I'd put the odds on. Lucknell, I figured, couldn't get past the idea that Bill was really in charge.

By the time Lucknell finally pushed open the door and deposited himself in a folding chair, I'd cataloged the chipped paint on the block walls, the scratches on the vinyl floor, and the water stains on the mismatched tile ceiling.

"Ma'am," Lucknell said. "Appreciate the patience."

"Anything to help in your investigation, Detective."

He looked at me, gave a short laugh, shook his head. "Yankee private eyes. Just when I thought I'd seen everything. So, ma'am, me and Mr. Smith, we just had us a very interesting conversation." Lucknell gave me his coyote grin and waited for my reaction.

"He's a very interesting guy."

I got the sense Lucknell was a little disappointed that I wasn't shaking in my boots about what Bill might have told him, but he went on. "That he is. He tells me you were hoping Tremaine McAdoo would have some information on what happened to Leland Tam."

"Not information, really. More like a theory."

"And what would that theory be?"

"I don't know. We didn't get to ask him."

"Still, y'all wouldn't have gone way out to Oldman's Brake without some idea what was there to find. How'd you know where Tremaine lives, by the way?"

"Pete told us."

"Why?"

I was tempted to say, *Because we asked him,* but I was getting hungry and I didn't want to be here all night.

"We wondered if what happened to Leland might be a hate crime, and Pete said as far as he knew, everyone liked Leland, except maybe the McAdoo family. Since the mother just died and the brother's at Parchman, we thought we'd try Tremaine."

"Ain't that something? That's just what Smith said."

"Because it's true."

"Or because y'all worked that story out in the car while we was waiting for the crime scene folks to show up."

The crime scene folks had turned out to be from the state police, Coahoma County not having a lab of its own. I'd tried not to be pleased at how annoyed they were by Lucknell's tromping all over the pathways. But though from inside the car we couldn't hear what was said, I'd found myself smiling when they pointed and barked orders. As Lucknell stomped back to the flat and out of their way, steam almost visibly poured from his ears. I could see some of the people of Oldman's Brake snickering on their porches.

A tech had come over and asked me and Bill to step out of the car so she could take our fingerprints and casts of our shoes. These requests were made politely, either because the techs didn't consider us suspects, or to irritate Lucknell. Either was fine with me. They did Lucknell's, Thomson's, and Big Bone Stafford's shoes, too, and the shoes of the people on the porches. During all this, Bill and I exchanged no words.

"If we'd worked our story out in the car, Detective," I said to Lucknell now, "you'd have it on tape already."

He paused and then got my meaning. "We don't bug our cars, ma'am."

I thought that was probably true, for budget reasons if nothing else; but I also thought it wouldn't hurt to flatter him a bit. "Come on, Detective. It's done everywhere. Leave the suspects alone and turn on the recorder. No legal expectation of privacy in a police car, but most people don't know that."

From his face, neither had Bert Lucknell. He recovered well, though. "All right, ma'am, I'll give you that. Not that y'all couldn't have worked out your story before we showed up, but let's just move along. I can't say I'm satisfied with your explanation of what y'all wanted with Tremaine. Don't suppose the truth is more like, he knew where to find Jefferson? And if he did, maybe Jefferson killed him to keep him from saying. Or maybe, being Jefferson's cousin, you did that yourself."

"That's ridiculous. But if you're planning to arrest me, I want a lawyer."

"No, ma'am, I'm not fixing to do that right now."

"Good, because I'm sure your medical examiner will find that Tremaine died a while ago."

"Nothing to say you couldn't have killed him *a while ago*, then gone away and come back. But how about we leave that until Dr. Delew finishes the autopsy? So, you never got the chance to ask Tremaine where Jefferson might be?"

If this was his sneaky attempt to trip me up on why we'd gone to Oldman's Brake, his technique needed polishing. "We wouldn't have anyway. That's not why we wanted to see him. If Tremaine McAdoo knew where to find Jefferson, it's news to me. And I don't know why he would, since the McAdoos don't like Chinese people."

"People get paid enough, they could like anybody."

I wasn't sure what that remark referred to, so I didn't answer it. Lucknell waited and then shrugged.

"Still and all," he said, "I suppose there's no shortage of people might have wanted Tremaine McAdoo dead. Man was in a dangerous profession, that's for sure. A customer might've felt cheated. Or some one of them Fergusons decided they been letting him slide long enough. Truth is, ma'am, I got no reason to connect up Tremaine's killing and Jefferson Tam except for y'all's being there."

"Which we explained."

He eyed me and switched tacks. "Now, another interesting thing. I got a witness swears a white guy wearing a hoodie and shades came to see Tremaine yesterday. Just after sundown. Strange time for sunglasses, wouldn't you say?"

"I never wear mine then."

"Does your cousin Jefferson?"

"I wouldn't know."

"The witness says you thought it might be Jefferson. Got to admit, with sunglasses on, Chinese look just like everybody else."

I ground my teeth. *Except in the other half of the world*, I thought, *where* you'd *have to wear sunglasses to look like everybody else.*

"I didn't say anything about Jefferson. I just asked if the 'white guy' might have been Asian."

"Why?"

"Just being thorough, Detective."

"Same witness says he heard gunshots right around that time. Deer season, so he didn't give it much thought."

"Yes, I understand deer season is big around here."

Shaking his head, Lucknell smiled. "Ma'am, you really are something. All right, you can go." He stood. "But I got to try one more time to make myself clear. I'm getting tired of seeing you and Smith every time I spin around." His face took on a thoughtful expression I hadn't seen before. "Still, looking on the sunny side, I suppose as long as y'all are hanging around Coahoma County, that most likely means Jefferson's still here, too."

"That only makes sense if you think Bill and I know more about where he is than you do."

"Is that so? Well, ma'am, when you're up to your neck in horseshit, probably there's a pony around someplace."

———

Bill was waiting for me downstairs in the sheriff's department lobby. "How'd it go?" he asked, lifting himself off an orange plastic chair.

"A peaceful interlude in an otherwise hectic day. I get the sense Lucknell still thinks we're hiding something, however."

"He made that suggestion to me, too."

"Did he tell you about the pony?"

"What pony?"

"Never mind. I'll call Pete."

Pete was home, having begged a ride from Henry. That was a good thing, since the Malibu was still back at Oldman's Brake.

Bill had just finished a cigarette when Pete pulled up in a red Miata.

"Nice ride," Bill said as we got in, me scrunched in the back because the car was so tiny.

"Midlife crisis. Well, that was its grandpa. This is Miata the Third. So tell me again how you folks just happened to be at Tremaine McAdoo's place right after he bought the farm."

"Again? We didn't tell you at all, yet."

"I was being polite. Not pointing out how you're keeping the client in the dark. And I better not find out you went to Oldman's Brake because you were in Burcell anyhow."

"We weren't. But, Pete—"

"But me no buts."

"How about," Bill broke in, "we discuss this over dinner? I'm starving. Pete, is there a place we can go?"

"Yeah," Pete grunted. "I know just the spot."

We backtracked to Oldman's Brake to pick up the Malibu, passing through Burcell, where nothing had changed except now Rupert's Bud sign was lit.

Rectangles of yellow light shone in windows in Oldman's Brake as Pete pulled onto the flat. The McAdoo place was dark, but it had its yellow accents: it was wrapped with crime scene tape.

"Damn," said Pete. "I haven't been in Oldman's Brake since I was a kid. Even then, hardly ever."

"You don't come out to visit Big Bone?"

"Nah. We socialize at Red's, or the Shacks, or up in Tunica. Neutral territory, so to speak. Out here, it's kind of like the Down Home Club. Place black folks can call their own."

A few faces appeared at windows, and a man opened his front door. He stood silhouetted, watching us, as if to prove Pete's point.

"But it was different when you were a kid?" I was still befuddled by the intricacies of Mississippi social structure. Maybe I should have paid more attention in cultural anthropology class.

"Well, Daddy had a customer here, way back when. He'd come out with a delivery most every week. Sunday afternoon, when the store was closed."

"H. Tam and Sons delivered?"

"Not so unusual, then. Those days, lots of folks without cars, so Daddy brought his customers the necessaries. Usually took Paul along to help him carry. If Paul had a ball game or something, he'd bring Jonas. Once or twice me, just so's I could feel big, too, but I was kind of useless." He peered around. "That house right there, I think."

I was surprised. "The McAdoo place?"

Pete's lips pursed. He sighed. "Long time ago, Cousin Lydia. I can't really say."

The man in the open door didn't move when Bill got out of the Miata and into the Malibu. He was still there watching as we drove out of Oldman's Brake.

We headed to Clarksdale. Before going on to whatever supper spot he had in mind, Pete, with Bill behind us, pulled into his own driveway. Not a bad idea, I thought; hungry as I was, I could still use a little freshening up. When I followed Pete through the front door, though, I understood about the supper spot.

"God, Pete, it smells great in here! I thought you didn't cook."

"Expected you might be hungry, so I scavenged the store. Came across a couple boxes of Ronzoni, some cans of spaghetti sauce, a pound of sausage in the freezer. Dump some oregano in there, throw cheese on top, and you could be in Rome. Found a package of dinner rolls in the freezer, too, made garlic bread. Cookies and ice cream for dessert. And plus, before we eat, how about a little moonshine?"

29

While the dinner-roll garlic bread baked, we settled into sofa and chairs to nibble on olives and drink moonshine. The crystal clear liquid made Bill say, "God, Pete, this is great!" It made me shudder and cough. Both reactions got a big grin from Pete.

"Fellow I know makes this stuff out behind his garage. Couldn't be more pure if it dripped straight from heaven."

That may have been, but no matter where it dripped from, I couldn't see the point of something that didn't have any flavor, just the ability to light your insides on fire. I gave up after the second taste and dumped what was left into Bill's glass. Drinking water to put out the flames, I filled Pete in on our visit to Callie Leblanc and why what we'd learned there had sent us to Oldman's Brake. He listened, frowning, sipping his moonshine, and when I was finished, he got up without a word and went to the kitchen. He brought out place mats and plates and set them on one end of the dining table, crowding Leland's photo and the flowers down to the other end. I tried to help, but he waved me to sit. I exchanged silent glances with Bill, and we watched through the opening while Pete drained the pasta, grated the cheese, and ladled the sauce. He took the garlic bread from the oven and beckoned us to the table.

Either I was ravenous, or Pete's cooking was better than he claimed, or both. The al dente spaghetti, spicy sauce, and buttery garlic bread all tasted as good as they smelled. Pete waited until Bill and I had made serious inroads into our meals before he spoke.

"Listen, you two. There's something we're not saying. According to Bert, maybe Jefferson killed Tremaine because Tremaine knew where he was hiding. That's ridiculous. For one thing, if you know someone knows where you're hiding, why don't you just go hide somewhere else? For another thing, a McAdoo's going to be the last person to know anything secret about a Tam. But"—he looked down at his spaghetti-wound fork—"a Tam might know something about a McAdoo. Tremaine might've killed Leland, and Jefferson found it out, and killed him because of it."

"Why would Tremaine do that?"

Pete shook his head. "I don't know."

"Then—" I started.

"But whyever," Pete pushed on, "it may be that Trevor knew what Tremaine was planning and wanted to sell the information to Reynold, and that's what that was about."

"Trevor's a lifer," I said. "What could be worth selling out your own brother for if you're never getting out anyway?"

"Getting out," said Bill. "Commuting his sentence, if Reynold gets elected. Roberson said congressmen have no influence at a state prison, and that's true. But governors do."

"Oh," I said. "That actually makes sense."

"Thanks."

"But Jefferson killing Tremaine—are you saying, Pete, that's why he escaped? To do that? But, come on. If Tremaine killed Leland and Jefferson knew that when he was arrested, why not tell the sheriff?"

"Might be he didn't know, but he thought it could be. Maybe he did say it and they all thought he was just trying to throw suspicion somewhere else. Or maybe he didn't find out until he was on the run." Pete shook his head. "Got to tell you, I don't like it. Or that guy with the sunglasses and hood turning up at Tremaine's yesterday. I don't like it at all."

"As long as you're not liking things," I said, "there's more." While we ate, Bill and I took turns telling Pete about our trip to Oxford: the lady on the porch next door who didn't approve of Jefferson's friends, and the outdoor laptop sessions at the Café Café.

"Anna Rae Ferguson? And Johnny Ferguson?" Pete's lips set into a tight line. "I don't believe it."

"Johnny and Jefferson went to school together, Pete." I tried to say that gently.

"I went to school with a lot of no-accounts myself. You don't find me hanging around with 'em now."

"We don't know what it means," Bill said reasonably. "And maybe Darlaine at the Café Café was wrong and it's not even Jefferson. But we have to consider that it might be. If Anna Rae Ferguson sicced Bert Lucknell on us, he'll come around to the idea there's a connection between Jefferson and the Fergusons eventually, too. Unclear what he'll want to do about it, if he's in their pocket, but I'd rather it was us who got there first."

"If by 'there' you mean Burcell—"

"I think—"

"Pete—"

"Just hold your horses, both of you. I've actually been giving this some thought while you were out racing around annoying live people and finding dead ones."

"Giving what some thought?"

"I didn't get the feeling you were fixing to give up on the idea of talking to Johnny Ferguson, even before what happened today. Closing in on him in Burcell's a nonstarter. But if you insist on exchanging words, some of them younger Fergusons like to take their breakfast out at Walid's."

"What's Walid's?"

"Lebanese diner out by the highway. Walid's Oasis. Y'all are about to drop your jaws and say '*Lebanese*'?, aren't you?"

"Okay, yes, I was."

"Me, too," Bill said. I didn't know if that was true, but I appreciated the support.

Pete sighed. "Chinese and Jews aren't the only folks who weren't white or black and came to the Delta. Lot of Italians came a hundred fifty years ago, and a whole bunch of Syrians and Lebanese came in the sixties, after some war they had over there. They set up restaurants. Not many left, same as with the Chinese grocers, but out at Walid's, you can still get a great plate of kibbe and grits."

Kibbe was a Middle Eastern meat, wheat, and spices patty. I'd eaten them at New York street fairs, but two days ago, I'd have said you'd never find them in the Mississippi Delta. Of course, two days ago, I'd have said you'd never find *me* in the Mississippi Delta.

"We'll go out there in the morning," Pete went on. "If we're lucky, we can eat before the Fergusons come in to spoil our appetites."

"Moonshine and spaghetti for dinner," Bill mused. "Kibbe and grits for breakfast. Remarkable place, the Delta."

"Remarkable, yes," I said. "But Pete. Jews, Italians, Lebanese—you wouldn't call them white? Lebanese, I guess you could say they're Middle Eastern, but still. I'm not sure Middle Eastern is a race classification."

"It is in Mississippi. Like Jew. And Italian."

—

The day had been exhausting, so after blue-frosted sugar cookies and fudge-swirl ice cream, Bill and I helped Pete clean up so we could all go to bed. "I'm sorry, Pete," I said as we loaded the dishwasher. "I know things aren't turning out the way you hoped."

"Not your fault. You and Bill, you're finding the facts. If they point to Jefferson not being the boy I thought he was, still, can't argue with the truth."

I knew someone who could, though. Once we were done, I headed to my room to call my mother.

"Ling Wan-ju. You are calling to report the progress you have made?"

"We haven't made a lot, Ma."

"It's been an entire day since we spoke. You have done nothing?"

"We've done lots of things. It's just that none of them have resulted in progress."

"Have you at least been able to find your cousin Jefferson Tam?"

At least. "No, Ma."

An exasperated sigh. "Ling Wan-ju, I didn't send you to the Delta of Mississippi to enjoy yourself."

"I get that, Ma. It's just, like I said yesterday, things are complicated down here."

"Things cannot be more complicated in the Delta of Mississippi than they are anywhere else. If they appear so, it is because you are looking at them the wrong way. Tell me, what is so complicated to you?"

I was not about to bring up the second homicide, much less that Bill and I had found the body; nor did I want to mention our fears that Jefferson was involved with the Fergusons' meth business until I had to.

"For one thing," I said, "there are a lot of people who seem to be connected but I don't know how."

"Do you mean connected to your case, or connected to each other?"

"To the case." And in some ways, to each other: Lucknell to the Fergusons, or the Fergusons to Jefferson, or Trevor McAdoo to Reynold Tam. But I didn't say that, either.

My mother made a wordless, but nevertheless easy to understand, sound. She said, "Have you discussed the situation with the White Baboon?"

Wait. Was my mother really asking me what Bill thought?

"Yes," I said cautiously. "He's—" I stopped myself before I said *stumped*. Why cap this new well at the moment it started to flow? "He doesn't see the answer yet, either. But we're working on it."

"Please continue to work on it." My mother paused, and I could have sworn her voice softened the tiniest bit as she said, "The Delta of Mississippi is no different from other places. Cuckoos do not hatch from robin's eggs there. This is only a case, Ling Wan-ju. It's more important than others because it involves family. Also because Jefferson Tam is innocent—" I bit my tongue. "—no matter how things look," she finished, as usual reading my mind. "But for all of that, this is no different from other cases you have solved. You must use the same detecting methods you have used in the past. Please call me tomorrow when you have made progress."

And she hung up.

I sighed, brushed my teeth, and climbed into bed. I was so tired I probably wouldn't have noticed an entire army of cicadas if they'd suddenly massed under my window and started to sing.

30

I wasn't destined to spend the long Southern night on the wings of sleep. Somewhere around 4:00 A.M., my phone rang. I've never known a wee-hours phone call to mean anything good, but I grabbed the thing, squinting at the screen to see who it was.

"Linus!" I half said, half coughed. "What's wrong?"

"Nothing! Did it!"

"Hi, Lydia!" Trella called.

"Hi, Trella. Did what? You guys, it's four in the morning."

"It is? Wow." I imagined Linus fact-checking me against the digital outputs in his crammed garage office. He and Trella had covered the windows to keep Wong Security's equipment from prying eyes. Plus, Cousin Linus had the family sleep-pattern genes. And he was a millennial with a taste for clubbing. I realized it was downright unreasonable to expect clock-time to mean anything to him at all.

"Did what?" I repeated, rubbing my face.

"Broke into your boy's laptop." His grin just about materialized in the air before me like the Cheshire cat's.

"Oh!" I said, fully awake now. Maybe a 4:00 A.M. phone call could, in fact, mean something good. "Oh, Linus, that's great! Thanks! What did you find?"

"A bunch of stuff. Not sure what you're looking for. A lot of games, but no email, blog, photos, anything like that. Hasn't accessed Facebook or Twitter or anything from here; probably does all that on his phone." Like any self-respecting millennial, was the implication. "He does have FanDuel and DraftKings on here. You can play them on the phone, but it's a pain." Linus hesitated and said, "You know, online gambling?"

It was sweet of him, and typical, to want to explain if I needed him to, but be worried he'd offend me by stating the obvious—which, to Linus, was just about anything that happened in cyberspace.

"Yes, I knew he did that," I said nonchalantly, as though online gambling were something that had floated into my awareness more than twenty-four hours ago. "Did you find anything else? Anything kind of private, personal? It seems weird he has no email on there." I'd been hoping for something that would give us an idea what Jefferson was like and had been up to. That hope had given me qualms, but I'd squelched them. Violating Jefferson's privacy, I reasoned, was better than letting him be sent up for a murder he didn't commit. Unless, a qualm argued back, he did commit it, and his email helped prove that. Or, a different qualm stuck in, what if the email had nothing to say about the murder but proved Jefferson was involved in the Fergusons' drug trade? Qualms everywhere. I tried to squelch them all, feeling like I was playing some bizarre game of Conscience Whac-A-Mole.

"Not so weird," said Linus. "If he needed to access his email from here, he could always go through his provider's website. Lots of people keep their business and personal accounts on different devices."

Not people I knew; but Linus and Jefferson ran with crowds different from mine and similar to one another's. I wondered if they'd like each other, and if they'd ever get a chance to meet.

"Are you looking for, like, who he emails with and who his friends are?"

"That would be handy, for sure. But what we really were wondering was why he took the trouble to hide it."

"Hide who his friends are? No, wait, you mean hide the laptop. Couldn't tell you. We did find one weird thing. But I don't know what it means yet."

"Weird how?"

"There's a bunch of spreadsheets on here, and complicated algorithms."

"For what?"

"I don't know. Some of the algorithms seem to, like, piggyback on others, but the others are conditional, too. They're full of if/thens and necessary/sufficients. I can run them by plugging in values, but all they do is give me a bunch of other values. I can't tell what it means."

"I can barely tell what you're saying. But listen, Linus." Might as well come out with it. "Could it have to do with a drug operation? Formulas, like for making meth, or maybe for tracking ingredients, output, sales, that kind of thing?"

"Wow. Like *Breaking Bad*? You think that's what cousin Jefferson's into?"

"I hope not. But could it?"

"Hmm. I can't see it. Unless each of these variables is a different ingredient, and if you use more of one you'd use less of another . . ." He trailed off, and I could hear him clicking keys. "No. No, it's too complex and interdependent. You know? I mean, I guess it could be, if the variables aren't just ingredients, they're temperature and time, purity, all the stuff that would go into making drugs. But they're not expressed that way. I mean," he said earnestly, and I could tell he knew he was losing me, "math has symbols for that stuff. Time and temperature, rate of change, those things. He's not using them."

"What's he using?"

"Letters. A, B, C. Numbers. If/thens, like I said. I need more time to work on this."

"Couldn't it be about sales? Suppliers, customers, dealers? You get more of A from B, you sell more of X to Y?"

"That would be even simpler, just a couple of spreadsheets. Maybe linked to each other or whatever, but nothing like this."

I took his word for it, since I was only making wild guesses based on what I was afraid of finding. "Okay, that's good news. Keep going, okay? And when you figure it out, let me know."

Again, he didn't comment on my *when*. "You got it. This is fun. See ya, cuz."

"Bye, Lydia!" Trella called.

"Goodbye, guys. Thanks."

My head full of complex, interdependent, and conditional algorithms, I turned over and went back to sleep.

31

I spent the next three hours in a slumber solid and peaceful. When I woke just after seven, I heard voices beyond my door, identified them as Bill's and Pete's, and realized, to my shock, that I was the last one up. Not that it mattered to anything but my pride. Our plan was to get to Walid's and eat before the Fergusons showed, if they did. According to Pete, they tended to arrive around nine. We had plenty of time.

I crossed the hall and proceeded through my morning bathroom routine. Pulling on my robe, I ambled into the living room. "Gentlemen," I said, "good day to you both."

"Same to you, Cousin Lydia," said Pete. He rose from his worn armchair and disappeared into the kitchen.

Bill, sipping coffee in the other chair, eyed me critically. "If I can't have a connecting door to your room, I protest you walking around in a bathrobe looking so adorable."

The bathrobe was a blue-and-white cotton affair that went to my ankles with a belt around the waist, and I had a tee shirt and running shorts under it, but as Pete came back carrying a mug of hot black tea, I said, "I'll put your protest on the record."

"No sugar in there," Pete said, handing me the mug. "Yankees. What protest?"

"Nothing," I said. "Yankee business. Listen, you guys, guess who I talked to last night?"

Pete sat and picked up his coffee. "You actually talked to someone?

In the middle of the night? I heard you, but I thought you were talking in your sleep."

"I started the conversation in my sleep, but it was on the phone. Linus called. He hacked into Jefferson's laptop."

Pete paused a moment before he said, "Is that good?" He looked like he was having the same qualms I'd had.

"It's why we sent it to him."

Pete shrugged. "I got HB next door to warn me about burglars, but I'm happiest when I don't hear from him."

The analogy wasn't precise, but I got it.

Bill was more to the point: "What did he find?"

I told them about the games, lack of email, and folder full of algorithms and formulas.

"Maybe it's got nothing to do with anything," Pete said. "Some client of Jefferson's, something like that."

"Could be. Linus is working on it."

Bill persisted. "He's sure it's not for a meth operation?"

"He's sure. That doesn't mean he's right."

"Well, here's hoping he is," said Pete. "Now we'd best get a move on. If we want to head out to Walid's, one of us better get dressed."

That had to be the only one still in a bathrobe, so I took my mug of tea and scurried off to my room.

—

Walid's Oasis, its '60s roadside sign promising *American-Italian-Lebanese*, sat back from a street that I'd bet hadn't been nearly this built up or well paved when Walid planted his flag. That flag, Lebanon circa 1960, I spotted as we walked in. It hung on the wall behind the tinsel-draped counter, where a black-haired woman was pouring coffee for a man chowing down on a pile of scrambled eggs. The woman looked up and smiled at Pete.

Half past eight was late for a Delta breakfast, according to Pete, but Walid's was close to full. Formica tables at no particular angle to each other dotted the checkerboard floor. Booths lined the two windowed walls, with the kitchen in the back. The air was full of the smells of toast and coffee, plus other more exotic, less diner-y scents. The pies in the glass cabinet included meringues so tall any New York eatery would be proud to display them.

We took the only empty booth. I slid in beside Pete, and it was a bumpy landing: decades of patronage had cracked and sagged Walid's vinyl upholstery. The counterwoman brought over menus and her coffee-pot. "Good to see you, Captain Pete. I'm so sorry about Leland. And Jefferson, that's nothing but nonsense. I'm sure they'll get it all get straightened out real soon."

After almost two full days with Pete, whose face was South China but whose accent was American South—not to mention my cousin Reynold, whose Mississippi speech was much more obvious than his half-Asian eyes—I shouldn't have been surprised to hear the Delta drawl coming from this woman who could have been Tony Shaloub's prettier sister. But the Deep South sound of her words caught me by surprise and I almost laughed. Luckily, she took the grin I wound up with as a friendly greeting.

"You got to be Jefferson's cousin I heard was in town."

"Yes, ma'am. Lydia Chin. This here's Bill Smith."

I didn't get an eye roll from Bill for *this here*, but that was probably because we were in polite company.

"Welcome to Clarksdale, y'all. Can I get you some coffee?"

"You sure can, Lizzie, and tell me something," Pete said. "Seen any of those young Fergusons today?"

"Not yet. Just about due, though. They haven't been here in two, three days, and those boys do love their grits." Lizzie poured coffee for Bill and Pete. When I shook my head she said, "You want sweet tea, hon?"

"Can I have hot tea?"

"Why, sure you can. Just be a minute."

"Yankee," Pete told her confidentially.

She smiled. "Takes all kinds."

We inspected our menus, which included kibbe, tabouli, and ravioli. Bill ordered eggs, toast, kibbe, and grits. Pete ordered eggs, toast, bacon, and lemon meringue pie. I ordered eggs and toast. I mean, come on, it was breakfast.

Just as the food arrived, so did the Fergusons.

I might have known even if Pete hadn't prodded me, from the way the three men rolled through the door. Twentysomethings, one with a thick mustache and a windbreaker, one balding, wearing a flannel shirt over a thermal, and one Johnny Ferguson himself. I didn't need Pete's additional poke to specify which he was. Johnny's resemblance to his kid sister, Anna Rae, was striking, though he'd pulled his blond hair into a scraggly ponytail and wore a couple of days' worth of stubble on that square Ferguson jaw. He moved with the same athletic confidence, nodding to Lizzie behind the counter, throwing some wisecrack over his shoulder that made the balding cousin grin. It struck me that these cousins, growing up together, playing in the grass and fishing in the river in their small Mississippi town, weren't that different from my brothers and me, who grew up chasing each other down the stairs of Chinatown apartment buildings and riding the subway with our own cousins and friends. That the adults in Burcell were in a dangerous, destructive business was something these boys hadn't known then, just as we'd known nothing about Chinatown's tongs and gangs.

There was no doubt my father had paid protection money to Old Jun, whose tong controlled the block his restaurant was on. Ba had managed otherwise to keep to the high ground, avoiding the treacherous criminal waters around him. But, I wondered now, what if he hadn't? What if he'd been seduced by the money, the sense of safety, the feeling of belonging? If he'd joined the tong and risen, as his charm and cleverness would surely have helped him do, to a position near the top? Would my brothers and I, if we'd grown up in that shadow sphere, now be like these younger Fergusons, part of and looking to expand the family criminal enterprise? Or would we, any of us, have had the clear-eyed strength of Anna Rae, to leave for something better?

And had my cousin Jefferson been given a choice in the Fergusons' world? If so, how had he chosen?

These thoughts swirled through my mind as I ate my eggs and wondered how to approach Johnny Ferguson. As it turned out, we didn't have to.

From the corner of my eye, I'd been watching the cousins demolish their mountains of pancakes, thatches of bacon, and piles of buttery grits. Just after Lizzie refreshed their coffee, the mustached cousin said something to Johnny. Johnny, whose back had been to us, turned in his chair. He stared, turned back, and spoke to the others.

"I think trouble's coming," I said.

"They'll finish eating first," said Bill, who'd also been watching. "These grits are too good to waste."

He was right; it was another couple of bites and gulps of coffee before Johnny Ferguson pushed back his chair. He ambled to our booth, his cousins flanking him, and stood looking down at Bill.

"You the guy who was over in Oxford yesterday, bothering my sister?"

"Actually," I said before Bill could answer, "that was me." Bill doesn't like to be hemmed in and loomed over. Not that anyone does, but he's been known to erupt, and I didn't want that before we could have a civilized conversation with these gentlemen.

"Yeah," said Johnny. "She said there was a Chinese girl, too. Jefferson Tam's cousin."

"Lydia Chin. Pleased to meet you." I stuck out my hand. Johnny Ferguson ignored it. I shrugged and picked up my tea instead. "It was Jefferson we were looking for," I went on, talking to all three of them. "We heard he was in Burcell a few weeks ago and we were wondering why." I looked right at Johnny. "And of course, we're wondering where he is now."

Johnny Ferguson stayed with the part that was making him mad: us messing with his little sister.

"Anna Rae don't live in Burcell anymore."

"I know, but we've heard she's a friend of Jefferson's."

The balding cousin snickered. "What's she saying there, Johnny-boy?"

"Shut up, Keith. Ma'am, what that sounds like, it better not be what you mean. Some people"—he looked at Bill—"might be all right with that sort of thing, but it don't go over here."

"I don't mean anything," I said. "I just thought if they're friends, she may know why he was there, or where to find him now. Or . . ." I paused, as though the idea had just occurred to me. "You might."

"Why the hell would I?"

"Well," I said reasonably, "if Anna Rae doesn't live in Burcell anymore and Jefferson was in Burcell, he must have been there to see someone else."

"Who says he was there?"

"The sheriff," said Bill. I could see him starting to steam. I kicked him under the table, but gently.

"The sheriff? He couldn't keep Jefferson in his own jail, now he thinks he's in Burcell? Why don't he come look, then?"

"No," I said, "the sheriff knows Jefferson *was* in Burcell, but before Leland Tam's murder." That might not be true, since it was Tolson Reeves's car that had been in Burcell, and we might be the only people besides Reeves himself—and Jefferson—who knew Jefferson had been driving it. Although if the Fergusons were as buddy-buddy with Bert Lucknell as we suspected, Lucknell might in fact know Jefferson had been in Burcell, as well as exactly where and why, and where he was right now, and what he was having for breakfast.

"And he told y'all about it?" Johnny sneered. "Don't make me laugh. Sheriff Bradley couldn't pour piss from a boot with directions on the heel, but he ain't about to say nothing about nothing to two Yankees and an old man Chinese gambler."

At that, Pete pursed his lips and gave a thoughtful frown.

"If it weren't true," I said, "he wouldn't have anything to say nothing about, would he? So, if Jefferson didn't go to Burcell to see Anna Rae, who did he go to see?"

For a moment, all three Fergusons looked confused. Pete's frown turned into a barely suppressed snort of laughter.

"Whoa!" said the mustached cousin. "Shit, Johnny, I think she's saying you and that Chinese boy got a thing going on." He dangled a limp wrist and laughed.

"Shut *up!*" Johnny took a step closer and poked a finger in my shoulder. "Girlie, you'd better—"

Smoothly, Bill slid out and stood chest-to-chest with Johnny. All three cousins, none of them as big as Bill, took a reflexive, choreographed-looking step back. I got up fast and put a hand on Bill's arm. I knew what the next scene was likely to be, and Johnny

Ferguson flying through a plate-glass window wasn't going to be much help to us in finding Jefferson.

"I'm sorry if you got the wrong impression," I said. "I'm just worried about my cousin, and I'm hoping you can tell us something that will help us find him."

"Your cousin and his troubles ain't my business, and my family ain't yours. I got nothing to say except y'all better keep my sister's name out of y'all's mouths from now on." Johnny stabbed his finger forward, stopping barely short of sticking it in Bill's chest.

That was enough for Bill. He shook off my hand and said, "Let's take this outside."

"Ain't nobody taking it outside, nor in here neither." Lizzie, still wielding her coffeepot, wedged herself between Bill and the Fergusons. "Anyone breaking up my place, and that includes my parking lot, better not plan on coming back. Now y'all know my grits are way too good to lose them to whatever it is y'all are fixing to fight over. Lord's sake, Captain Pete, put down that pie!"

I turned to Pete, still in the booth but standing. He held the plate with his slice of lemon meringue by his shoulder like a javelin ready to launch.

The Fergusons stared, dumbfounded. An old Chinese man was ready to hit them with a pie and a large Yankee who'd called them out was practically toe-to-toe with Johnny, with just a middle-aged Lebanese woman and her coffeepot between. It made a pretty funny freeze-frame, but I didn't dare smile. The Fergusons weren't sure which way was up, but any hint that the joke was on them and fists would fly.

"Captain Pete!" Lizzie said again, and then, "Okay, boys, y'all's finished up, breakfast's on me, git on out of here now."

Pete put the pie down. After a moment, he sat. I decided that was a good, defusing idea and sat, too. Bill stayed standing, but he unclenched his fists.

Johnny Ferguson glared at Bill, then at me. "Stay out my way from now on," he snarled. He strode back to his table, dug two twenty-dollar bills from his pocket, and slapped them down. He pushed out the door, flanked by his cousins.

32

"Well," said Pete, when the door closed behind the three Fergusons, "I can't see where that got us very far."

"I disagree." I spoke as the rest of Walid's breakfast crowd—with a certain degree of disappointment, it seemed to me—turned back to their own tables and booths. "For one thing, Bill and I learned how far you're willing to go to protect friends and family. I, for one, am humbled to learn that if need be, you'd sacrifice a slice of pie."

"Can't tell you how happy I am it didn't come to that." Pete stuck a fork in the weapon's crust.

"I am, too," said Lizzie, now with a pot in each hand. She topped off Bill's and Pete's coffee, and when she refilled my cup with hot water, she put down another tea bag. She cast a suspicious eye on Bill. "I don't know y'all, but you're with Captain Pete, so I'll cut y'all some slack. I'll say this for free—y'all don't want to be messing with those boys."

"I apologize for disrupting your place of business, ma'am," Bill said, his face contrite and his voice dripping Southern honey. "I shouldn't have let them get under my skin."

"They do make that a specialty." She seemed mollified. Breaking into a smile, she added, "And I gotta admit it was a hoot to see Johnny Ferguson not knowing whether to scratch his watch or wind his behind." She grew serious. "But whatever it was about, y'all best be on the lookout for them now. They don't like to be worsted." Lizzie threw a significant glance at Pete and left to bring the blessing of caffeine to another table.

Bill drank some coffee, put it down, and said to me, "I apologize to you, too."

"Accepted."

"For what?" Pete asked.

"My knight-in-shining-armor routine. Lydia doesn't like it when I do that, and she's right. She can take care of herself."

Pete stared at me. "That's ridiculous. Everyone could use a little help sometimes. I'd be grateful, have someone rescue me like that, if I needed it."

"Well, I didn't, right then." I smiled. "But to know I would if I did, yes, I am."

Bill smiled back and turned to Pete. "And, Captain Pete, if you ever find you do need it, you've got it."

Pete broke into that giant smile, and we all sat there grinning like idiots.

Bill, reaching for his coffee, interrupted the lovefest. "Actually, I think we might have learned something else."

I considered that. "That you, in fact, can control yourself and not automatically beat on anyone who invades your personal space?"

"Yes, and I hope you remember that next time you feel like invading my personal space. But besides that, while you were running verbal rings around the Fergusons, I was watching. From Johnny's reaction to the idea of Anna Rae and Jefferson as an item, it didn't seem like it was something he knew and was trying to hide, from his cousins or anyone else. It seemed to genuinely piss him off."

"I got that same impression. Which unfortunately makes it more likely that Jefferson was in Burcell for business, not romance. I'm sorry, Pete."

Pete shook his head. "Not like we hadn't thought of that. But what do we plan to do about it?"

"I'm not sure. I did notice that Johnny invited the sheriff to come on over to Burcell and look for Jefferson, but he didn't invite us."

"And you're not going."

"It's either us or the sheriff. The objections to him going are the same as before."

"And the objections to you two going are worse. Now you've crossed them. They find you on their patch, they're not going to stop for a howdy-doo. If you think I plan to explain that to your mama, you got your head screwed on funny."

"I understand. But—"

"But maybe we should take *this* outside," said Bill.

I looked at him and then around the room. You can feel people's attention on you even when they're not looking at you, and Walid's was full of that feeling.

In an echo of Johnny Ferguson, Bill dropped two twenties on our table. It was far more than breakfast cost, even with a generous tip, but we had disturbed the peace of the morning.

Out in the parking lot, we began to discuss a plan for the day. We were about to put one of our ideas into action—to have Bill, as a man and a Southerner, call down to Parchman and try to finagle a way to speak with Trevor McAdoo before his stretch in solitary was up—when my phone rang.

I checked the screen and put phone to ear. "Linus, don't you ever sleep?"

"Why, is it some weird time again? Trella just made coffee. I thought it was morning."

Through the speakerphone echo, Trella called, "Hi, Lydia."

"Hi, Trella. Yes, Linus, it's morning. Never mind. What's up?"

"Me!" he said brightly. "No, seriously, cuz, I got it. Your boy's algorithms."

"Linus! You deciphered them?"

I almost put him on speaker at this end, too, so Bill and Pete could be part of this revelation, but I realized that whatever was coming might not be something I wanted Pete to hear first from a stranger on the phone in a parking lot. Instead, I walked away, one finger in my other ear, as though the road noise was making it hard to hear.

"Well, not me," Linus said. "Can't lie, bad karma. I farmed them out. See, Trella and I were getting nowhere and it was driving me nuts. Trella said maybe it needed fresh eyes. That worked for me, so I sent a couple of Jefferson's files around to some friends of mine and asked if they looked familiar, or if anyone had any good guesses. This one guy— Azarael, I think he's in the Bahamas or something—he was all over it."

Trust Linus to call people he's never met, only knows by their screen names, and can't even geographically locate, "friends of mine."

"And? I'm holding my breath here."

"They're for online sports gambling." He took a breath the way he does when he's about to explain something. "Remember I said I found DraftKings and FanDuel on here? The way they work—"

"No, I'm actually good with that. You make lineups from players from lots of teams and however they do that week combined, that's how you do."

"Oh. That's right. Do you play them?" He sounded like I'd told him I'd enrolled in culinary school: not outside the bounds of possibility, but nothing he'd ever considered.

"Can't lie, bad karma. Bill explained it to me yesterday."

"Aha! How come?"

"Because someone told us Jefferson did it. I hate to say this, but so far you haven't told me anything we don't already know."

"Ah, but I'm about to. So you know the way the gambling part actually works?"

"You play other people who picked other lineups?"

"Right. But you don't choose who the other people are. The gambling site puts you against them. And it's always other people you're playing. Nobody plays the house. The site just takes a cut for, like, being the place where it happens." He started to bellow, '*I wanna be in the room where it happens, the room where it happens*—' Anyway, they make it sound scientific and complicated, how they connect people, but no matter what they say about newbies playing newbies, Azarael says the sites make the most money off people losing to whales, and the whales only keep coming back if they win, so you're always playing whales. That's—"

"Big, big fish."

"Right. Good." I felt like he'd patted me on the head. "Now, Azarael says a lot of whales pick their teams mathematically. That's what the base algorithms on Jefferson's computer are, they're for picking teams. Using algorithms is against the sites' rules, but Azarael says whales do it all the time and it's almost impossible to catch them at it. If the sites even try. Mostly, they don't."

"So, Jefferson's writing algorithms for whales?"

"No. Better. Those are the *base* algorithms. I don't think he wrote those. He must have hacked them, or maybe he even bought them from wherever the whales get theirs. I mean, someone must write and sell these things, right?"

I could hear his wheels turning. "Don't even think about it," I said. "Bad karma. Go back to what you were telling me."

"Oh. Okay." If he was disappointed, I couldn't hear it. I've often wondered if ideas pop into Linus's head so fast that he's used to chucking out ones that for whatever reason—like his cousin warning him off—don't seem worth working on. "So the base algorithms. I think they're not his because they have—they're—the way their code reads—"

"It's okay, I'll go with blind faith. You have reasons to think Jefferson didn't write them. What about the others?"

"I think he wrote those. And they're for busting the base ones." Linus's triumphal grin just about blazed through the phone.

Except: "I don't understand."

"Yeah," he said. "Okay. You're a whale. Your algorithms pick teams of players. Maybe you don't pay much attention. Maybe you're not even a sports fan, you're just a gambler. You don't give a—you don't care who you have, you just check at the end of the day to see how you did. You lost a few, maybe, but overall you did great. Because the algorithms, they consider every player from every angle: their stats, their past seasons, how they do in the rain, 'cause that's what's predicted IRL on Sunday."

"IRL?" I interrupted.

"In real life. So the algorithms match your players up really well. That's what they're written to do. So, say, if the algorithm picks you a quarterback who's killer accurate but not strong enough for a really long distance, it'll pick you a receiver who's great at finding a gap. If your quarterback can throw for ninety yards, it'll pick you a fast receiver who can be there by the time the football gets there. See? That's how the algorithm works."

"And those are the ones you're calling the base algorithms on Jefferson's laptop?"

"Yes, they are."

"So what about the others? The ones he wrote?"

"Well. So what if every time your algorithm picked Player X, some other algorithm snuck in and replaced him with Player Y? In fact, what if the second algorithm started going around sticking random players, irregardless of their stats, into all a whale's algorithms?"

"Um . . . I don't know. What if?"

He took his explaining breath. "Well, what does an algorithm know? If you stick in random players instead of the ones it picked, it'll play those. Then, if you're the newbie playing against its teams and you pick players for *your* teams based on actual talent, stats, whatever—the way the algorithm was supposed to do it, the way these sites tell the newbies to do it—you'll beat the algorithm's now-random lineups all to little pieces. And mostly, the whales will never know, because they didn't even know who they had to begin with."

"So what Jefferson was doing was writing algorithms to defeat the algorithms the whales use?"

"Not really defeat, more like screw up. Make them trip over themselves. Throw a monkey wrench into their works. Because, see, when they—"

"Yes!" Trella called from across the room. "Lydia, that's what they're for. Linus, she doesn't need to know how they work."

"Oh. Okay," Linus said. "But the thing is, I don't think they do work. Yet. They need a couple more iterations. If you want me to, I'll work on them, but I'm not sure there's enough time."

"Why is time an issue? Especially for a guy who doesn't sleep?"

"It's not my time. It's NFL time. I'd have to make changes and then see if they work for this Sunday's games. Then make more changes if I need to. But this whole online gambling thing, it's really only good in the regular season, or, if you push it, maybe into the first round of the playoffs. After teams start getting eliminated you don't have a big enough player pool to draw from, and the ones you do have are all on the top teams, so there's not enough differential in their stats to make the odds worthwhile. By the second round, Azarael says, the whales all quit football until next season. They go gamble on other sports."

I thought about that. "So if these monkey wrench algorithms are going to be useful this season, they have to be finished soon?"

"Real soon. Next week or week after, latest."

"Linus, you're a genius. Thanks."

"Hey, it's what I'm here for, cuz. You want me to see if I can make them work?"

"No, I don't think we need that." Although I wouldn't be surprised if Linus did it anyway, just to see if he could.

"That's it, then? Nothing else Wong Security can do for you?"

"Don't sound so disappointed, you were a huge help. If there is something more, I'll let you know. Again, thanks, and Trella, thank you, too. And thank Azarael for me, whoever he is."

"Actually," Linus said, "I think he's a girl."

33

We piled into the Malibu. "Where to?" Bill asked.

I was thinking, so I didn't answer. I wanted to chew over with him what I'd just learned from Linus, but, until we really knew what it meant, not with Pete around. After a few moments, Pete spoke from the back: "Unless you detectives have another plan for where we can go get into a fistfight, I'd like to head to the store. Lord knows there's enough to do there."

"Good idea." I buckled my seat belt. "I'd like to see what you accomplished yesterday."

"Oh, now, missy, don't think you can breeze right past that phone call you just got. That was from that New York computer geek cousin, right? He said something you're not sure you want me to know about. Well, spill it."

I turned to face him. "Can't slip anything over on you, can I, Pete?"

Pete gave a righteous *harrumph* and leaned forward. As we crossed Clarksdale to H. Tam and Sons, I delivered a condensed version of Linus's report.

The car was silent a moment when I finished. Then, "Hot damn!" Pete slapped his palm on his knee and laughed. "See? Kid really is a genius, isn't he?"

"He might be," I said. "Though I'm not sure what he's doing is legal."

"Well," Bill said, "online sports betting is only legal because it's supposed to be a game of skill. So using the base algorithms might well be illegal to begin with."

"And if it isn't," declared Pete, "it oughta be. That there's the kind of thing gives gamblers a bad name. Jefferson screwing them up to give the little guys the edge, like he's Robin Hood—"

"Would be just hacker fun and games," I said, "if it were theoretical. But I'm willing to bet—ha-ha—that Jefferson isn't doing this to entertain himself."

We parked in front of H. Tam and Sons. The bench and the stoop were empty. "Where's the E Street Band?"

"Henry and them? It's a touch early. They'll be along." Pete unlocked the store and we went in.

"Wow," I said. "Pete, honestly, the place looks great."

Possibly better, I suspected, than it had in years. The floors had been scrubbed, and though worn, the vinyl now read as green. Light no longer had to shove its way in but slanted gently through the newly clean strip windows, as though pleased to be invited back. Even the neon-blue pickle jar had been righted and set on the counter beside the ancient cash register. The scattering of goods on the shelves was conspicuously thin, but the store looked ready, even eager, to welcome customers.

The living quarters in the back had not fared as well, though they'd been neatened up. The gutted furniture and mattresses had been dragged out back, to await garbage pickup beside the boxes of broken dishes. What could be salvaged had been replaced in cabinets and drawers. With half the furniture gone and the walls practically bare, the little apartment looked more spacious, but sadder. It had been the Tam family home, even with the Tam family's belongings strewn and shattered in it. Now it seemed like a thread had been broken.

"Still work to be done back here, sorting things out," Pete said. "I put piles of stuff in that closet there. Couldn't stand to look at it. Peculiar, though, haven't seen a sign of the scrapbooks and all. Wanted to show them to you, Cousin Lydia. I think maybe even there's a Polaroid or two of your daddy that time he came down. Leland had all that stuff, but it hasn't turned up yet."

Pete squared his shoulders, looking at the closet that held the day's task. This was my opening. "We need to go over to see Tolson Reeves. You want to stay here, and I'll call you later?"

"Yeah." Pete nodded without looking at me. I kissed him on the cheek, and Bill and I headed back through the store, leaving Pete standing in the house where he was born.

34

"We're not going to see Tolson Reeves, are we?" Bill asked as we steered away from H. Tam and Sons.

"Sure we are. First."

"And then we're going to Burcell."

"Yup."

"Because that's what the rush was to get Jefferson out of jail. Finishing the algorithms, so they can be used this season."

"Yup."

"Because that's the diversification the younger Fergusons are looking at."

"Yup." I turned to face him. "Don't you think? Take the drug money, which is complicated, time-consuming, and risky to make, and invest it in a scheme to fleece online whales. Safer, quicker, more productive. And the only cost is whatever stake you start your online account with."

"And," Bill said, "the cost of your computer-geek algorithm writer."

"Oh." I sat back. "Right. That."

I called the Public Defender's Office, to be told neither Tolson Reeves nor Callie Leblanc was in. According to the receptionist, Tolson was scheduled to be in court with a couple of clients this morning and had gone to the courthouse straight away. "He'll be done in an hour or so," she said. "Should I tell him to call you?"

"No, thanks, we'll catch him later." With Tolson, an ambush might work better than a warning. Besides, my sense of urgency was directed elsewhere right then.

As we drove, we kicked around some open questions. Was the older generation of Fergusons party to the cyber sports-book scam? Unlikely, according to what Big Bone Stafford had said. Did they even know about it? Probably not. If the younger Fergusons had broken Jefferson out—the focus required for the elaborately detailed escape, according to Bill, marked the scheme as classic tweaker—they'd likely want to wait until the algorithms were finished and the scheme was a proven moneymaker before they mentioned to their elders that they had a price-on-his-head cop-magnet stashed in the woodshed.

Burcell was its pretty, sleepy self when we rolled in. As we were parking, the door to Rupert's Bar opened and a scruffy guy with bad teeth scuttled out, stuffing something into his pocket. He loped around a corner and out of sight.

"Well," I said. "I see business is booming."

Heads turned and cold stares fell on us as we pushed into Rupert's. Shades of the Down Home Club. Except for three booths along the left side and the desultory string of multicolored lights behind the bar, the look was pretty much the same, too, dimness and dilapidation being the guiding design principles. Cigarette smoke, thick enough to make me blink, spoke of a robust disregard for the minutiae of public health laws.

Bill ambled to the wooden bar, with me a few steps behind, scanning the room, watching for any movement beyond the lifting of a beer.

"How you doing?" Bill asked the T-shirted, goateed bartender. "Looking for Johnny Ferguson."

The bartender, narrow-eyed, asked, "And who might you be?"

"Might be anybody, but my name's Bill Smith. This here's Lydia Chin." I stepped up beside him, still watching the room, as it was watching us. "Met Johnny this morning over breakfast," Bill went on. "Wanted to talk some more. We believe we owe him an apology."

The bartender's stare didn't change. Finally, he said, "Johnny ain't here."

"If you could tell us where to find him, we'd be obliged."

Now the bartender, barely shifting his gaze, called over his shoulder, "Fisheye! These folks are looking for Johnny. What's your pleasure?"

So that was Fisheye Ferguson holding down the back booth. I peered through the dimness and smoke, but I couldn't make him out. I could, though, make out the two men who stood up off their barstools. I guessed they were ready in case Fisheye's pleasure was to have us tossed into the street.

"That a fact?" came a lazy, raspy voice. "What do they want with him?"

"Say they owe him an apology."

"Aw, ain't that nice?" The voice's sneer drained all the nice out of *nice*. But it went on to say, "Send 'em on back."

Under the glowers of everyone else in Rupert's Bar, Bill and I made our way to Fisheye Ferguson's booth. Fisheye was smoking and fiddling with that indispensable tool of the drug trade, a cell phone. Bill didn't even break stride, just slid into the booth opposite Fisheye. I slid in next to Bill.

The possibility of having to deal with Fisheye Ferguson himself had been something we'd accepted, though nothing we'd wanted. We were aware that we could be wrong about our hypothesis, in whole or in part. The monkey wrench algorithms on Jefferson's computer might have nothing to do with the Fergusons, Johnny and Jefferson whiling away the afternoon over a computer at Café Café notwithstanding. But if we were right, it would do neither us nor Jefferson any good to alert Fisheye to what his son and nephews had going behind his back.

And yet, here we were, sitting across a scarred tabletop from him, speared by his one-eyed stare.

Fisheye Ferguson had a droopy gray mustache, droopy gray hair, and vertical anger lines between his droopy gray eyebrows. And then, those eyes. Both of them, the one fixed on us and the one that appeared to be looking at the bartender, seemed about to pop out of their sockets on springs, like in a cartoon. The thought of growing up with that glare almost made me feel sorry for Johnny Ferguson.

"How y'all doing?" Fisheye asked, looking like he hoped the answer would be "poorly."

"Fine, sir," Bill said. "Yourself?"

"I'll do. Can't say what I'll do, but I'll do." Fisheye cackled at his own funniness. Then his face iced over. "What y'all want with my boy?"

"Like I told that gentleman," Bill nodded in the bartender's direction, "we met Johnny out at Walid's this morning. Got into a little disagreement, and I lost my temper. Come to apologize."

"That a fact? What's she doing here?"

"Lydia Chin. She was the subject of the disagreement. I'm Bill Smith, by the way."

Fisheye gave a laugh that devolved into a cigarette cough. "Sure, you are. Smith. Do she talk?"

"I do," I said. "I'm the one who suggested we find Johnny and apologize. I have relations around here, and I don't want to be the cause of any hard feelings."

"What relations?"

"Captain Pete Tam. The late Leland Tam. And Jefferson Tam." I didn't invoke Congressman Reynold Tam. I had a feeling that in Rupert's, that would be counterproductive.

"Jefferson Tam. Went to school with Johnny. Shows you about affirmative action. The reason Leland Tam's late is Number One Son drove a knife into him, ain't that right?"

"No, sir, I don't think it is, but it's the general opinion. I wonder what Johnny thinks." I turned to Bill. "Let's ask him when we find him."

Fisheye said, "Johnny? Likely Johnny ain't had one thought in his head about Jefferson Tam since their school years."

Many things were likely, but not that. "Well, if Johnny's not here, I guess we'll be going. Could you tell him we stopped by? I'd like him to call me, just so we can put this all behind us." Like Bill's, my wallet carries a variety of business cards. The one I gave Fisheye had only my mailing address and phone number. He read it, snickered, and slipped it into his shirt pocket. I was sliding out of the booth when his cell phone rang.

"Yeah? Shit, I know it's you, get to the point. Say what? *What? Anna Rae?* You little bastard, I'll shove that . . . I don't believe . . . That ain't what I'm paying you for. No, you— *Shit.* Okay, mother-fucker, you better hope you got that right, because if you ain't, I'm gonna come over there and make you wish you was never born."

He lowered the phone just enough to punch another button, then brought it back to his ear. "Johnny? Johnny, you got Keith and Howie with you? Get over here, we got business to attend to. I don't give a shit! Listen, I just got a call from that little weasel over in Oxford. No, Freddie. Yeah. He says—" Fisheye looked up and noticed me, half out of the booth. "Get the fuck out of here! Go on, get!"

"Sorry," I murmured. "Leaving."

We strode quickly through the smoke of Rupert's. Everyone ignored us, intent on the rage radiating from the back booth.

35

Bill and I climbed into the car and hightailed it out of town. At a thickly overgrown curve, we pulled off and waited. "Freddie," I said. "The manager at the Café Café."

"Keeping an eye on Fisheye's little girl." Bill opened his window and lit a cigarette. The breeze rattled bare branches and brought the scent of damp and decay.

"Her daddy has people spying on her? Ugh, how creepy."

"Well, Fergusons don't usually go far," Bill pointed out. "Fisheye might've just wanted to make sure she was okay."

"Still. That's one of the things about leaving home—you get to screw up unobserved, not have your boss call your family to report on you."

"What, you don't think I've been calling your mother every day since we got here?"

"Who made you boss?"

"Good point."

"And in case you're interested, *I've* been calling my mother to report on *you*. So you'd better behave." I watched a little brown bird hop from branch to branch. "I guess what this says is, even if you leave Burcell, you never really leave."

"I think," Bill said, "that's true of every family. Even if you leave, you never really leave."

About five minutes later, a dark blue car with silver rims came barreling toward Burcell. A Camaro, I saw, as it whizzed past. It had three men inside and a Confederate flag sticker on the back bumper.

"Holy cow," I said. "The car that the guys from the Down Home Club saw tearing away from the store?"

"Betcha. Lizzie should have let me take the fight out into the parking lot, we'd have known it was the Fergusons sooner."

"I'll remember that next time someone's trying to stop you from getting yourself clobbered. Did they go there to get Jefferson's computer, do you think?"

"I'd put money on it."

We sat there waiting. Whatever the immediate crisis involving Anna Rae, eventually Johnny would leave Burcell again, and since this was the only way out of town, we'd be ready to follow. My focus was on getting Johnny to cough up Jefferson. Still, a part of my mind was interested to know what the big emergency was.

After a peaceful few minutes of waving branches and chirping birds, the growl of an engine made us both straighten up. The Camaro came charging out again, Johnny at the wheel, Keith and Howie in the back, and Fisheye riding shotgun. As they passed, I could see Fisheye talking into his cell phone. He and Johnny both looked grim, but the two cousins wore wide impatient smiles, like kids on their way to someplace exciting.

"Hmm," I said. "Doesn't look good. Someone's in trouble."

Bill gave them a big lead, then pulled out. We stayed back; until the larger road we didn't need to be close because there were no turnoffs. Once there, we'd shorten the distance and see which direction they chose. My money was on Route 278 to Oxford. As it turned out, I was wrong.

Johnny Ferguson took a sharp corner in the other direction. Bill swung in a few car lengths back. It was Clarksdale they were making for, and Clarksdale they entered ten minutes later. Cutting through town, they ended up in the last place I would've predicted: the parking lot behind the courthouse.

"Wouldn't you think this is somewhere Fergusons might avoid?"

"They don't seem to be in much of a hurry to get out of the car, now that they're here," Bill said.

The four men sat, Keith grinning, Howie smoking, Johnny scowling, Fisheye on the phone again. He pocketed it, said something, and they waited. From where they were, they could see through the courthouse's double glass doors to the inside. From where we were, behind two rows of cars on the lot's other side, we couldn't. It wasn't until Johnny sat up sharply and Keith slapped Howie's arm that we knew their person of interest had arrived.

Johnny started the car and screeched up to the door. I was out of our car already, shouting and running, but I was too late. Keith and Howie jumped out, grabbed Tolson Reeves, shoved him in the car, and the Camaro peeled away.

36

Bill slid the car up and I jumped in. The Fergusons hurtled out of the lot and out of Clarksdale, not the way they'd come but into the fields and woods outside town.

"Tolson didn't hear me," I said. "Damn!"

"It looks like they didn't, either. I don't think they know we're here."

That was good, anyway. I called 911, reported a kidnapping, and said we were following a dark blue Camaro along Old Highway 61. A minute later, we weren't. Johnny Ferguson took a turn and raced down a tree-shaded road beside the levee. Now there was no point in hanging back. I called 911 again while Bill sped up. The trees grew thicker and dense with undergrowth.

When Bill slammed on the brakes, I jackknifed forward, grateful for my seat belt. The Camaro had sprayed mud in a one-eighty skid and rocked to a stop in a clearing.

Our cars were grill-to-grill. From the back seat of the Camaro, the cousins threw an already-bruised Tolson into the mud. They jumped out after him. Johnny and Fisheye each boiled out a front door. Bill and I did the same.

Johnny's side was mine. Before he could get a bead on what was happening, I launched into a tackle. He punched empty air and thudded on his back. Astride him and adrenaline-flooded, I slammed my fist down on the bridge of his nose. Then I jumped up and stomped his knee, same place three fast times. I raced back around our car, leaving Johnny howling. He'd get up, but I'd slowed him down, and the point wasn't to win this fight. It was to grab Tolson and get the hell out of here.

Tolson, eye swollen, shirt torn, was on one knee, breathing heavily and pushing to stand while Keith and Howie piled onto Bill. That was because Bill had Fisheye pinned against the Camaro. As I watched, Howie's fist connected with the side of Bill's head. Keith was closest to me, so I front-kicked his butt. I felt the jolt all the way to my hip, and he clearly felt it worse. He spun to attack me but threw himself so off-balance that when I slammed my shoulder into him, I knocked him smack into the mud. Howie abandoned Bill and leaped at me. I danced out of reach. Bill wrenched Fisheye off the car and flung him into Howie. They crashed down together in a tangle of flailing limbs.

"Come on!" I shouted, and pulled Tolson to his feet.

We made it two steps. Then the angry wrecking ball that was Keith thumped into my back. I staggered and flew forward, landing hard. My breath was gone, and I couldn't get it back. Hands pushed on the back of my head, grinding my face into a mud puddle. I twisted, desperate for air. Then suddenly the weight lifted. I rolled over, gasping, in time to see Tolson and Keith grapple until Tolson broke free and decked Keith with a huge fist to the chin.

Tolson dove into the battle between Bill and Howie. Fisheye was in there, too, trying to hold Bill so Howie could land blows, but Bill's not an easy guy to hold and Fisheye dropped to his knees after a single kidney punch from Tolson's giant fist. Tolson sliced an uppercut into Howie's jaw at the same time Bill punched the guy in the stomach.

There was, briefly, not a Ferguson standing.

"Let's go!" I scrambled to my feet and grabbed Tolson again.

"I'll kill them!" he roared.

"Not a good idea." I clamped on to his arm through his ruined suit jacket. Bill clinched Tolson's other arm and we hustled him into our car. Bill started the engine and slammed into reverse, K-turning to charge back down the levee road.

We didn't get ten yards before sirens and red and blue lights announced the arrival, on the road ahead of us, of the Coahoma County Sheriff's Department.

—

"Well, well. What do we got here?" Bert Lucknell, hands on hips, looked around the clearing like a kid on the playground wondering where to have fun first. "Whole pile of my unfavoritest people all in the same place." He looked at Tolson Reeves. "Except you. We ain't acquainted. So how about you be the one to tell me what the hell is going on?"

Not an unreasonable question, even coming from Bert Lucknell. Tolson in suit, tie, and swollen eye; Bill, with blood down the side of his face from a gash on his temple; me, mud from scalp to shoes; and four Fergusons in various states of disrepair. Not that I believed Lucknell about his unfavoritest people, except for me and Bill. Still, I understood why he had to say it.

Lucknell had brought with him Tom Thomson, of course, and another pair of uniformed deputies in a second car. Thomson and one of the new folks, a skinny white woman, had the Fergusons corralled over by the Camaro. The other, a stocky black man, stood guard over me, Bill, and Tolson. No one was handcuffed yet and no one was under arrest, but I would be surprised if the morning ended with both those things still true.

Tolson stood straighter, and I could see he was aching. "Tolson Reeves. I'm with the Coahoma County Public Defender's Office.

Those men"—he pointed at the Fergusons—"abducted me outside the courthouse. They assaulted me, punching me and using racial slurs. These folks"—now his arm moved to me and Bill—"must have seen what happened and came to help."

"That's exactly—" I began.

Lucknell wheeled on me. "I'd be obliged if the rest of y'all would exercise y'all's constitutional right to remain silent." He turned back to Tolson. "Abducted, is that a fact? And why would these gents be wanting to do that?"

"I have no idea."

"That's bullshit!" Fisheye lunged forward. Tom Thomson seized him from behind in a body lock. Fisheye thrashed, yelling, "Bullshit!"

Johnny, who'd made it to his feet and around the car while we were driving our ten yards, now started limping toward Thomson with clenched fists. He stopped short when the female deputy pulled her gun and said, "I'd stay right there."

"Damn good idea, Johnny," Lucknell said, winking. "Beth Ann's a helluva shot. Now, Fisheye, you telling me this gent ain't being truthful when he says all y'all abducted him, or when he says he don't know why?"

"Of course he know why!" Fisheye glared at Tolson with the forward-facing eye, and at Lucknell with the other. "That colored son of a bitch been chasing after my daughter!"

37

I stared at Tolson Reeves. My eyes were wide with disbelief, but not at him. How dumb was I? If Anna Rae Ferguson did indeed have a boyfriend she wasn't willing to go public about, it seemed it wasn't Jefferson.

Lucknell needed a minute to take this in, too. "Well," he said, adjusting his hat. "Well. I'll be." He turned to Tolson. "That true?"

Fisheye Ferguson squirmed, but Tom Thomson managed to clink his wrists behind him into handcuffs and then vise-grip onto his arm. Tolson, gaze locked on Fisheye's straight-staring, popping eye, said, "First, that's no one's business but mine. Second, if it were true, would that give them the right to abduct and assault me?"

Lucknell appeared to be considering this. "No, sir," he said. "No, it would not. Excepting, if your advances happened to be unwelcome and—"

"Unwelcome?" howled Fisheye. "What the hell, Bert? Of course they're unwelcome! Bet your fat ass they're *unwelcome*!"

"Fisheye, calm yourself down, there." Lucknell regarded the hand-cuffed man. "You got a way to get in touch with Anna Rae?"

"'Course I do! Number's on my speed dial." His chin gestured toward his shirt pocket. "Tell this chimpanzee to leave me go, I'll call her."

Lucknell said nothing until he'd walked over, slid Fisheye's phone from his pocket, and poked it on. Then he asked for the password.

"The fuck? No way. Use your own damn phone!"

"What's to say she'll answer? She don't know my number."

Wait, I thought. *She don't—doesn't? Then how had she called to tell you we were heading back from Oxford?*

"Give it here, Fisheye," Lucknell said, "or I'm taking y'all in."

"On what charge?"

"Kidnapping. Assault. Looking ugly. Any shit I can think of."

Sullenly, Fisheye murmured a string of numbers. Lucknell, grinning, tapped them into the phone and put it to his ear. He waited, then, "Hi there, Anna Rae. No, it ain't your daddy, this here's Detective Bert Lucknell down here in Coahoma County. How you doing? No, he's fine, but there's been a little disturbance and I got something to ask you."

Lucknell walked until he was out of earshot. We all watched, no one saying a word, while Lucknell, his back to us, conversed with Anna Rae. Finally, lowering the phone, he turned. He treated us all to his noxious smile. Walking back, he slipped the phone into Fisheye's pocket and patted it. In the tense silence, Lucknell sauntered over to Tolson and looked him up and down. Then he spoke.

"You willing to press charges? Abduction, assault, whatever the hell went on?"

"You bet I am."

"And y'all," he said to me and Bill, "you willing to testify, being witnesses and such? Maybe even"—he eyed the blood on Bill's face—"press a charge or two yourselves?"

"Yes, sir," I said, and Bill nodded.

"What?" roared Fisheye. "Listen here, Bert—"

"I'd advise you to shut it, Fisheye. Tom, read these boys their rights. See, Fisheye, what I was thinking, it would've been one thing if this fellow was bothering Anna Rae, wouldn't leave her alone, and she called her daddy for help. But Anna Rae, she says it ain't like that. She tells me she and Mr. Reeves here, they been seeing each other since school started. It's true love, so she tells me, or at least it ain't nothing she's about to call her family concerning. Because she knew for a fact that if any of y'all found out, you'd beat the crap out of him."

Fisheye paled. "My Anna Rae, with this monkey? Bert, shut your lying mouth!"

Howie flushed rage-red, and Keith snarled wordlessly. Johnny just kept a grim stare fastened on Lucknell.

Lucknell gazed over the Fergusons, and a sly grin spread across his face. "Now, I ain't saying what Anna Rae and him are doing is anything I like. Y'all know my feelings on that kind of subject. But they ain't neither of them children, and Fisheye, you're the one let her go away to Oxford. And what this here gives me, it gives me some of that—what's the fancy word?—serendipity. 'Cause right here, I got something I been wanting a long time. I'm gonna arrest me a bunch of Fergusons for a damn big crime, and I'm gonna make it stick."

38

The next hour passed predictably enough, though I was variously confused, skeptical, and furiously thinking.

Everyone was either arrested (the Fergusons) or more or less politely requested to accompany the deputies back to the Sheriff's Office (Tolson, Bill, and me). Paramedics were waiting at the station to examine those who needed examining. The skinny female deputy, whose full name turned out to be Beth Ann McGee, took me off to take my statement. Bill went with the stocky man, whose name tag gave his last name as Waters. Tolson, as the kidnap-and-assault victim, was escorted by Tom Thomson, the senior deputy. Bert Lucknell took the honor of dealing with the Fergusons for himself.

Lucknell made it to my interview room just as I finished giving my statement to Beth Ann McGee. I was feeling right at home, having become so familiar with the place yesterday. Lucknell told McGee to go ahead and scoot, and when she left, he pulled out a chair and sat.

Grinning, Lucknell shook his head. "You people sure are something. Two Yankee private eyes—one a Oriental girl—and a colored lawyer, whaling on four Fergusons. Johnny tells me it was you jumped him yourself, while the menfolk were busy with his kin."

"I wouldn't say I 'jumped him.' But yes, that was a one-on-one match."

"I'll be a son of a spotted pup. Now, ma'am," he said, and his grin faded, "I'd very much appreciate knowing what all this morning's ruckus has to do with Jefferson Tam."

"I would, too," I said. "Though probably, it doesn't."

Oh, Lydia, I thought, *a technical truth like that is exactly what your mother hates about your job.* While Tolson's romance with Anna Rae might, strictly speaking, have nothing to do with Jefferson, Bill's and my presence on the scene had everything to do with him.

Lucknell sighed. "Still, ma'am, I'd be obliged to hear what story you got to tell me."

So I told him. Everything I said was true, but I didn't say everything. I left out the part about us following the Fergusons, because if we'd really been in Burcell just to apologize, that wouldn't have made sense. I could only hope Bill had thought of that, too.

Lucknell sat, arms folded on the mound of his belly, and when I was done he asked, "So what you're are saying is, y'all just happened to decide to go to the courthouse to find Mr. Reeves to talk to him at the same time as Fisheye and his boys decided to go find him, too, for their own reasons? There ain't no chance y'all overheard him say that on the phone?"

"No, sir, we didn't. The call he took seemed to have to do with Anna Rae, and he called Johnny right after, furious. We did figure it was possible he'd go running out and do something about whatever he'd just learned. But he threw us out before we heard anything else. And honestly, I thought they'd go to Oxford, if they went anywhere. Fisheye told Johnny he'd just heard from Freddie. That's the name of Anna Rae's manager." I added helpfully, "Where she works."

Lucknell eyed me. "That's pretty much exactly the way Smith told it." He shifted in his chair. "Seems Fisheye's been employing one or two folks up there in Oxford to keep an eye on his little girl. This Freddie fellow saw Anna Rae and Reeves together after her shift last night. Him and Anna Rae weren't holding hands, nothing like that, so Freddie wasn't sure what he was seeing, but he's had his suspicions before. Reeves drops into the café from time to time, get himself a cup of coffee. Always, so happens, on Anna Rae's shifts. When Freddie heard Anna Rae on the phone this morning, cooing like a lovebird, talking about 'when you come in tomorrow,' he thought he'd let Fisheye know." Lucknell folded his hands on the table. "Thing that interests me, ma'am, is Freddie's never seen the two of them alone before. Usually they have another student or two with them. Like, for example, Jefferson Tam."

To his pointed look, I said, "I knew they were friends."

"If someone had shared that information with me, I might've discussed with Mr. Reeves the question of where Jefferson Tam had got to."

"I guess I assumed you knew everything of importance that went on in Coahoma County. Anyway, we asked Mr. Reeves. He says he doesn't know."

"I'm sure he did say that." When I didn't reply, Lucknell shrugged and went on. "He just told me the same, in a room down the hall there. I dropped in to mention that Anna Rae's on her way down here now, all worried about her sweetheart and madder'n a wet hen at her daddy."

Talk about a guy's girlfriend to soften him up and then sandbag him with the question you really want the answer to—not a bad interrogation technique. I looked at Lucknell with new respect as I said, "I guess the Fergusons have some family issues to work out."

"Oh, yes, ma'am, they got some *issues*, for sure." Lucknell nodded. "And in the matter of family, so you're telling me y'all ain't no closer to finding Jefferson Tam than any of us was yesterday, that right?"

I wasn't sure, actually, if that was right, but I was sure I didn't want to explain to Lucknell why it might not be. I settled for, "I think so."

For a time, he sat gazing at me. Finally, he hefted himself up out of his chair. "Ma'am," he said, "I got to admit that from the day we met,

I saw y'all being here as adding to my headaches. Now in a way I'm indebted, because I got four Fergusons sitting in a jail cell I'm thinking they ain't gonna easily get out of. If I can get Fisheye's ass locked up— begging your pardon, ma'am—then that whole sweet operation they got down there in Burcell is gonna go straight to hell, 'cause there ain't another one of them with brains enough to run it. That's why I told you about Freddie just now. A way of paying off that debt.

"But," he said. "But. I wouldn't want anyone thinking that rounding up a pile of Fergusons is about to take my mind off looking for Jefferson Tam. Looking for, and I'm here to say, finding. So, ma'am, whatever really did happen this morning, and however much my boss would be pleased to see Congressman Reynold Tam and all them Democrats happy down there in Jackson, please keep it mind that none of this gives any y'all any license to come between the Coahoma County Sheriff's Department and Jefferson Tam. Have a nice day."

Lucknell left the interview room door open, which I took as permission to leave. As I was walking the corridor to the stairway, my phone rang.

"Me," Pete said when I answered. "Where are you two at?"

"We're in Clarksdale," I said. "Long story."

"Any chance you could come over and tell it? I got something to show you."

"Sure. To the store?"

"No, I got Henry to drop me home, like yesterday."

"Be there as soon as we can."

Not surprisingly—by now it was almost a tradition—Bill was waiting for me in the reception area by the door. He had a gauze pad taped to his temple—under the circumstances, also not surprising. The new factor was that Tolson, rumpled, bruised, one eye swollen half-shut, sat beside him.

"Wow," I said. "You two look like ten miles of dirt road."

Tolson grinned at my Southernism.

"Don't do that," Bill warned him. "It will only encourage her. Although I must say," he surveyed me, "dried mud is a good look for you."

They lifted themselves off their plastic chairs and we walked into the midday sun together. Bill lit a cigarette as soon as we got outside.

"Waited around to thank you," Tolson said. "Probably you folks saved my life back there. I think those boys were gearing up for an old-fashioned lynching."

His voice was as matter-of-fact as it had been two days ago when we'd first heard him say "colored folk." I got a chill up my spine. I wanted to think it wasn't true, that the Fergusons were planning to give Tolson a beatdown but not actually kill him. But this was Mississippi.

"If we did, I'm glad," I said. "Though I wish we'd known earlier what was going on."

He looked at me a moment before he answered. "Grateful as I am, I don't see how my relationship with Anna Rae has anything to do with Jefferson, either what happened to Leland, or Jefferson breaking out of jail. Him taking my car to Burcell did put me in a bad position, like I said, and not just with my uncle Montel. I didn't want anybody in Burcell having any thought in their heads about me at all."

"I can understand why. Though Bill and I did think Anna Rae was hiding something. Knowing about you two would have saved us from thinking it was a romance with Jefferson. He knew, though, didn't he? He was your beard in Oxford."

"That's right. We didn't know Fisheye had spies in Oxford he was actually paying, but it still would've been crazy for us to just up and go to Anna Rae's apartment. We don't even like to walk down the street alone together. When I stay in Oxford after class, I crash with friends—sometimes Jefferson. When Anna Rae and I started seeing each other, it tickled him to give us the use of his place."

"So you and Jefferson are closer friends than you led us to believe."

"Yes, ma'am. We are."

"Another thing I wish we'd known."

"Ma'am, if I thought telling you that, or telling you about me and Anna Rae, would help you find Jefferson, I'd have done it." He added, "I swear to you, I don't know where he is."

"I believe you." We started toward the Malibu. "I hear Anna Rae's on her way down here now."

"She called me. This is going to be hard on her. She loves her daddy, and Johnny, too. She always knew the business they were in was risky, but they'd never been caught yet. I guess she figured she could hope their luck would hold up. Now it's run out in a whole different way."

"Has it? Or what I really mean is, was it ever luck? We were thinking the Fergusons had a line into the Sheriff's Department, and we were thinking it was Bert Lucknell."

"We were just talking about that," said Bill. "Before you came down."

"Fact is," Tolson said, "like I told you folks before, the Sheriff's Department leaks like a rusty bucket, and if it's not just an accident of flapping gums—and around here, you can't count that out—but if it's not, then I was thinking the same. I was surprised to hear Lucknell say how happy he was to have netted the Fergusons. Could be that's just smoke, because truth is, they'll have a hard time worming out of this, so he might as well distance himself. But I swear, the man practically did a dance."

Bill unlocked the car. "Can we give you a ride?"

"I'd appreciate it. Can you take me back to the office? They're expecting me. I have some things to finish up."

"Wow, a tough guy," I said. "Not going home to rest?"

"It's not me who's tough." Tolson smiled. "It's Callie."

"I can see that. Still, she wouldn't take being beat up by a bunch of Fergusons as a good enough reason to call in sick for half a day?"

"Oh, she would. But I want to be done with work by the time Anna Rae gets here. She's going to need a little help."

———

We dropped Tolson at the Public Defender's Office and watched from the car as he walked in. Through the glass we could see everyone stop work to stare at him. Then a young woman started to applaud. The applause spread, Tolson grinned, and Callie Leblanc came out to see what was going on. She shook Tolson's hand.

"Look at that," Bill said. "If I didn't know better, I'd swear she was smiling. Where to now?"

"Good question. My first instinct is to charge out to Burcell and find Jefferson while the Fergusons are locked up."

"Want to?"

I looked at the bandage on Bill's head and the blood on his shirt and I had to smile.

"What?" he said. "You think you're the only one who likes a good fight?"

"Clearly not." I leaned back against the seat. "But no, not Burcell. For one thing, Pete called, and he wants us to come back to the house. He has something to show us."

"Really? What?"

"He didn't say. Maybe he found Leland's scrapbooks. And for another thing, if we're right that it's Johnny and the cousins who have this online sports-book thing going with Jefferson, there may be no one else in Burcell who even knows he's there."

"If he is."

"If that. But the four in jail aren't the only Fergusons, and they do know *us*, at least in that bar. We'd be even less popular than we were before. And I don't know about you, but I'm not feeling my usual sharp self at the moment. Let's go back, clean up, and think about what to do next."

We pulled up in front of Pete's, where we got our greeting barks from HB next door. The drapes on Pete's living room windows were closed. I knocked instead of ringing the defunct bell. I saw the curtain move. A moment later Pete pulled open the door. He stopped still when he saw us.

"Holy cats! What the hell have you two been up to?"

"We found that fistfight, Pete. Took some looking, though. We'll tell you all about it. Are we too much of a mess, or are you going to let us in?"

"Huh? Yeah, of course." Pete stepped back.

And now it was our turn to stop still.

There, standing in the living room, was what Pete must have meant when he said he had something to show us.

A handsome young Chinese man.

My cousin Jefferson Tam.

39

I stared at this young man, this cousin for whom I'd been searching for days, who last week I didn't even know existed. He didn't look like all that much, given the trouble swirling around him. Sharp cheekbones and a fine nose, yes, but short and thin, like Pete's side of the family, not tall like Reynold's. And right now, haggard, like he hadn't had a good night's sleep in a while. Still, unmistakably a Tam. Therefore, a Chin. Family.

"Lydia Chin, Bill Smith," said Captain Pete, "this here's Jefferson Tam."

"That was superfluous, Pete." I turned to Jefferson. "Your cousin Lydia, from New York. My partner, Bill. We're private investigators."

Jefferson offered his hand in an automatic, well-trained way, and a sudden surge of anger erupted in me.

"Where the hell have you been and how the hell did you get here? For days we've—"

"All right, now, Cousin Lydia, Jefferson's got his story to tell. Sorta looks like you've got a doozy of your own, too. Let's all sit down and tell stories, what do you say? I got tea all made." Pete looked us up and down. "Except it wouldn't surprise me if you'd rather a couple of beers."

I didn't take my eyes off Jefferson, who'd withdrawn his hand and was looking at the carpet. The hoodie and jeans he wore seemed a size too big, and scruffy, as if, say, he'd been in jailhouse orange and had to borrow clothes after he escaped. He lifted his eyes and returned my gaze with a look both apologetic and hopeful, but I wasn't ready to buy it yet.

"I got hot water on for you," Pete said, cajoling. "Come on, sit down."

"Pete, please don't tell me you've known where Jefferson's been all along."

"Don't be ridiculous. I had no idea about anything until he knocked on my kitchen door. I called you right away. I haven't even heard his story yet. If you keep carrying on like this, none of us ever will."

I looked over at Bill. His shrug was one I'd seen before; it meant I might consider a pause to see if I really needed to explode. I glared at him, but sat abruptly in the non-Pete armchair and said, "Okay. I can't wait." Jefferson moved tentatively to the couch, and Bill sat beside him.

Pete asked, "So what'll it be?"

Bill chose the beer option. In the grip of a post-adrenaline crash, I was desperate for caffeine. Pete came out from the kitchen and set down a tray that held something for everyone, including a heaped-high plate of cookies. I picked up the steaming mug. The cookies—walnut chocolate chip—looked great, and I took two. Bill laughed.

"What's funny?"

"You're hungry. You're always hungry after a fight. I'm surprised we didn't have to stop for ice cream on the way here."

I looked at the cookies in my hand, then melted back in the chair, aching and exhausted. "Okay, Jefferson, give."

Jefferson Tam, the man at the center of this convoluted storm, wrapped his hands around his glass of sweet tea. "First," he said, "I didn't kill my daddy. I didn't."

I nodded. "Who did?"

"I don't know. When I found him he was . . . barely conscious." Jefferson swallowed. "I must have come just after the fight, but no one else was there."

"How do you know there was a fight? Did Leland tell you that?"

"He hardly said anything. But that's the knife we use when there's trouble in the store. If someone came in and started acting up, Daddy would take it up and run them off. When I got there, the front counter area was kind of wrecked, so I figured there must've been a fight and the other guy took the knife away and . . . cut him."

Jefferson looked down. He took a gulp of tea, and I gave him time.

When he seemed ready, I went on. "'He hardly said anything.' What did he say?"

"He was pretty much whispering, but it sounded like, 'He has the picture.'"

"He was telling you he has the picture? Leland had a picture of the killer?"

"No, no. '*He* has the picture.' Those words, that's what he said. Like someone else, the killer, I don't know who, had a picture."

"Of what?"

"I don't know. It was really important to Daddy, I guess, because he could hardly talk but he said it twice. Or, I don't know, maybe he was just . . ."

Jefferson wiped his eyes with a napkin. Awkwardly, Pete patted Jefferson's shoulder. The guy had just lost his father, I reminded myself, and he looked like the rest of his week hadn't been real good, either.

I picked up a cookie from my plate, and that made the plate empty. I didn't remember eating the first one, but it was gone. Between the sugar and the caffeine, though, I was beginning to sharpen up.

"Okay," I said to Jefferson, trying to be a little more gentle. "Then what?"

"I tried to stop him bleeding and I called 911. But he . . . I could tell he passed before they got there."

I drank some tea. "And?" I said finally.

"And what? I waited for them."

"You didn't do anything else?"

Jefferson looked to Pete, then back to me with a face of confusion.

"Your laptop," Pete said.

"Pete!" I said.

"Leading the witness, Pete," said Bill, and it was a good thing he did, because he said it with a smile and everyone else smiled a little bit, too. That cut down the tension, which I knew mostly came from me. I needed to hear the story Jefferson wanted to tell, not the story Pete wanted Jefferson to tell. I wanted to trust my cousin and I wanted him to be innocent. But you don't always get what you want.

"Oh," Jefferson said. "My laptop? I hid my laptop."

"Where?"

"There's a shelf under the register. Did you guys find it? How do you know about it?"

"Why did you hide it?"

Jefferson took a long pause. "What's on it has nothing to do with what happened to Daddy, but it was still . . ."

"Still what?"

"It's . . . I was afraid the deputies who came would take it for whatever reason and I was working on something I didn't want them screwing up."

"Tell us about it," I said. "What you were working on. But start by telling us why you escaped from jail."

"I didn't."

"Oh, come on!"

Bill shot me a look.

"Lay off!" To Jefferson, I said, "Don't give me that. You're sitting right here, and you're supposed to be in jail."

"No, what I mean is," Jefferson said, "*escape*'s not the right word.

It wasn't my idea. These guys came to get me, in uniform and everything. They said I had to go to the courthouse. They put me in this prisoner transport van, and then we just kept going. Ended up in Burcell. Then I got it."

"Got what?"

"Who they were, why I was out."

"Who were they?"

"Well, I mean, I don't know who they were, not them personally. They were just hired help. But I knew who they were working for. See, what I'd been doing"—he glanced at Pete, looking worried—"on the laptop, was working on a way to defeat the whales who game the online sports-book sites." Jefferson drew a breath, exactly the way Linus does when he's about to explain something. "Whales, that's—"

"We know," I said. "How?"

"Oh, Cousin Lydia, give the kid a break!" Pete sputtered. "We know all this. Jefferson, you were making algorithms to screw up their algorithms. Like Robin Hood. I love it. The only thing we want to know is, why in the hell were you doing it all tied up with the Fergusons?"

"Because," Jefferson said. "I was trying to help a friend."

40

Sipping tea in Captain Pete's living room, I echoed my cousin Jefferson. 'Help a friend.' I thought of Fisheye's angry, stabbing, pop-eyed glare. "Johnny Ferguson?"

"Johnny? God, no. He's no friend of mine."

"Really? You didn't hang out together in Oxford playing Draft-Kings on your laptop at the Café Café?"

"Of course we did. As I made progress on the algorithms, he'd come check it out."

"Bringing his sister's dog as cover," said Bill. "So she wouldn't know why he was really there."

"Yes. But how do you know that?"

"For God's sake, Jefferson, we're detectives," I snapped. "We've been looking for you for days. So you were working on this algo-rithm project with Johnny Ferguson, but you're telling us he's not your friend."

"No," Bill said. He spoke to me, but his eyes were on Jefferson. "The friend is Tolson."

I looked from Bill to Jefferson, sitting side by side on the couch. "Wait. Tolson Reeves is in on this?"

"No," said Jefferson quickly. "He doesn't know anything about it. But Johnny—" He paused. "Johnny found out Tolson was seeing Anna Rae. He knew his daddy and his cousins would blow a gasket if he told them. He said if I worked out these algorithms for him, he'd keep quiet." Jefferson gave a cold laugh. "Not that Johnny knew the word algorithm. Now he knows it, but he still can't pronounce it. But he figured the whales were cheating. He said no one would bet the kind of money whales do on these sites, blind, unless they've rigged the game. And he figured it had to do with math. He tried to work it out but, my God, he had no idea. The Fergusons use spreadsheet programs to keep track of the business, but this is a whole other level."

"So Johnny came to you. Why, if you aren't friends?"

Jefferson put his mug down. "In high school, early on, he used to make me do his math homework. After a while I got up the guts to say no, but he beat me up. I told Daddy I fell down the riverbank."

"I remember Leland telling me about that!" Pete said. "He said you were climbing around on some rocks by the creek and you took a bad tumble. He ran you to the emergency room."

"I never told him what really happened. You know how he got when family was involved. I didn't want him thundering over to school. That would only make it worse for me."

"But Tolson knew," Bill said.

Jefferson nodded. "A few day later, he cornered Johnny in an empty classroom. He never told me what went on. But I can pretty much guess, because I didn't have to do Johnny's math homework after that."

Jefferson picked up his sweet tea. Bill drank his beer. I reached for a third cookie.

"When Johnny found out about Tolson and Anna Rae, that's when he came to you?"

"He was grinning like it was Christmas. He said I'd better find out what the whales were up to and then turn it into a way to make him rich, or he'd . . . he'd stomp that suit-wearing fancy-ass monkey to a pulp."

"So you agreed?"

"What else could I do?"

"See?" Pete's eyes glowed with triumph. "I told you Jefferson's all right. My gut said so." He patted his astute belly.

"So did my mother."

"Your mother?" Jefferson looked at me quizzically. "Have I met your mother?"

"No. But you're related to my father, therefore incapable of a crime." He still looked confused. It might have been my mother's logic, but in case it was our relationship, I said, "Your great-grandfather— the original H. Tam—was my grandfather's brother."

"My great-grandfather. Uncle Pete's father?"

"Yes," I said. "Pete, Jonas, and Paul's father. Leland and Congressman Reynold Tam's grandfather. Let's not get distracted here. The Fergusons sprang you so you could finish the algorithms?"

"It's late in the season," Jefferson said. "They have to be ready in the next week or two or they're no use until next year."

"All right," I said. "That's how you got to Burcell. How did you get out?"

Pete poured Jefferson more tea. Jefferson said, "I mean, it's not like they were keeping me locked up. Besides what they'd do to Tolson, Johnny kept reminding me I was an escaped murder suspect. Nobody would believe me if I said the escape wasn't my idea. All Johnny would have to do if I ran away was call the sheriff—who's Tolson's uncle, not that that matters—and say they saw me near Burcell."

"Actually," I said, "it does matter, because that's what started us connecting you up with the Fergusons to begin with. But we'll tell you about that later. Keep going."

"What do you—" he started, but this was the time for his story, not ours. I shook my head.

"Yeah, okay." He went on. "They stashed me in Johnny's cousin

Keith's house. These are Keith's clothes." Jefferson raised his arms. "Keith said he couldn't stand to look at the jail jumpsuit, it reminded him of a spell he did himself."

"Did they—Keith and Howie—know why you were there? Did Fisheye?"

"Fisheye doesn't know anything. I gather he's against the whole online-gambling thing in the first place. And he'd be mad if he knew I was in Burcell, because the law was looking for me. Keith and Howie know about the algorithms but not about Tolson and Anna Rae. That's Johnny's private thing. What I was really afraid of was that after I finished the algorithms, he'd turn me in to the sheriff and go after Tolson anyway. But I couldn't think what to do about that."

"So you stayed and worked. But now you're here. What changed?"

"Keith's wife got a phone call. She sounded upset, so I listened in. After she hung up, she called a lawyer. She told him they all got arrested—Johnny, Keith, Howie, and Fisheye—for, quote, 'beating up some colored boy.' She said she wanted Keith to have his own lawyer, not for them all to have the same one, because the colored boy was the sheriff's nephew, so this could be real trouble. I don't know why they went after Tolson now, but obviously I can't protect him anymore." He shook his head slowly. "I guess I didn't do all that good a job. I hope he's okay."

I said, "He is." Jefferson and Pete both opened their mouths to speak, so I told them, "That's the fight we found." I gestured to my mud and Bill's bandage. "We'll tell you later. But it wasn't your fault." *Except*, I thought, *you weren't in Oxford to provide cover, which is why they got spotted*, but this might not have been the time to mention that. "Tolson will be fine. So then what?"

"I slipped out the back and a few houses down, I grabbed some kid's bike. I pulled up my hood and prayed I could make it here without being seen. When I got to the creek, I ditched the bike, snuck along through the brush, and came here." Since it was about twelve miles from Burcell to Pete's house, and that was if you used the roads, it was kind of unnecessary when Jefferson added, "I'm exhausted."

"Good," said Pete. "You can stop talking. I want these two to tell me whose dirt they've been rolling around in."

It was a fair question. Bill and I took turns filling the Tams in on our visit to Rupert's and the subsequent excitement. The tea, the cookies, and all of us were pretty much done by the time the story was over.

41

We took a break from the confessional so three of the four of us could get cleaned up. I grabbed my robe and headed for the bathroom while Jefferson and Bill went to the basement. Pete collected everyone's clothes to stick in the washer in the utility room.

I was glad for the water, the soap, and the chance to think. I didn't like the way I'd snapped at Bill before; all he'd been doing, really, was asking me to keep a lid on it until Jefferson explained himself. If I didn't believe Jefferson, I could bark at him then.

The problem, of course, was how deeply I wanted to believe Jefferson. I wanted him to have not killed his father so I could tell my mother she was right. It would be even better if his tale of selfless cyberheroism was true. That would make my mother strut like a rooster. But, except for Pete's gut, we had no way of knowing. Maybe Jefferson really had been blackmailed into making the algorithms and surprised when he was broken out of jail. Or maybe he'd been a partner in the plan all along and was changing his story now that the Fergusons were in deep doo-doo.

What Fisheye and company had tried to do to Tolson argued for Jefferson's story. And Johnny, now that I thought about it, had been grim-faced as he drove past us on the way out of Burcell, as opposed to the eager anticipation I saw on his cousins. He might have been seeing his golden goose about to be cooked for dinner, with himself as part of the kitchen staff. After all, he couldn't very well stop them by telling his father he'd known for a while about his sister's interracial affair and was using it for leverage on a scheme Fisheye had already vetoed. On the other hand, it wouldn't have been hard for Jefferson, full partner, to concoct his story once he learned Fisheye and the others had found out about Tolson and Anna Rae.

As I scrubbed red Mississippi dirt from my skin and hair, I reflected that the truth might come out soon, if the Fergusons were even now jockeying for position in the prosecution steeplechase. Which, if they all had separate lawyers, they well might be. It would be interesting to see how deep Ferguson family feeling ran when long jail terms were on the table.

But even if every word Jefferson said was true, that still left us with the original problem: who'd killed Leland? When all this Ferguson dust cleared, Jefferson would still be the chief suspect in that crime. If I were a Ferguson in the sellout scramble, I'd try to use Jefferson's whereabouts as a bargaining chip. If I were Bert Lucknell and that happened, and a raid on Burcell didn't pan out, Pete's would be the next place I'd come. If I were me, I wouldn't give too much for the chances of anyone in this house once Lucknell arrived.

I dried off and, with Bill's objection to my bathrobe in mind, put on brown corduroys and a white cotton sweater before I headed back to the living room. The guys were there already, Bill in jeans, dark blue T-shirt, and a spiffy new white bandage. Jefferson wore clothes that had to be Pete's. They fit him fairly well, both of them being in the slight-Tam, not lanky-Tam, mold; but the chinos and striped shirt that looked so sharp on Pete gave Jefferson the air of a fresh-off-the-boat immigrant hoping to come across as "American." *Odd*, I thought. Here was Jefferson, born in Clarksdale, wearing his uncle's clothes and looking like he's pretending to be what he actually is. Somewhere in there was a comment on paper sons, but I had other things on my mind.

"So," I said to Jefferson as I sat again, "to get all the details straight: the Fergusons broke you out of jail, but to work on the algorithms you needed your laptop. You told them where you'd hidden it and they went to the store for it, but they couldn't get past Pete's new alarm locks before the Down Home Club guys chased them away. Before they broke you out, they had tried to come for it, too, the night after— after Leland died, but they didn't know where it was, so they tore the store apart looking."

Jefferson looked confused. "The first part's right but the second's wrong. Someone tore the store apart?"

"Made a helluva mess," said Pete.

"Why?"

"Looking for something."

"Well, if it was before I was busted out, it wasn't the Fergusons. They only went there after I was in Burcell, when I told them I needed my own laptop, so I didn't have to reconstruct what I'd done on the one they had. That was Lucky Culligan's. Remember, Uncle Pete, I helped him set it up?"

"It was a Ferguson lifted Lucky Culligan's laptop?"

"Johnny himself. He stole it out of Lucky's car because he'd heard him bragging about how he was going to beat the other whales on the online sports books."

"The *other* whales? Lucky thought he was a whale?" Pete sounded incredulous.

"He'd bought some of the team-picking algorithms. Anybody can. Johnny thought if he had Lucky's laptop, he could figure it out. Hah. Anyway, you're right, they couldn't get into the store. So I've been trying to reconstruct what I had, using Lucky's machine." He gave us a slight smile. "Got pretty close, too. A couple more days, I'd have had it."

Pete frowned. "Jefferson, I gotta say, you were doing some pretty shady work for meth cookers on a stolen laptop. Least you could do is feel bad about it."

"You can skip the finger-shaking-uncle routine," I said to Pete. "Anyone can see you're as proud of Jefferson as he is of himself. But I'd like to bring you guys' attention to another matter, if no one minds? Forget the whole sports-book thing. If Jefferson didn't kill Leland, who did? And if the Fergusons didn't turn the store over the night Leland was killed, who did, and what were they looking for?"

Everyone was silent.

"I mean," I added reluctantly, "I guess it's possible it was really just a burglary, someone grabbing the chance because the place was empty."

"No way." Pete shook his head. "Like you said before, why make such a mess? Nope. Someone was looking for something."

"Did Leland keep a lot of cash in the store?" Bill asked. "Or were there rumors that he did?"

"Not that I ever heard," said Pete, and Jefferson shook his head. "Listen, I get that you detectives are trying to cover the bases, but if Leland was so upset about some picture that he said it with his dying words, don't you suppose it might be the picture that's at the bottom of this?"

"Okay," I said. "Let's look at that. Leland said, 'He has the picture.' He was telling Jefferson someone, most likely the killer, has some really important picture. Of what, we don't know, but maybe whoever broke in that night was also looking for it. Someone who didn't know the killer already had it."

"Or it was the killer, coming back to make sure there weren't more copies," said Bill. "At least at the store."

"If it matters so much," I said, "it must be pretty explosive. So then, did Leland actually have another copy, and did the searcher find it?"

"And," Pete said, "was Leland killed because of it? Or was that an accident?"

"Callie Leblanc made it pretty clear it was an accident during the struggle," Bill said. "Maybe they were fighting over the picture."

"Callie Leblanc?" Jefferson, after all this talk about Leland's death, was beginning to look a little ashen. "You talked to her?"

"She's not happy with you," I told him.

"No, I guess not. Will she still be my lawyer, after . . . ?" He trailed off.

"We're not going to worry about that right now," Pete said firmly, planting both hands on his knees. "First, we're going to figure out this business. You'll stay here with me until we do." He glared, daring me to object, but I couldn't think of a better idea. "Don't worry." Pete softened. "I got hiding places and such."

"Uh-huh," I said. "I hope so. But this picture. Do you guys have any idea—?" I stopped, because Pete and Jefferson were both shaking their heads. "Well, what was important enough to Leland that it would be on his mind at the end?"

After a few moments, Jefferson said, "Family. That's what Daddy cared about most."

"And," Pete said, "that's what I haven't found. Leland's scrap-books, the family pictures, all of that. They haven't turned up."

42

"Scrapbooks," I said. "That would make sense, if we're talking about a picture so important Leland would say it twice with his last breath. Except who'd keep a picture that explosive in a scrapbook?"

"Maybe he didn't," said Pete. "Maybe whoever it was just wanted to make sure."

"Pete, could we have a look at your scrapbook again?"

Pete was ahead of me, already pulling it out of the drawer. We all bent over it, examining each photo: the parents, stocky H. Tam and his pretty wife, both looking dignified and formal in the first photo, relaxed and smiling in the last. The three boys, lanky Paul, pudgy Jonas, sprightly little Pete. Bikes, baseball bats, the store, Paul's long arm sticking out of his car. We looked, discussed, and examined, but in the end, we had no blinding insights.

"Okay," Pete announced, "lunch. No one can think on an empty belly. Bologna-and-cheese sandwiches okay with everyone?"

Bologna's never okay with me. But it wasn't like we could go out as long as we were harboring a fugitive, so I negotiated to plain cheese. Jefferson went into the kitchen to help Pete slap the sandwiches together, and Bill went out for a smoke. I went with him. Maybe some fresh air would help.

"Do we believe him?" I asked as we crunched the dry grass down the backyard slope.

"He's your cousin."

"Which doesn't mean I have any better sense of him than you do."

"No, I think it means the opposite. You distrust how much you want to trust him, so you trust him less than you feel you can."

"You're making my eyes cross."

"Yes, I believe him. For one thing, he could've tried to just plain run, leave the state entirely, but he didn't. For another, he doesn't seem in any hurry to use the algorithms himself, not even to finish them, now that the Ferguson pressure is off. And plus, there's Pete's gut."

"Oh, great. I'm not trusting my gut and you're trusting Pete's." We reached the edge of the marsh and I watched the water inch downstream. "But really, someone killed Leland over a picture? What could it possibly show?"

"Something to do with H. Tam being a paper son? Proving, I don't know, that the family doesn't really own the store?"

"Would someone really kill for Clarksdale real estate? It looks like there are plenty of storefronts you could pick up for a dollar, and better located ones, too. And the paper son thing doesn't even worry Frank about Reynold's campaign. So how explosive could it be?"

A gust of wind rattled the bare trees. We'd been down here with Frank Roberson, who'd looked over the brown water and the waving branches and said, "This is home."

"Reynold," I said. "He's family, too. Maybe this has something to do with him. Although Leland hardly knew him. Reynold hadn't been down here in years, until the day before yesterday."

"Your mother's never been down here. She doesn't know any of these people and the one she's in contact with—Pete—she doesn't approve of. But when he called and told her family was in trouble, she sent family to straighten it out."

I looked at him. "Sometimes," I said, "you're really smart."

He shrugged. "Tell your mother."

"She knows. It's not your brains she's worried about. I'm calling Frank."

"Cousin Lydia," Frank said cheerfully after the second ring. "How's it going?"

"Hi, Frank. Got a minute?"

"Sure. How can I help?"

I didn't want to mention Jefferson, so I told him we had new information that a witness had turned up who claimed he'd heard Leland's dying words.

"A picture?" Frank sounded skeptical. "Of what?"

"We have no idea. We were hoping you could think of something."

"Well, I never met Leland—never met any of the Delta Tams before. I can't think what kind of picture that could possibly be."

"We were thinking maybe it had to do with Reynold."

"Reynold? How?"

"If Leland was trying to protect family, well, Reynold's family."

"But they hardly knew each other."

"Still."

Frank sighed. "You're right. Family's family."

Except, I realized, in cases like Frank's own father, who'd written off his one-eighth Chinese grandchildren, and with them, his son.

"I'm sorry," I said. "I know that's a sore point."

"My daddy, you're thinking of? That's all right. I have a new family now. But as to what this picture might be, or what it might have to do with Reynold, I have to tell you I'm drawing a total blank."

"That's too bad. It might strike some chord with Reynold, though. I'll call him next."

"He's right here. I'll just give him my phone."

Cousin Reynold was delighted to hear from me, according to Cousin Reynold, but he could offer no more insight into what the picture might be than his son-in-law had. "I wish I could help. I'll give it some thought. Is there any word on young Jefferson?"

"The law hasn't found him yet." Putting it that way kept me from having to lie to my relations. "If anything comes to mind about this picture, could you let me know right away?"

"Of course. Good luck. I hope we'll see you again soon."

Frank took his phone back, echoed Reynold's hope, and we hung up.

"Damn."

Bill peered at me over imaginary glasses.

"What?" I demanded.

"Aren't you going to apologize? For using a bad word? Everyone else around here does."

"That word wasn't nearly as bad as the one I wanted to use. What's our next move?"

Our next move, apparently, was to stand still, feeling the cool but still soft Mississippi breeze and watching a few yellow leaves drift into the water. Birds sang songs unfamiliar to me, and two squirrels, smaller than the ones up north, scrabbled around a cottonwood tree.

"Hey," I said.

"Hey, what?"

"There's still something we don't know."

"I'd say there are a lot of things we don't know."

"Yes, and this one may be a dead end, but—Trevor McAdoo, down at Parchman. We still don't know what he wanted with Reynold. And since Reynold's family . . ."

"It's a stretch," Bill said. "But it's worth following up."

"Especially since we don't seem to have much of anything else to follow up. Go ahead, call the prison and lay that brotherhood of Southern white guys thing on thick."

Bill took out his phone, but before he could start, Pete appeared at the kitchen window and hollered, "Lunch!"

Before we sat down, Bill called Parchman Farm. As it turned out, the call was as unsatisfying as my American cheese on white bread. He poured on the charm, which can be considerable—one of the things my mother distrusts about him—but without result. The gist, as reported by Bill as we started on the sandwiches, chips, and sweet tea, was that Trevor McAdoo was a troublemaker who'd lately been particularly pleased with himself and disruptive. This had landed him in solitary—again—and he was going to damn well stay there until his stretch was up—another four days—unless the governor, the president, or God himself decreed otherwise. Did Bill want to make an appointment to come down then? If Trevor McAdoo would see him, of course. He might choose not to. Because he wasn't an easy prisoner. He was a troublemaker who'd lately—

At that point, Bill had thanked the warden and hung up. "So," he said. "Four days?"

"I don't think we have four hours before Bert Lucknell figures out we're harboring a fugitive."

Pete spoke through his sandwich. "I'm harboring my nephew and I'll harbor who I please."

Jefferson shook his head. "Uncle Pete, if they come with a warrant—"

"Oh, shut your piehole. I have an ace or two up my sleeve. Let 'em come."

I could see that argument was going nowhere. Sure, let 'em come; but after they came, I wondered how I was going to explain to my mother that not only hadn't I gotten Jefferson out of jail, but Pete was in now, too. And, for knowing about it and not alerting the law, Bill and me.

Briefly the room was full of nothing but the grunts of men chowing down on nasty sandwiches, and me, nibbling. Good thing I'd had those cookies. I looked at Bill. I knew he was thinking as hard as I was. I hoped he was coming up with something, because I also knew that Pete was counting on us. Me, I had nothing.

It was Pete, though, who broke the silence. He issued a garbled sound through a mouthful of bologna, swallowed, and said, "Hey! There's still a McAdoo left!"

"What?"

"Old Miz McAdoo's gone, Tremaine's gone, Trevor's in solitary, but old Miz McAdoo's sister is in some nursing home somewhere. Remember, Henry and them were talking about it, and Big Bone, too? How sad it was that she come down here to spend her last days with family and now she's all alone in a nursing home?"

"Hmm," I said. "Dubious. But it's something. Pete, do you know where?"

"No. But those layabouts might."

Bill was on his feet, grabbing the car keys with the hand not holding his sandwich, before I could tell Pete and Jefferson, "Stay here."

43

Henry, Sam, and Bobby Lee were sitting out in front of H. Tam and Sons, smoking and watching the traffic, which, foot or vehicle, didn't offer a lot to look at.

"Hey," said Sam as Bill and I got out of the car. "Lookee here, it's Pete's detectives. How y'all doing? Gonna open up?"

"We don't have a key, Sam, sorry."

"Dang. I been sitting here waiting for Pete so I could get my malt. Where's he at?"

"He might be along later," I said. Unlikely, I reasoned, but possible. "We have a question, though. About old Miz McAdoo's sister."

"Lunetta?" said Henry. "She up in a nursing home, ever since her stroke. What y'all want with Lunetta?"

"We have a few questions we thought she might be able to answer. Do you know the name of the home? Where it is?"

"Questions have to do with Jefferson?" Henry and Sam looked baffled, but Bobby Lee smiled.

"Hey, they're detecting," he said. "They ain't about to tell you why. I expect when they solve this thing they gonna let us in on it"—he looked at me; I nodded—"so, Henry, you go on and tell them where Lunetta staying, if you know. Let them get on with it."

Henry grunted. "Lunetta's over at the Villanova Home, in Crenshaw. Married name is Briggs, Lunetta Briggs. Can't see she gonna tell you much. Even before her stroke, she ain't spent much time in

Clarksdale. Don't know as I ever seen her in the store. Probably she ain't never met Jefferson at all."

"Still," I said.

Bill grinned at Bobby Lee. "Thanks, little brother."

Bobby Lee grinned back. "Anything for family."

———

Set back from the street, the Villanova Senior Home sprawled behind a grassy yard in the decrepit, dusty town of Crenshaw. Long and low, built of brick, bordered by bushes, with geraniums waving in boxes under white-trimmed windows, the unexpected cheeriness of the place made me smile. Then I laughed.

"What's funny?" Bill asked as we walked up the concrete path.

"I was just wondering if this might be not such a bad kind of place to spend your twilight years after all. And then I heard my mother saying, 'Don't even think about it.'"

Bill grinned, too, and pulled open the wreath-hung door into the home. Tinsel draped the front of the laminate counter and a corn-rowed receptionist sat behind it. I asked her if we might see Lunetta Briggs.

"Sure can. Just sign in here." She gave us a curious, though not unfriendly, head-tilt. "Are y'all friends of Miz Briggs?"

I guessed young Chinese women in the company of middle-aged white men didn't come calling on elderly black ladies very often. "We haven't met her yet. We're doing some research, though, Mississippi history. We have questions about her family."

The receptionist looked dubious. "Well, I hope y'all's questions is about the old days. Miz Briggs a mighty nice lady, and she can tell stories about them days till the cows come home, but she don't necessarily recall what she had for breakfast." She waved to an orderly who was walking down the hall and asked her to show us to Lunetta Briggs's room.

The orderly led us along a vinyl-tiled, fluorescent-lit corridor, where a thick coat of glossy white paint brightened but didn't disguise the concrete block walls. Bulletin boards announced movie nights and upcoming school group visits. A Christmas party was in the offing. Posters reminded staff to wash their hands and illustrated the Heimlich maneuver.

The smells of disinfectant, air freshener, and baby powder almost, but not quite, covered the scents of urine, institutional food, and decay. A slack-jawed man whose wheelchair was tucked into a sunny niche followed us with his eyes as we passed; except for those eyes, bright and large, he could have been a statue.

Near the end of the hallway, the orderly knocked on an open door and said, "Miz Briggs? I brought you some friends."

In a wheelchair by the window, a nightgown-clothed woman sat gazing out past the geraniums to the front yard and near-deserted street. She turned her head and smiled when the orderly spoke. Her mahogany face, her coiled white hair, her arms and fingers, everything about her was long and thin. She looked like she'd probably been tough and energetic before the stroke that had paralyzed her left side. Her right hand, I noticed, absently rubbed the left, smoothing out the fingers, massaging the palm.

The orderly went around the bed to turn the wheelchair to face us, without asking whether that was what the occupant wanted. Still, Lunetta Briggs said, "Thank you, child," and smiled.

The orderly smiled back and departed. Lunetta Briggs looked from Bill to me. "Good afternoon." Her voice was strong but slightly slurred. "I'm sorry. I'm sure I know y'all but I can't recall just now."

"No, ma'am. We haven't met. I'm Lydia Chin, and this is Bill Smith."

"Pleasure, Miz Briggs," Bill said. He took her extended hand and cupped it briefly in both of his. I shook hands with her the standard way, but I tempered my usual I-am-Woman-don't-mess-with-me squash so as to avoid ninety-six-year-old broken bones.

She looked at us quizzically through heavy glasses. "Are y'all doctors? Is it time for more of them e-valuation tests? Where's y'all's white coats?"

I breathed a sigh of relief. Lunetta Briggs wasn't displaying any signs of her older sister's reported animosity toward Chinese people. That meant Bill and I wouldn't have to put plan B into effect, which would have been to good-cop-bad-cop it, winding up with him suggesting I go wait in the hallway while he talked to the nice lady my presence was upsetting.

"No, ma'am, we're not doctors. We came to ask you some questions, something we're hoping you can help us with. But first, we've brought you this." I held out the box of candy we'd stopped for on the way.

Behind the glasses, Lunetta Briggs's eyes lit up. "Oh, ain't y'all just the sweetest things? Yes, I surely do like me some fudge." She shakily took the box and balanced it on her lap. One-handed, she started picking at the cellophane wrapping.

"Might I do that for you, ma'am?" Bill asked, his Southern speech once again in full bloom.

"That's very kind, young man."

Bill ripped off the cellophane, lifted the cardboard top and fit the bottom into it, and replaced the box on Lunetta Briggs's lap. She examined the pieces with care, though they all looked the same to me. "Please. Y'all help yourselves," she said, selecting one and popping it in her mouth. Bill, naturally, took a piece. I thanked her but declined.

"Child, you don't know what's good. Now. What kind of doctors did y'all say you are?"

I said, "We're not doctors, ma'am. We came to ask you some questions."

"Questions? About what? Must be important, y'all's bribing me with chocolate."

I smiled. "It is important. But the fudge, that's because Big Bone Stafford told us you liked fudge." I said that so Lunetta Briggs would know we had mutual friends.

"Big Bone Stafford?" Confusion clouded her eyes; then they cleared. "Oh, you mean Li'l Billy Stafford. I recall someone tell me they calling him 'Big Bone' now." She nodded, as if re-registering that information. "I believe he still live down to Oldman's Brake. I ain't seen him in some time." I glanced at Bill. Big Bone Stafford had said he'd been visiting Lunetta Briggs regularly. "Y'all got questions about Li'l Billy, probably best ask Lentitia."

Uh-oh. Had Lunetta Briggs not been told her older sister had died? Or had that fact also not made it into her failing memory?

"The questions aren't about Mr. Stafford," I said. "We want to ask you about your nephew Trevor."

"Trevor. Lentitia's boy. Can't come visit me no more, Trevor's down on Parchman." She frowned in disgust and reached for another chocolate.

"Yes, ma'am. Can you think of a reason he'd want to talk to a man running for governor?"

She blinked. "Why who'd want to do what?"

"The candidate's name is Reynold Tam. Trevor wants to talk to him."

She bit into the fudge and gazed at me.

"Ma'am," I said, "have you heard of Reynold Tam?"

"I don't believe I have. Who might he be?"

"He's a congressman, running for governor of Mississippi."

"Democrat or Republican?"

"Democrat."

"Well, then, y'all can tell him he's got my vote. And thank him for the fudge."

My heart sank. As Bill had said, it was a stretch, anyway, to think Lunetta Briggs might know what her criminal nephew wanted with Reynold Tam. Clearly we were going to have to wait until Trevor was out of solitary to talk to him. Meanwhile, what? I didn't know.

Oh, well. At least we'd made an old lady happy by visiting and bringing chocolate.

I shrugged at Bill, who was obviously thinking the same thing, and I cast an eye over the room. Opposite the bed hung a print of a sunny garden with robins and masses of—aha!—bougainvillea. A lavender sweater draped from a hook on the wall, a quilt was folded neatly over the room's guest chair, and a pair of fuzzy pink slippers sat by the door. The bed table held a well-worn Bible and two old, framed photos. In a faded Kodachrome, Lunetta Briggs, in late middle age, held a baby on her lap. A man her age sat beside her, and a younger man and woman—the man in an army uniform—stood behind. The other photo, black-and-white, had clearly been taken much longer ago, in a yard with a wooden shack to one side and chickens pecking the grass. A stocky man stood with his arm around the shoulders of a gangly woman an inch or two taller than he was. Two girls and a boy, thin and loose-limbed like the woman, were arrayed in front of them. It reminded me of the photo Pete had of him with his parents and brothers, except all these people, adults and kids both, wore wide grins. Leaning down to look more closely, I felt an electric jolt.

The similarity to Pete's photo was based on more than the setup.

While the girls shared the woman's dark skin and curly hair, the boy, who was the youngest and palest of the children, had the man's features.

Asian features.

Chinese, really. I'd seen that man before—in Pete's photo. He was my great-grandfather's brother, Chin Song-Zhao, called, in Mississippi, Tam Hong-Bo. The original H. Tam.

I caught Bill's eye and nodded toward the photo. Bill glanced at it. His eyes widened.

"Mrs. Briggs," I said, "may I look at this?"

"Look at what? Oh, my pictures? Of course, child. Just be a tad bit careful, if you don't mind. They pretty much all I got left of the old times. That one there, that's me and my Walter before he passed, and our Ralphie with Carla and little Mason. Ralphie, he's career army, live over in Germany. Fixing to retire soon, likely going to stay there, he like it so much. Don't know why, never been there myself. Little Mason, I don't rightly know how old he'd be by now. Grown man, for sure, married with his own family. Over there, too, somewheres in Europe, 'cause he grow up there. Get a letter from him on my birthday and Christmas, every year."

"You must be very proud of them, ma'am," Bill said, as I lifted the black-and-white photo for a closer look. "What about the other picture, who's that?"

"Oh, that so long ago." She shook her head with a little smile. "That there in the middle, that skinny thing, that's me. Don't look like much, do I?"

"I think you look lovely. Who are the others?"

"Mama, and Daddy, and Lentitia—she's bigger than me—and Paulie."

"This man," I said, keeping my voice calm though my skin was sizzling, "he's your daddy? And this is your brother, Paul?"

"Yes, child."

I looked at her eyes behind her thick glasses. Like Reynold Tam's glasses. Her eyes slanted just slightly. Like Reynold Tam's eyes. "What was your daddy's name?"

"Harry Tam. 'Course, Harry not his name for real. He have some Chinese name, but Mama the only one ever call him that, and only when she mad with him. She don't say never it right, though, so he laugh, and then she laugh, and then she can't stay mad no more." Lunetta Briggs reached for the photo. I handed it to her, making sure she had a firm grip, and watched her smile as she gazed into it. "This from way back before the flood, all of us still living in that broke-down shack." She laughed. "Flood took that away, for sure." Her face grew more thoughtful. "Took Daddy and Paulie away, too. They come back, but they live somewheres else after that. Don't stop with us no more."

"The flood, you mean the Great Flood of 1927?"

She laughed again. "I surely do. Ain't no other flood like it before or since, excepting the one the Lord sent Noah."

"Mrs. Briggs," I asked, still trying to keep my voice steady, "can you tell us the story of the flood? About how it took your daddy and Paulie away?"

"Why, of course I can, y'all want to hear it. Y'all best sit down and be comfortable, though." She looked around at the room's sparse furnishings. "Or I got a better idea. Down past the community room, they got a little porch. We can all go set there, if this young man would be kind enough to push my chair." Her face was glowing. The receptionist had said Lunetta Briggs could tell stories about the past until the cows came home, but I wondered how often anyone gave her the chance.

"Of course." Bill went around behind her. "Should we take the chocolates?"

"No, we should not. Them people be jumping on that fudge like a duck on a june bug. My special friends, gonna invite them in, maybe after supper. Have me a little chocolate party."

44

Bill pushed Lunetta Briggs's wheelchair along the corridor. In the community room, a group of elderly men and women, both black and white, sat watching or not watching a blaring TV. I guessed a nursing home was like an airport. Even if you wanted to, you couldn't control who was there with you.

We navigated to a screened porch facing the side street. Lunetta Briggs's room looked onto the main road, but the view was essentially the same: dilapidated buildings, cracked sidewalks, parked cars, the occasional person sitting in the sun.

Lunetta Briggs had asked that I bring her lavender sweater, and now I helped her into it. "These people here, they freeze themselves in weather like this," she said, with what sounded like a chortle of satisfaction. "Me, I been more of my life in Chicago than here. This don't even seem like December to me."

"What sent you to Chicago, Miz Briggs?" Bill asked, settling onto a steel-framed chair beside her. I was dying to hear the flood story, but it occurred to me Bill might be priming the pump, starting Lunetta Briggs off delving into the past. I pulled a chair around to face her.

"Well, like for lots of folks, it the war. They have work in Chicago because of the war. Down here, we was sharecroppers. Wasn't no way to get out from under, anyone could see that. Walter Briggs, he go on up north, in 1942, that was. We was married just before he leave. Couple months, he find himself a job and send for me. End up to be a electrician, that's how come I got my union pension." Her pride in her man was evident. "Quite some time before we have Ralphie. We think we gonna have more, but the Lord say, Ralphie enough for anyone. Now, Lentitia and them, I want them to come, too, but Mama want to stay, and Lentitia don't like to leave Mama. She say someone got to take care of her, since Daddy gone."

"Your father had died by the time you went north?"

"No, no, by 'gone' I mean they living elsewhere. Oh, but y'all got to understand, Daddy be taking care of us all along, even when him and Paulie be over in Clarksdale. That's why we come to live at Oldman's Brake, make it easier for them to come see us on Sundays. I always be happy to see him, happy to see Paulie, too. But Lentitia, she so mad with him even Mama couldn't never make her like him no more. She ain't want nothing to do with him, nor with Paulie neither, after that."

"After what?" I said.

"Well, after the flood take him away."

"Mrs. Briggs, we'd like to hear all about that. If you don't mind."

"Don't mind a bit. Haven't talked about those times in a dog's age." She looked at the floor and frowned, as if deciding how to begin. "See, we all living in that shack, the one in the picture. Place called Preacher's Hollow, north of here. Don't suppose young people like y'all even remember them days. Got no electric, the kitchen be outside, we have a outhouse, chickens and a garden, a cow. Some years we have a pig, too." She wrinkled her brow. "What y'all ask me about?"

"Your whole family, living in the shack."

"Oh, I recall now. Well. Most folks down to Preacher's Hollow, they sharecroppers, but Daddy go off in the morning in that rattly old truck, leave Mama to do the farming. Mama say he work at a store, but me being so little then, I got no more than a hazy idea what a store might be. All I know is the shed off the kitchen, Mama call that the storeroom. I can't think what Daddy might be doing in a place like that all day. Lentitia laugh, she think I'm funny." Lunetta Briggs smiled. "Tell the truth, it make me glad when Paulie come along, 'cause Lentitia, after that, sometime she laugh at him instead of me."

"I have older brothers," I said. "I know about being laughed at. And then, there was the flood?"

"Well, not right away. Paulie be walking and talking some by the time the flood come. Still, Lentitia put him on top the cow, so we can go faster. Mama pull the cow along, and Lentitia and me got the cook-pots and all. Have to leave them chickens, but Mama say they gonna be fine 'cause they can fly. People be laughing at us, dragging that cow down the road. It ain't raining yet, you see. Mama say the river gonna top the levee soon as the rain start. People be saying, 'Ma'am, you gone crazy. Levee ain't never broke, and we miles from that levee, anyhow.' But Mama, she have her this feeling, like she get sometime. About weather and all. She say, 'Ain't never seen rain like that what's coming, neither.'

"And see what happen? Rain come the next day. By then we be walking all day, half the night, too. We make it to Aunt Hetty's house, mama's sister. Got a little hill there, her place. Well, I tell you, that hill turn itself into a island and we was up there for weeks, us and Aunt Hetty and Uncle Toby, and them three boys of theirs. Around us there be water everywhere you look, trees and house roofs sticking right up through it. Dead animals come floating, one time a man, too. We eat right through Aunt Hetty's grits and all the vegetables she put by. That cow, she don't have enough to eat to be making much milk, and all what she have we be giving to Paulie and to Caleb, Aunt Hetty's youngest. People come by in boats, even white men from the army, they say come on, they got a tent camp, they got food for folks an' all. But Mama and Aunt Hetty and Uncle Toby, they don't like to leave, go live in no tent camp. Mama, she worried crazy about Daddy, but ain't no way of knowing where he be.

Finally, water start to go down. Uncle Toby and the older boys and Lentitia, they walk through the mud to one of them camps, come back two days later with sacks of grits and rice and a couple of boxes of that dried milk. Ain't nothing never tasted so good, I tell you." Lunetta Briggs, with a smile, looked through the screen to a past I couldn't see.

"And your daddy?" I said. "What happened to your daddy?"

She brought her eyes back to me as though she'd forgotten I was there. "Daddy?"

"In the flood. Where did your daddy go in the flood, when you were on the island?"

"Oh, Daddy get himself to one of them camps and he wait. After the water go down, he go back to Preacher's Hollow. Ain't nothing there, no shack, no chickens. No neighbors to ask, neither. Everything been washed away. He get all scared, but he study on the problem and it occur to him, just maybe, mama think to make for Aunt Hetty's. So he head over there. Tell you, we was so excited, see him slogging through that mud where the cornfield used to be! This before Lentitia get mad with him, so she go running down the hill, slipping, sliding, jump on him with a big hug. Me, too, and Mama and Paulie. Everybody be crying and laughing, even Aunt Hetty and Uncle Toby, even they never think too much of Daddy because . . ."

"It's all right," I said. "Because he was Chinese?"

She gave me a grateful smile. "Yes, child. A shame, how people sometimes just want to keep to their own." She moved her eyes from me to Bill and included him in her smile. He grinned and winked. I felt myself blush.

Back to business. "That sounds like a wonderful reunion. But if he came back, what do you mean the flood took him away?"

"Well, see, after the water go down, we stop with Aunt Hetty and Uncle Toby for a bit, 'cause we got no shack to go back to. We all of us be out in the mud all day, digging and clearing and trying to plant the garden, plant them fields again. At night, Mama and Daddy have them some of them long talks. You know how grown folks do and children don't never know what's going on. Lentitia and me, we hear them sometimes." She gave me a sly look. "Ain't gonna lie, one time we hear them because we be pressing our ears to the floor of the attic while they talking in the kitchen. Mama, she saying Daddy got to do it, Jesus give Paulie this chance. Daddy say no, he ain't going. Mama say, look at the child, he don't look colored, now all the records been washed away, ain't nothing no more to say who he be. He can go to school with white folk, get him a education. Daddy say even if he ain't colored, he Chinese, he ain't never gonna be white. Mama say, this Mississippi, they a world of difference between colored and any other kind of not white. Then she say Paulie her son, he got this chance, and Daddy gonna take it for him. Now, me and Lentitia, we got no idea what they talking about, but Mama, she have a voice that say that the end and no more arguing. Daddy don't say nothing after that, just we hear them sounds that mean they doing huggy-kissy stuff, so we giggle and we fall asleep.

"Couple days after, Daddy leave again. He tell us be good, he be back. Few weeks, he do come back, bring everybody presents, even Uncle Toby, Aunt Hetty, them boys, like it Christmas. When he leave, he take Paulie with him. Me and Mama and Lentitia, we stay at Aunt Hetty's place all winter. Lentitia and me waiting and waiting for Daddy and Paulie to come back, but Mama say they can't come right now. Sometime she seem sad, but then she smile when she see us looking at her. In the springtime, we pack up what little we got, tie the cow to the wagon, and Uncle Toby take us downriver to Oldman's Brake. Daddy and Paulie be there, standing on the porch of a blue house. Daddy say, this y'all's house, y'all gonna live here now. Lentitia and me ain't never seen nothing like it. We get all happy, running around, but then after lunch, when Uncle Toby head back in the wagon, Daddy and Paulie go with him. Daddy don't never live with us in the blue house. He come to visit lots of times, especially Sundays, bring sacks of flour and cans of beans and presents, and he do repairs and such, but he don't never even stay the night."

Lunetta Briggs fell silent. Her right hand rubbed her left. I was concerned she was tiring, but I had to hear the rest.

"Is that why Lentitia was always mad at him?"

She gazed at me. "Lentitia?"

"Why Lentitia was mad at your daddy. Because he went away, after the flood?"

"Oh. Yes, no question. And take Paulie with him." Lunetta Briggs nodded. "Mama, she miss him so bad, and Paulie, too, sometimes she be crying and all. Lentitia say, Daddy done a bad thing, shouldn't of went away. But Mama say it her idea, she the one say they got to go. Lentitia, she just stay mad. Mama say, but see, this way, Paulie can go to school. Make something of himself. Ain't no one to say he colored." Lunetta paused, pressing out the curling fingers of her left hand. "Daddy, he bring him another wife from over there in China. He be telling everybody she bring Paulie with her, she Paulie's mama. That's why Daddy go on down to start him a store in Clarksdale, where don't no one know him—so they believe all what he say. And why we come to be in Oldman's Brake, us and Mama. 'Cause it nearby to Clarksdale.

"Now, ain't hardly no schooling for colored girls in them days. Lentitia say it ain't fair. Me and her, we just as Chinese as Paulie, he just as colored as us, but he going to school down in Cleveland and we working in the fields. Mama say, hush, in this world, it ain't what's true, and for sure it ain't what's fair, it what folks *think* is true. She make us promise to never tell nobody. When Daddy come visit, she tell folks he that nice Chinaman shopkeeper from over in Clarksdale, take pity on a poor widow woman and bring her groceries. When he stop for a bit, she say it's 'cause least she could do be offer him a cup of coffee.

"Could be, if Mama ain't so sad after Daddy and Paulie go away, day might have come when Lentitia stop being mad. Or if Lentitia come on up to Chicago, like I want her to do, her life be different, so maybe then she could feel some kindness toward him. But she stay right in that blue house and just get more and more bitter, all her days. She always keep her promise to Mama, even after Mama pass, don't never tell nobody, but it just grow into a rotten thing inside of her. Have her two babies with that no-good man who run off on her. Both her sons turn out bad, too. It like she expecting everyone to be a disappointment and everyone oblige."

Lunetta trailed off. Sunlight hit a corner of the screened porch and laid angled patterns on the floor. I thought she was finished, lost in the past, but she spoke again. "That picture, I ain't seen it in years, until I come back from Chicago. I ain't even know Lentitia have it, but for seeing it on her table. So sad, she keep that all these years, but she can't keep no love in her heart for Daddy nor Paulie." She sighed and added, "Don't know why she send it to me, neither."

"She sent you this picture?"

"Last week, or some such. Come in the mail. With a letter. Next time she come up to see me, gonna ask her why she send it, why she don't just bring it."

I let that go. "What did the letter say?"

Lunetta frowned thoughtfully, and then gave me a sad smile. "Can't remember."

"Do you still have it?"

"I don't know, child. I can look, you want me to."

"I'd appreciate it."

I wasn't sure Lunetta heard me say that. She sat staring through the screen into the day.

"Miz Briggs, I think we should be getting you back to your room," Bill said, standing. "I believe we might have tired you out."

Lunetta roused herself and smiled at Bill. "That y'all did, young man. Talking about the old days, yes, that's really something. If y'all would be kind enough to take me back to my room now, I'd be obliged." She surprised me by saying, "I can look for that letter before y'all go, you want me to."

"Yes, please," I said.

She held the photo on her lap and looked at Bill and then at me. "Y'all going on over to Oldman's Brake, I wouldn't ask Lentitia about them days. Matter of fact"—and for a moment, her gaze sharpened—"could be y'all don't want to be going to see Lentitia at all."

45

On the short trip back through the hallways, Lunetta faded again, but she perked up when we reached her room and insisted on searching for Lentitia's letter. It wasn't a long search; a paw through the night table drawer produced an envelope with shaky handwriting, inside of which were two sheets of paper covered with the same.

"May I read this?" I asked.

Lunetta laughed. "Child, that's why I went looking for it. I wouldn't want you to go running off with it, but if y'all want to ask that nice young lady up at the front desk to make a copy, I wouldn't have no objection."

"The photo, too?"

"Why, I guess so."

Bill left to take the photo and letter to the receptionist. Lunetta cocked her head at me. "Might I ask, what give y'all such a interest in the old days?"

I hesitated; but really, there was no reason not to tell her. "Mrs. Briggs, if Tam Hong-Bo—Harry Tam—was your daddy, then I'm your distant cousin."

Her eyes widened, as did her smile. "Well, now. Is that God's truth?"

"Yes, ma'am. Your daddy was my great-grandfather's brother." I took her good hand in both of mine. "Your cousin Lydia," I said. "I'm so happy to know you."

"I'm just tickled pink to meet you, too, child. Sometime when I ain't tired myself out by talking, you got to come back and tell me some stories. Promise to do that?"

"Yes, ma'am, I will."

Bill returned with a manila envelope. He slipped the letter back into the drawer and stood the photo on the night table.

"Well, then," said Lunetta. "I believe I'll take me a nap. But now that we relations, you gonna come back, is that right? Good, that's good. And if it ain't too much trouble, bring some more fudge."

—

We jumped in the car outside the Villanova Home. As Bill started the engine, I scrabbled the envelope open. I began to read out loud.

> Dear Lunetta,
>
>   If you reading this letter it mean I passed. I gone on to glory in the arms of Jesus. I be back with Mama again, and together we waiting for you, too. Until then I hope you don't suffer none.
>
>   Why I'm sending this letter is to explain what I done.
>
>   Long time ago, we promised Mama we wouldn't never speak of Daddy, who he really be, or either of Paulie, that he our little brother. All my life I keep that promise, but now that I can see that light shining ahead of me I'm fixing to break it and I want you to know why.
>
>   My two boys, they men now but they gone to the bad from a young age. I know that and it always grieve me. Some of that, it cause of their daddy, a man I shouldn't never have had nothing to do with. But still and all, whatever they done, both my boys be more than they think and I want them to

know it now. I want them to understand they can take Jesus into their hearts and turn themselves around, even no matter what they been until now. No man done such terrible things but God will forgive him if he truly asks.

A person who refuse to come home to the Lord, though, going to suffer all the trials and tribulations the Devil got to offer. I don't wish that on nobody, and me so close to the final door I ever step through, the thought of it be putting fear into me. All my life I been speaking with bitterness about Daddy. Also all of his people, which maybe ain't right, judging them all on him. Now I'm dying, I have open my heart and forgive him. Not because what he done was right in any way, shape, or form. But I want to spread my wings and fly to my Savior without no hate nor anger weighing me down. So what he done, denying us and Mama, I forgive him for. Mama love him till the end, so could be he have more good in him than maybe I ever could see. He support us, which was true as she always remind me. But when he visit, with little Paulie, and y'all be playing and laughing, I always be so mad at him I can't help but run off the other way. But now I forgive him in my heart.

Lunetta, I be sending this picture I always have by my bed, and I want to tell you I have sent one to Tremaine, and one to Trevor down there on Parchman. This is not to cause them to hold anger like I done. Just, I think it ain't fair that they don't know. Especially now I hear Paulie's son, Reynold, he making something big out of himself, might be our next governor. Good for him, I say, and what I want my boys to know is, we got the exact same blood running in our veins as Paulie had, and it the same as Reynold Tam got, and my boys got it, too, and that mean they can be more, so much more, than what they is now.

Lunetta, I hope you understand why I have broke this promise. I prayed on it, and this what Jesus tell me to do, to try to bring my boys to Him.

Now I say goodbye, until me and Mama welcome you on that sanctified shore.

Your sister, Lentitia

46

I lowered Lentitia's letter to my lap. "My God," I said. "Lunetta doesn't know who Reynold Tam is. But he's her—her nephew. Right? Her brother Paul's son."

"Right."

"Paul wasn't born in China. He was born in Preacher's Hollow. His mother was black. Reynold Tam's grandmother was black." I slid the letter back into the envelope, next to the photograph. "These could explain why Trevor wanted to see Reynold."

"Blackmail, you're thinking."

"I sure am. But not for money. Like you said before—for freedom. If Reynold's elected, Trevor gets a pardon."

Bare branches and fallow fields slid by. I thought of Lentitia McAdoo, bitter all her days, reaching out from beyond the grave to reveal to her family the secret she'd promised her mother she never would.

My heart lurched. "Oh my God."

"What?"

"Family. Frank. He said they didn't know what Trevor wanted. But what if it's just that *he* doesn't know? What if Reynold did talk to Trevor, on the sly? Read the letter, saw the picture?"

Bill was silent for a moment. "It's the picture that makes the difference," he finally said. "The rest would only be rumors."

"But the letter."

"In the South, every family has stories about hidden branches on the family tree. The letter could just be a crazy old lady rambling on.

But the picture—it's not proof, but with the letter, it could be ammunition."

My thoughts swayed from bitter Lentitia to hopeful Reynold, a long shot making an unexpectedly strong showing. He and his chief aide son-in-law, as well as Pete, had said his only chance to win would be to draw in conservative voters. Like those Family First people he'd gone to meet with. Family First. If only they knew. And that was the problem right there: *if they knew*.

"Reynold's opponent," I said. "This Stirling Mallory. Reynold said he was worried his grandfather being a paper son would be a problem. Frank said it wouldn't. But this is his *father*. This is a whole other kind of paper son." I laughed, without humor. "A paper son of a different color. But Bill—even if Mallory's the kind of guy everyone says he is, would he really come out and say, 'Don't vote for this guy, it's not just that he's Chinese, he's also part black?'"

"No, that would be bad form. But he wouldn't have to. He'd just say that Reynold had been *hiding* the fact that he was part black. That would alienate Reynold's black voters. And Reynold's one-quarter blackness would alienate the, um, conservative vote without Mallory having to hammer on it. He'd give voters the perfect out, because they could say it wasn't Reynold's racial makeup that turned them off, it was that they couldn't trust a politician who would lie about something like that."

I looked out the window at the gray December sky, at the Mississippi that wasn't what I'd expected.

"Especially," Bill went on, "considering who Reynold's black relatives are. The McAdoo brothers are not what Tolson Reeves called 'the right class of colored folk.'"

"All of what you just said—that's the real meaning of *this is Mississippi*, isn't it?"

He didn't answer me.

I thought about my mother, telling me Mississippi wasn't different from anywhere else, that cuckoos don't hatch from robin's eggs here. But didn't the cuckoo lay its eggs in other birds' nests and leave them there to be raised?

Bill asked, "What do you want to do?"

"All of this could be wrong. Reynold might have nothing to do with it." Though the vision of Reynold making an off-the-radar trip to Clarksdale, walking into the family store, asking his cousin Leland whom he hadn't seen in decades about a family photo that Leland either knew nothing about, or had been hiding until that moment, a photo that totally changed the family story . . .

And Leland, dutiful and quietly resentful all his life, feeling a surge of hot anger, perhaps, and no one nearby but Reynold, and nothing nearby but the knife . . .

An argument, an accident, who knows what happened? Then Tremaine—a white guy went to see Tremaine. Or, at least, a guy who wasn't black.

I felt sick.

After a few deep breaths, I took out my phone, put it on speaker, and called Frank.

"Cousin Lydia! How are you? What's up?"

"Hi, Frank. Tell me something. With the campaign reaching such a critical point, are you and Reynold together pretty much twenty-four-seven these days?"

He laughed. "It sure seems like it. Not really, though. There are times I need to be in the office and he's out pressing the flesh, that kind of thing. Today he's down in Natchez, but not me. Why? You have reports of Reynold on the loose, misbehaving?" He said that with the teasing tone of a man who knew it couldn't be true.

I tried to match his lightness. "No, of course not. Just wondering about something. And you have no idea what Trevor McAdoo wanted with him?"

"Trevor—the convict at Parchman? No, we haven't heard from him again."

"And you're sure Reynold never talked to him?"

"I'm sure. You don't mind me asking, what's this about?"

"Nothing really, just working something out. Okay, thanks. Give my love to Reynold." I cut the call before he could ask anything else.

"We have to talk to Trevor McAdoo," I said to Bill. "We have to get into Parchman."

"You want me to call again?"

"No, that didn't work the first time. Let me think." After a few minutes I asked, "The number's in your phone?"

He slid it out and handed it to me. I had my story all ready, that I was with Reynold Tam's campaign and one of their convicts had reached out to us with an urgent request. I was going to heavily imply it would be an obstruction of Trevor McAdoo's rights and ours not to let me talk to him and I was all primed to sound completely convincing. It might have worked, except I hadn't noticed how much of the day had gone by. It was after five and all calls to the state prison went to voice mail. *Leave us a message and we'll get back to you. If you have an emergency, call 911. Have a nice day.*

"Maybe we should go down anyway," said Bill. "They may not be in the office, but it's not like there's no one there. Maybe we can get the guard at the gate to call the night warden for us."

"How likely is that? And if he did, how likely is it the night warden would let us talk to a guy in solitary?"

"Not very."

"You're humoring me, right?"

"A little," he admitted.

I flopped back on my seat. "We do have to talk to Trevor. But I guess it can wait until tomorrow. Let's go back to Pete's. I need to think some more, anyway."

It was Reynold, my mother, and my father's sainted family I needed to think about. I was silent and preoccupied for the rest of the drive, and Bill being Bill, he opened a window, lit a cigarette, and said nothing as we rolled from the Mississippi twilight into the Mississippi night.

I was still thinking, and it was fully dark, when we parked in front of Pete's. Light gleamed around the drawn shades in Pete's living room windows. HB gave one greeting yip from behind his fence and quieted down. I guessed we'd become familiar pretty fast.

Another car also stood along the curb, one I didn't recognize, so I wasn't entirely surprised to find someone else in the living room when Pete answered my knock.

I was surprised, though, that it was Frank.

47

I took a quick glance around to assure myself that Jefferson was not in evidence. It was bad enough that Pete, Bill, and I were harboring a fugitive. For Reynold Tam's chief aide son-in-law to know about it would put him in an impossible position.

Jefferson, though, was apparently not on Frank Roberson's mind. "I was up by Tunica when you called," he said as Pete went into the kitchen. "I pass near here on my way back to Jackson, so I thought I'd stop. I wanted to talk a little more about what you called about. Surprised I got here first, though. You weren't nearby?"

"Rooting around the county, to see what we could find." It wasn't that I didn't trust Frank, but until I figured out what to do, the fewer people who knew about Lunetta Briggs and the rest of Reynold's other relations, the better. Pete came back with a glass for Bill, so he could partake of the sweet tea on the coffee table, next to, of course, the cookies.

"Your hot water won't be a minute, Cousin Lydia," Pete said. I tried to figure out if he'd told Frank anything about where we'd gone, or about who else was in the house, but his face was a perfect mask of friendly blandness. I could see how he made a living.

Frank pointed to the manila envelope I'd brought in. "What've you got there?"

"Just some papers."

"Something you picked up rooting around the county?"

I shrugged.

"Um." Frank looked at me, at Bill, at Pete. Quietly, he said, "It's the photo, isn't it? You went to Parchman, you talked to Trevor. You know."

I stared. So much for trusting Frank.

"How did you get to see him?" Frank went on. "He's supposed to be in solitary. When you called me, you were fishing, asking about Reynold. So Trevor must not have told you I'd been there. But he shouldn't have talked to you at all. That wasn't the deal."

"The deal," I said. "I guess that means we were right."

Pete said, "What are you—?" but the whistling of the tea kettle cut him off. "No one say anything!" he commanded, and strode to the kitchen. He came back in seconds, plunked a steaming mug down beside me, plunked himself back in his chair, and said, "Okay, go ahead."

Frank stayed silent, his expression both patient and oddly satisfied, as if he already knew what was coming and had his answer prepared. It must be a technique he used in high-level meetings; it made me feel defensive, which is how you want your opponent to feel. I didn't like the idea that I was Frank Roberson's opponent, but right now that seemed hard to deny.

While I tried to decide what to say I felt a change in Bill. His breathing slowed, his focus seemed to sharpen. This was my case, my *family*, my call, and whatever I wanted, he was ready. This was how we worked, not reading each other's minds but trusting each other's instincts, having each other's backs, whatever happened. This, I suddenly realized, was something my mother knew full well, though she'd never admitted it. This was why she'd sent him with me.

Bill. My mother. I felt myself back on solid ground. I reached for my tea, took a long sip. Then I picked up the envelope and slid the photo out. "Yes, we know. And I guess, so do you. You and Reynold both know."

"Know what?" Pete demanded.

"Not Reynold. Just me." Frank took the photo. Pete leaned forward to look.

"Just you?" I wasn't quite willing to believe that.

"I went down to Parchman without telling Reynold. Protecting him is my job. I had to make sure Trevor McAdoo didn't have anything that could bite us later. Good thing I did."

Pete's forehead creased as he stared into the photo. "What the heck is this? That's Daddy. And Paul, right? Who're these people?"

Frank waited for me, but I was waiting for him.

"That's Aletta McAdoo, Pete," Frank said. "Your daddy's first wife. Those are your half sisters."

"First wife? What are you talking about?"

"Before your mother came from China, your daddy married this woman here. Your brother Paul, your mother wasn't his mother. This is Paul's mother."

Pete looked up. "Wait—McAdoo? Any relation to old Miz McAdoo, just passed?"

Frank tapped the older girl in the photo. "That's her."

"Holy cats, what are you telling me?"

No one spoke.

"*This* lady is Paul's mother?" Pete said. "My mama's not?" A long pause. "Paul's mother . . . I'm not sure what . . . Oh, Lordy. *Oh*. If this is true, Reynold's grandma was a black lady."

"That's correct." Frank nodded. "And if anyone else in the state of Mississippi finds this out, Reynold's political career is over."

Pete stared at Frank, at the photo, back to Frank. I didn't speak, afraid of the answer to the next question. Bill asked it. "But Leland found out, didn't he?"

After a pause, Frank said, "In the end, yes."

Now I spoke. In a big way. My words came out as a shout. "So you killed him?"

"Oh my God, no." Frank's hands went up. "I didn't. That wasn't me."

Pete jumped up. "Just hold on here! What in the hell are you people talking about? What do you mean, Leland found out? Who killed him? And for God's sake, why? Someone slow down and explain this to me!"

"Pete," I said, "that story your daddy told over and over, about how your family came here? It's not true. He had a first family, in a place called Preacher's Hollow. When your daddy sent for your mother from China, she pretended she'd brought Paul with her."

"That's crazy. You can't just pretend stuff like that. There'd be papers, records—"

"There are," Frank said calmly. "I checked. Your mother came through Angel Island, alone."

"But Paul's birth certificate, if he was born here. Church records from where he was baptized. Or what about—?"

"The Great Flood." I said. "Nineteen twenty-seven. Town halls, churches, doctors' offices, all destroyed. Buildings and their records. That's what must have happened," I added, so Frank wouldn't get the idea anyone had told us that.

Pete dropped back into his chair as Frank said, "That's what I figured, too. Trevor McAdoo didn't say that, but the timing's right. Things like the flood, bad as they are, can give folks a chance to start over."

"But why the hell—?"

"So Paul wouldn't be black, Pete," I said. "Turned out he couldn't go to the white school, but he went to the Chinese school your father helped start. Then he could go on to college, and law school. He wasn't white, but in Mississippi he was better off as pure Chinese than half black."

Pete looked at the photo for a long time. "These folks. Daddy just up and left them?"

"No. He supported them. He went out to see them in Oldman's Brake. You were right about the blue house. But Pete, that's why old Miz McAdoo hated Chinese people. She felt abandoned, left behind to work in the fields while her little brother Paul had a whole better life."

"My mama," said Pete. "She and Daddy grew up together in the village back home. Friends since they were little. And they were so sweet to each other."

"I'm sure he really cared for her, Pete."

"But this lady. Old Miz McAdoo's mama. She was his true love, wasn't she? See how happy he looks. Never saw him grin like that, all my life."

For a few minutes, no one spoke. Then Pete sighed and said, "Did my mama know?"

"I don't know. Maybe. Or maybe your daddy told her Paul's mother died in the flood."

Pete rubbed his chin. "So where did this picture come from?"

I decided to take that before Frank could. Let him try to deny or amend the story, rather than tell it himself. "Old Miz McAdoo had letters ready to go to her sons when she died. That photo was in them. When Trevor got his, he realized what he had and offered to keep quiet if Reynold would pardon him once he was elected."

That was still technically theory, but I didn't doubt it. I said it as fact to bolster Frank's impression that our information and photo came from Trevor. I didn't know if Frank knew Lunetta Briggs was alive and nearby. I also didn't know if I believed him that he wasn't Leland's killer.

Which was apparently the question on Pete's mind, too. He took off his cap, smoothed back his hair, and said, "So in the middle of all this, who in the hell killed Leland?"

Frank said, "Tremaine McAdoo. Lentitia's other son."

48

Bill, Pete, and I stared at Frank, digesting what he'd just told us. Headlights slid past Pete's lowered blinds.

"Far as I know, them McAdoos hardly knew Leland." Pete frowned at Frank. "Why would Tremaine kill him? And how do *you* know?"

Frank stayed calm, as though this were a tough political meeting and we were rowdy constituents. "Tremaine got the photo and the letter, too. Did you see Trevor's letter, Lydia? They were pretty much the same. Telling the two of them they were more than they thought they were, they had the same blood in their veins as the congressman, the man running for governor, because they all had the same granddaddy. She told them to let Jesus into their hearts. She didn't mean any harm. She wanted to help her sons to a better life."

Pete kept the frown going.

"But they each had their own ideas about a better life," Frank went on. "More immediate than Jesus. Trevor wanted to get out. Tremaine, he wanted a place he could deal drugs from. So he went over to his newly found nephew's store."

"Leland would never—"

"He didn't."

"Then—"

"Tremaine showed Leland the photo and the letter and told him what he wanted. He offered Leland a cut. When that didn't work, he tried the same thing as Trevor. He said he'd let this out and ruin Reynold's chances of being governor, probably ruin his whole career."

Pete narrowed his eyes. Grudgingly, he said, "Threatening a relation, even one he hadn't seen in years—that would've set Leland off,
for sure."

"It did. He grabbed up the knife and tried to run Tremaine out of
the store."

Frank didn't go on, but he didn't have to.

What he did have to do, though, was answer Pete's other question,
so I asked it again. "How do you know all this?"

"Tremaine told me."

Oh. "You were the white man who went to see Tremaine," I said.

Frank raised his eyebrows. I said, "We've been in Oldman's Brake.
Rooting around. People saw you."

As far as we knew, really only one person, Hardison Lambert. I
threw in the exaggeration in the service of cutting off any must-be-a-
mistake argument.

Frank didn't seem disposed to argue. "Once I'd talked to Trevor, I
had to see Tremaine. Yes, I gave Trevor the promise he wanted. I'm
sure that's just the beginning, but if he's trouble later, I'll figure it out.
It's all about the next ten weeks. It's all about Reynold's primary."
Frank's demeanor didn't change, but his voice grew harder. "When I
got to Tremaine's, he was high as a kite. He opened the door holding
a gun. 'Who the hell're you?' he said. He pulled me inside. 'Neighbors
don't like me doing my business up in here.' I told him I wasn't there
to buy drugs. I offered money for the photo, starting low, expecting
to have to negotiate up. But he stared like I was speaking a foreign
language, then laughed. He took the photo and letter from a drawer,
tossed them on the table, and said 'That old Chinaman want that
picture, he pull a knife on me. White boy ain't got balls enough to do
nothing but flash a few dollars? Damn.'

"I asked if 'that old Chinaman' was Leland. He said, 'Hell, yeah.'

When I asked why he'd gone to see Leland, he leaned back on the sink, waved the gun around, and started telling me about it. Like we were just hanging out, swapping stories. At the end he said something like, 'Surprised he died, though. Didn't stick him nowhere but the leg.' Then he said maybe Chinamen had all their parts in different places. He laughed like crazy over that. His eyes were wild. What a mistake I made, going there. I wondered if I could turn and bolt. But he was between me and the door. I couldn't think what else to do, so I doubled my offer. He laughed and fired a shot over my head.

"I was terrified. He fired again. He was so high he was swaying, laughing and swaying. Maybe he wasn't trying to shoot me, just scare me, but he was so unsteady it didn't matter. I tried for the door, but he shot right into it. I ducked, turned the table over, knocked him backwards. He was laughing so hard . . . I grabbed for the gun. We fought. It went off. I swear, that's the truth."

In my cousin Pete's living room in Clarksdale, Mississippi, I stared at my cousin-by-marriage, Frank Roberson, who'd killed my cousin, Pete's nephew, Tremaine McAdoo. If what Frank was saying was true, Tremaine had killed his own cousin and mine, another of Pete's nephews, Leland Tam.

Mississippians put stock in family, Frank had said the day we'd met. *A man can't disavow his kin.*

Chinese families can be messy. This, though, was chaos on an order I'd never seen.

Maybe because he was raised in the South so he was less thrown by this, or maybe because it wasn't his family, or maybe to give Pete and me time to absorb what we'd heard, Bill started asking practical questions.

"Where's the gun now?"

"In the Mississippi."

"Tremaine's letter and photo?"

"I have them."

"With you?"

"No."

"It was you who broke into the store after Leland was killed?"

"Yes. I didn't know if Leland had a photo, too. I couldn't take the chance."

"Did he?"

"Yes. But it seemed he'd just gotten it. It was in an envelope with a letter from Lentitia McAdoo. She asked Leland to forgive her for all the hate she'd held, and hoped the photo would explain why, because his granddaddy was her daddy who'd denied her. There was one addressed to you, too, Pete," Frank added.

"Me? What are you saying, Leland had a— Oh." Pete looked around. "That's what he called me about, up in Tunica. He got a strange letter, asked did I get one, too. I said to be my guest, come look. He must've taken it because he wasn't so sure he wanted me to see it. And it's what he meant when he told Duverne he had something of old Miz McAdoo's. Damn." Pete let out a long sigh. Suddenly he sat up. "The scrapbooks!" he yelped. "You took the damn family scrapbooks!"

"They're safe, Pete. That's where the letters were, tucked into one. It's been worrying me, how to return them."

"Well, slap my face. That's why you asked to see what photos I had, when you and Reynold came here?"

"I had to make sure you didn't have another one."

"I see." Pete took off his cap again to run his hand over his scalp. "But seriously, son, did you have to slice up all the blessed furniture?"

"I'm sorry, Pete. I'm new at this."

Pete grinned. "Not that anyone's going to miss that broke-down old couch, tell you the truth."

Frank smiled. Pete's grin widened.

Family.

And that was the issue.

"Assuming all this is true, Frank," I asked, "what are you going to do?"

"I know." He rubbed his face, suddenly looking exhausted. "Now that I know who killed Leland, I can't let the law keep thinking it was Jefferson. But how do I explain how I came to be in Tremaine McAdoo's kitchen getting shot at, or why Tremaine killed Leland, without ruining Reynold's career? And why would anyone believe me? I'm family to Jefferson. Why wouldn't I lie to get him out of trouble?"

"Still," I said.

"And where the hell even is he? Why did he run? Why did he make it so much harder?"

I had my own questions about where Jefferson was at the moment, but none of anyone's questions were about to be answered.

49

Pete's alarm system, HB next door, suddenly started barking up a racket. Pete went to peek through the blinds. He just had time to mutter, "Hell and damnation!" before knuckles rapped hard on the door. Pete opened it a few inches. "Good to see you, but we're busy right now. Could you—?"

"Nope. Sorry." Deputy Tom Thomson strong-armed the door and pushed past Pete into the room. "Evening, folks."

Pete peered out the door and then shut it. "Where's your other half?"

"I'm here on my own, Captain Pete."

"Thank God for little favors. But I don't recall inviting you over."

Thomson looked around the room. "Didn't realize y'all were throwing a party or I'd have brought a cake. I know the New York detectives here, but would you care to introduce me to this gent?"

"Not particularly."

"Frank Roberson." Frank stood and offered his hand. "From Congressman Tam's staff. Pleased to meet you. You are?"

"Tom Thomson, Coahoma County sheriff's deputy. I'm here to pick up Jefferson Tam."

"Jefferson?" Pete sputtered. "What fool sent you here?"

"Been doing a little thinking, Captain Pete." Thomson folded his thick arms. "Those Ferguson boys, they're spinning all kinds of tales back there in the lockup. Not so easy to tell true from false, and anyhow each of 'em's innocent as a lamb, anything bad went on must've been the others doing it. Now, ain't none of them Einsteins, but my money was on Howie to break down first, him being dumber than dirt. So I leaned on him some, after Bert went home to his dinner. Might be I told him some things that wasn't true, might be he told me the same, but he finally got himself so confused he said he wished Johnny had just up and said about Anna Rae and that Reeves fellow instead of trying to get all fancy with Jefferson and all. 'Course I jumped on that and he spilled the beans.

"I went on down to Burcell and talked to Keith's wife. She told me Jefferson was there, but he's gone now. She claims she doesn't know why or when or where. I didn't buy a nickel's worth of it, but I let it go and wandered around Burcell, asking this and that. Ain't no one seen a Chinese fellow, but it seems some kid's fancy new bike is missing and his ma is all up in my face, how can the law just be letting thieves walk the streets of Burcell and did I think it was this Chinaman did it? Now, folks, when you think about it, who's gonna steal a bike in Burcell? Fisheye, he don't hold with that kind of thing, and that's enough for anyone down there. I asked the lady if someone might have borrowed it, some cousin or friend, and she said the kid asked around and no one had it.

"So I started considering, and what came to me was this. Was I a fugitive, trying to get out of Burcell, I might run off with a bike, and ride like hell for the river"—Thomson cocked his finger like a gun toward Pete's back window—"and ditch the bike and walk my way along the bank. If I did all that, I'd be mighty tired by the time the river brought me into Clarksdale, to my uncle Pete's backyard." He slid the finger-gun toward the coffee table, and said, "Pete, could I trouble you for some of that sweet tea?"

Pete snorted, but he went to the kitchen and came back with a glass.

"I took myself to the first place between Burcell and here where the road drops close to the river. And damn if there ain't a bike there! Nice fancy one, too. Thanks, Pete, much obliged." Thomson poured from the pitcher. "Got that bike in the trunk of my car right now, gonna have it printed and such by the crime lab boys. Also went and checked the riverbank. Lots of broken reeds all along it, like someone's been bushwhacking down there." He took a long swig and said, "Now, Pete, here's the situation. I'm going to take the boy in. Y'all—all y'all, including the detectives and the congressman's boy here—got a fugitive from the law stowed away someplace. That ain't legal in the state of Mississippi."

"Now just a—"

"Come on, Pete. We got no time for this. I can take y'all in, or I can take Jefferson in and we can pretend I found him down by the river and y'all didn't know a thing about it. Which'll it be?"

I could guess what Pete was going to say but he didn't get a chance to say it. Four things happened in quick succession.

HB erupted in frenzied yowling.

Sirens screamed as blue and red flashing lights slid behind the blinds and stopped in front of the house.

The front door shook with loud pounding.

And Jefferson Tam, coming through the back door, appeared in the kitchen.

50

Bill, Frank, and I shot to our feet. Frank wore an expression of wonderment and worry. Of course: he didn't know Jefferson, and he didn't know Jefferson was here. The sirens stopped, but the lights still pulsed. The pounding went on, and so did HB's wild barking.

"They're here for me, Uncle Pete," Jefferson said, walking into the living room. "I saw them drive up. I can't let you get in trouble like that. I'll tell them you didn't know—" He stopped when he saw Frank Roberson and Tom Thomson. "Oh God."

"Well, now, look who's here." Thomson grinned and took the handcuffs from his belt.

A too-familiar voice from outside shouted, "Open this door or we're gonna break it down. I got a warrant, Pete."

"Oh, shut up, Bert!" Pete yelled. He took a quick look around the living room, shook his head, and opened the front door to Bert Lucknell.

Lucknell's gun was drawn. Striding in, he swung it up.

My heart froze. "*No!*" I shouted.

It took me a second to realize he wasn't pointing it at Jefferson.

Though he was pointing it in that direction. At the man who'd just finished clicking the handcuffs on Jefferson.

"Back off, Tom," Lucknell said. "And put those hands in the air or I swear I'll drop you right here."

Funny how a room can spin and be completely motionless at the same time. No one moved, no one spoke. HB's nonstop barking was the only sound.

Pete didn't seem any more on top of things than I was, but he could at least talk. "Bert, what in the hell is going on here?"

"Damn good question," Tom Thomson said. "Bert, I don't appreciate that gun up in my face. Maybe I didn't get me a warrant, and so I'm sorry, but I came here to pick up this fugitive we been hunting all over creation for the last few days."

"Uh-huh. And I do happen to have a warrant, and I came here to pick up the Fergusons' pipeline to law enforcement I been hunting for more than a year."

I drew in a sharp breath.

"Bert, you lost your mind?" Thomson tightened his grip on Jefferson's arm.

"Not hardly. Had my eye on you for a while now, Tom, but wasn't nothing I could prove. Then suddenly I got me a jailhouse full of Fergusons. I asked each of 'em, who's y'all's inside guy? But Fisheye and Johnny are too smart to answer, and Keith and Howie are too dumb to know." Lucknell shook his head. "So then, I think to myself, well, maybe it's Tom and maybe it ain't, but if it is, maybe he'll do something interesting right now. 'Cause if it was me, I'd want to up my credit on the good-guy side of the ledger by, say, grabbing me a fugitive who was hiding someplace I knew all along. Then maybe folks would buy my innocent act when the Fergusons start fingering me. I been trailing you all afternoon. You went down to Burcell soon's I said good night, but that didn't prove nothing. We been collecting Fergusons, so maybe you was headed out on some business related to that. But then from there you came straight here."

"Because Howie said Jefferson was hiding out in Burcell. When he was gone from there, it wasn't hard to figure where he must've come."

"And when did Howie say this?"

"I talked to him back at the jail."

"You did nothing of the kind, Tom. I got them cells bugged." Lucknell winked at me. "And the interview rooms, well, you know everything goes on in them is recorded. You never asked nobody nothing, not even a by-your-leave. And yet, seems like you knew just where to go. Now, I can't think of too many people who'd go to Burcell to look for Jefferson Tam—except maybe the guy who supplied the paperwork to spring him."

"That thinking, it's none of it right, Bert."

"Yeah, well, I guess that's possible. When Johnny and Fisheye see the light and sell out whoever they got on the inside, could be it'll turn out to be someone I never even thought of. In that case, I'll buy you a steak dinner. In the meantime, I'd be obliged if you'd let go that boy, lift up them hands, and come with me."

Thomson opened his mouth as if to keep the argument going, but after a moment all he said was, "I'm sorry, Bert, I can't do that."

"Tom, I got four deputies out front—and one of them's Beth Ann, fresh from the pistol range—and more out back. And plus, Sheriff Bradley's hopping mad, on account of these Fergusons was fixing to lynch his kin. I come here without mentioning it to him because right now he'd shoot you soon as look at you, for signing on with them. This ain't no time to be doing something stupid."

"If Sheriff Bradley had thought to make me a detective, or just given me another partner, instead of sticking me in a car with a potty-mouth tub of lard—"

"I asked for you, Tom. Said I wanted a talented officer with me. Best way I could think of to keep an eye on you. Now, let's go."

Thomson yanked Jefferson between himself and Lucknell's gun. He pulled his own pistol and pressed the barrel against Jefferson's head. Lucknell didn't move. Thomson looked at Bill. "Where's your car keys?"

"Right here." Bill, one hand raised, slowly slipped the other into his pocket and slid the keys out.

"Give them to her," he said, indicating me. As though the thought had just occurred to him, he added, "You can drive, right?"

"Of course I can." I took the keys from Bill.

"Good. You go first, hands up. I'm coming right after with the boy here. Bert, put that gun down there by that good sweet tea. Uh-huh. Anyone else armed?" Headshakes all around. "Now, Bert, tell them deputies to stand down. This is no bluff. I'd prefer to end my days here and now rather than spend even one in a Mississippi prison."

"That's where you're headed, Tom, believe me."

"Maybe. But I got a pile of that fine Ferguson cash and I got hostages here. I know the protocol. I suggest once we're gone, you call Dispatch and say to clear the roads, because I see even one headlight behind me, I'll figure the chase is on and I'll get rid of the baggage here so's I can travel light."

After another staring moment, Lucknell opened the door and boomed, "Hold y'all's fire! Hostages coming out!"

"Thanks, Bert," said Thomson. "I'd say what a pleasure it's been working together, but it ain't. Now, y'all"—he spoke to Lucknell, Bill, Pete, and Frank—"sit y'all's asses on the floor with your hands on your heads. That's right. Now everyone pray Beth Ann and them don't have itchy fingers, because it won't be me goes down first."

He looked at me. Hands up, I walked slowly out the door. Attenuated silhouettes stood in the glare of headlights. I couldn't tell where their guns pointed. The street was silent. Even HB had stopped, as though waiting for something to happen.

And it did.

A car alarm screamed, with blaring horn and flashing lights. HB yowled. In that second of distraction, I turned and yanked Jefferson's arm, hoping if Thomson fired at least his gun wouldn't be at Jefferson's head. But he didn't fire. He crashed hard to the ground, brought down by a flying back-of-the-knee tackle that, had this been a football game, would've gotten Frank Roberson thrown out of it.

51

The Coahoma County Jail, already well-stocked with Fergusons, just about burst at the seams when all of us were brought in and stuffed into various corners. Tom Thomson had been arrested back at Pete's, Beth Ann McGee hauling him to his feet and giving him a sad head-shake as she cuffed him. Lucknell ordered everyone else swept up and brought in. We all went meekly, even Pete.

At the jail, Jefferson was rearrested, for the original homicide and for escaping custody. Pete, Bill, and I weren't arrested, but Bert Lucknell made it clear that could happen at any moment, and therefore he would recommend cooperating. Starting with, until we were questioned, shutting up.

Frank, though, being the hero of the hour and, equally important, Reynold Tam's son-in-law, was offered Lucknell's thanks and the opportunity to head home.

"No," Frank said. "I appreciate it, but really, I'm the one you need."

"Needed you back at the house, that's for sure," Lucknell said. "Got to remember that car alarm trick." He scratched his head. "Concerning the tackle, though, I honestly can't say's I recall you showing that much quickness on the field back in the day."

"If you remember my football career at all, you're one in a million, Detective. May I call my wife before I give my statement?"

"Sir, in all seriousness, you don't have to—"

"Yes. I do."

I was escorted into an interview room new to me. That gave me a whole new set of scratches, paint chips, and ceiling stains to catalog before Lucknell finally issued through the door.

"Well," he said, settling in a worn chair and dropping his hat on the table. "Here I was thinking that tripping over Yankee amateurs every step I took was complicating my life. But now it seems I owe y'all a debt of gratitude."

"Glad to help."

"Oh, it ain't that I think helping was on y'all's mind. Probably if Jefferson had turned up sooner, y'all would've rushed him up to New York. As it is, y'all were hiding him and I could lock up all y'all, including Captain Pete, for that." I started to protest. Lucknell waved my words away. "But I had my eye on Tom. When he said we should wait on the road out of Oxford because one of his snitches said y'all was up there, I had to ask myself, why would Tom ask a snitch in Oxford to look out for y'all? And why would y'all go there except to take a look at Jefferson Tam's apartment, where there ain't nothing to find? But if it so happened that Tom was in the Fergusons' pocket, and if for some reason y'all was bothering Anna Rae, then the call likely wasn't from no snitch, but either Anna Rae, or maybe Fisheye. Now that I got a warrant for Tom's phone, we'll know soon enough."

"I see. Detective," I said, to head off any additional lengthy explanations and get to the questions that were bothering me, "what happens now? To Jefferson, but also, to Frank and Pete?"

Lucknell nodded. "Worrying about kin, that's admirable." He smiled. "Fishing for information about what they told me and what I told them is maybe a touch less admirable."

I didn't deny it. He stretched and reorganized himself in his chair. "But I'm feeling bighearted tonight. My report'll go something like this. Convict name of Trevor McAdoo down on Parchman got in touch with Mr. Roberson, asked him to come down. What they talked about, I couldn't say, there being some kind of confidentiality thing involved so Mr. Roberson, he don't have to tell me. But probably, it had to do with Trevor knowing his brother Tremaine was planning to get into some bad business with Leland Tam, because after that, Mr. Roberson went to see Tremaine. Tremaine told him this story about wanting to deal drugs from out Leland's store. Seems Leland tried to run him off with a knife, and Tremaine grabbed it up and sliced Leland in the leg. Then, for some reason, Mr. Roberson and Tremaine got in a tussle. Tremaine, he was that type, to tell a man a story and then kill him for hearing it. But it was Tremaine got killed."

Lucknell stopped and gave me a long look. I didn't say anything, waiting for the other shoe to drop.

"So we're looking at the knife now, see if we can find Tremaine's prints somewhere on it. To my way of thinking, even if we can't, the D.A.'ll drop the charges against Jefferson. Mr. Roberson, he's a pretty reliable witness."

Meaning, I thought, he's white, middle class, and works for a congressman.

"What Tremaine told him, you could call it hearsay, but there's also such a thing called a 'dying declaration.' Since it ain't a hundred percent clear when Tremaine said all this in relation to when he died, it might be one of those, so it would be admissible in a court of law. As to Jefferson, there's still the jailbreak, but he claims he wasn't in on it, didn't even know what was going on until they got him to Burcell, and I'm inclined to think that's true. D.A.'s got to sort all that out, but meanwhile, judge set bail and Captain Pete already went it.

"Now, then, there's Captain Pete himself. He was harboring Jefferson. And you and Smith knew about it and didn't say a thing." Lucknell leered, giving me a moment to wonder about the Coahoma County Jail's women's wing. Then he grinned broadly and went on.

"But I ain't disposed to bother with that. Sheriff's feeling real warm toward y'all for saving his nephew, and as to Pete, I don't know's it would do anybody any good for him to spend time as a guest of the county. Now, Mr. Roberson, he should've reported Tremaine's death, of course. He could be charged with leaving the scene, even with manslaughter, but I do understand the delicate position the boy was in and I doubt if the D.A. will bother to make anything of it. It ain't like Tremaine McAdoo was a prize citizen of Coahoma County."

Lucknell gave me another long look, then stood and put his hat back on. "That right there is pretty much it. Anything else you got to talk about with kin, anything to do with old photographs and family records, the Great Flood and suchlike, none of that's my business, and it's just a story, anyway, so it won't be in my report. You're free to go." Lucknell walked out, leaving the door open.

My mouth was open, too. I closed it and scuttled out before Lucknell changed his mind.

As I expected, I found Bill waiting on an orange chair by the entrance. Frank sat on one side of him and Pete and Jefferson on the other. They all stood, and nobody said a word as we turned and left.

52

The silence thing ended when we got to Pete's. The hospitality of the Sheriff's Department had included two patrol cars to take us home. I couldn't swear Pete's neighbors were watching from behind their curtains, but it seemed to me porch lights went on and people stepped out even before HB's greeting barks cracked open the night.

"Everything's fine," Pete hollered, ushering the rest of us through the front door. "No casualties. Tell you about it in the morning. Thanks for your concern." He shut the door, threw the bolt, and turned the porch light off. "Now," he said, hands on hips, eyeing us all. He opened a cabinet and took out a bottle and four shot glasses. "Cousin Lydia, you want some tea?"

"Is that moonshine?"

"The best there ever was."

"Then I believe I'll join you. I mean," I said, looking around at these three men who were related to me, and the one who wasn't but whom I knew so well, "all y'all."

Pete grinned, took out another glass, and poured. Moonshine was handed around. Then the questions and answers started.

Jefferson had gotten caught up on some things—like who Frank was—while they were waiting for me at the jail, but he was still behind on some others, like what had happened in Pete's living room while Jefferson was hiding in the secret room behind the basement water heater.

"For the times when I win big," Pete explained.

Jefferson replied, "Room's empty, Uncle Pete."

Pete took off his cap and whacked Jefferson on the arm with it.

After Jefferson was up to speed, all three of my relatives started talking at once. I pretty much just sat back and let them, as Bill was doing. I sipped at my moonshine, trying not to cough, deciding the warm glow I was beginning to feel was worth the struggle.

The guys finally ran out of steam. The pace of conversation slowed and the room quieted. As Pete poured more moonshine, I said, "All right, I have a question. Lucknell made it clear he knows the whole story—about the photo, about Reynold's grandmother. But he's not going to say anything."

Frank nodded. "We are, though. Is that the question? I spoke to Reynold while we waited for you." Frank rolled his shot glass between his palms. "For one thing, there's still Trevor McAdoo. My promise to him—" Frank grinned. "It only worked as long as Reynold didn't know about it. He just about blew his top."

"He won't pardon Trevor?"

"I never thought he would. I had to say it, to keep Trevor quiet until after the primary. I figured once Reynold was governor, Trevor could say what he wanted and we'd deal with it."

"A politician whose staff tells lies?" Bill shook his head. "What's the world coming to?"

Frank lifted his glass in acknowledgment. "But Reynold's pretty shaken, about who his grandmother was. He wants to see the photo and hear all the details."

"Then what?" I asked.

"Then we'll have a press conference. He's already decided. He's going to tell the voters the truth—that he just found this out and he doesn't want to hide it. In fact, he'll say, he's proud because it makes him the perfect candidate—now he knows he represents *all* of Mississippi."

"Will that work?"

"Unlikely. I think we're finished. Mallory'll sink his teeth into this. But Reynold's weakness as a candidate has always been a certain . . . sense of honor. It's a hard sell, these days." He rose. "I'd better go."

"It's late to drive all the way to Jackson," Pete said. "Why not stay here?"

"Thanks, but my family's used to my hours. I do like to get home to them, if I can." He shook his head. "It's just a shame we've discovered a whole new branch of the family tree, and there's no one left to ask about it but a guy like Trevor McAdoo."

"Oh," I said, "but there is." I pointed to the manila envelope, left behind when we all were carted off. I told Frank where we got it, and finished, "I'm sure Lunetta Briggs would be thrilled to meet Reynold. And all the rest of you, especially your kids. When you go, bring some fudge."

53

Everyone slept late the next morning, and everyone seemed to ease slowly into the new day, sipping coffee and tea, speaking little, waiting for the grits and eggs Bill had been working on in the kitchen. When finally the table was loaded, the toast buttered and fresh coffee poured, Pete said to me, "Your mama must be happy, how things worked out."

"She will be. But I didn't call her yet. I was a little . . . tired last night."

Bill tried to hide a grin behind his coffee cup.

"Don't pick on my mother!"

"I'm just being supportive. Your mother could make a tweaker tired."

"I'd back off, was I you," Pete warned Bill.

"Thank you," I replied with great dignity. "Besides," I said to Pete, "I want to be able to tell my mother the rest of the story. You know, what happens now."

Pete looked at Jefferson. "Well," he said. "What does happen now? Once the legal mess gets taken care of, I mean?"

Jefferson shrugged. "I'm not sure, Uncle Pete. Right now, like, after breakfast, I'd kind of like to go to the store. Just because . . . I mean, the last time I was there . . ."

"Yeah," Pete said. "We get it."

"But then . . . I know Daddy would've wanted me to stay here and take it over—heck, he wanted that for a long time—but it's just not right. I can't do that. Shopkeeping, it's not for me."

"Yeah," Pete said again. "Was never for me, either."

"I feel bad. Because the store's so old, has so much history."

"Still useful, too."

"I guess."

"As it happens," Pete said, "I've been studying on this problem."

"What problem? Me and the store?"

"Finish up. We got someplace to go."

That place, of course, was H. Tam and Sons, and sitting in the sun out front, of course, were Henry Watson, Sam Shoemaker, and Bobby Lee Smith.

"Welcome back, Jefferson," said Henry, as we got out of the car. "Word is, you're in the clear. That so?"

"Close enough," Pete said. "Sheriff would've taken up Tremaine McAdoo for killing Leland, but the devil saved him the trouble."

"That's good every which way, then."

The other two men echoed the sentiment, and Sam, rubbing his bald head, added, to Jefferson, "So. You gonna open?"

"Sam wants his malt," Pete explained, unlocking the front door. He stood aside for Jefferson, who stepped in, stopped, and whistled.

"Well, I'll— Uncle Pete, what *happened* here? The place hasn't looked this good in—in ever!"

"Your staff took care of things."

"My what?"

"See," Pete said, "right now, these worthless layabouts, they do nothing but sit out front and scare business away. They got their talents, though. Henry, when he gets up offa his butt, he's pretty good at organizing and such."

Henry turned around and stuck his butt out at Pete.

"Bobby Lee, he's got a mind for carpentry, electric, like that."

Bobby Lee waved a modest hand.

"And Sam—okay, Sam's kind of useless, but he can stock shelves long as you don't let him be the one puts the malts in the cooler. Point is, Jefferson, you got here a store you don't want to run, and you also got here three vagrants with nothing to do. Maybe there's a deal could be made?"

Jefferson looked from Pete to the three men, who looked at each other. Henry shrugged and nodded. "I don't believe I got any objection."

"Me neither," said Bobby Lee.

"Me neither," Sam agreed. "And now that I'm a employee, I gotta go check on the stock. Starting with the malts."

54

Bill and I left the Tams and their new hires to work things out. "We'll come back for you later, Cousin Pete," I said.

"Nah, Henry'll run me home in the truck. You kids run along. Now you got no murders to solve, maybe you could find other things to do."

"Kids, huh?" Bill said as we got in the car.

"It's all relative. And I have nice relatives."

"You do."

"Even my mother?"

"Especially your mother. Where to?"

"Well," I said, "everyone keeps telling me *this is Mississippi*. So I'd kind of like to see the Mississippi. Are we allowed to go up on the levee?"

"Who's going to stop us?"

We drove out of Clarksdale, past the occupied storefronts, the empty ones, the lamppost flowerpots and the draped tinsel. Brown frosted fields waiting for next year's cotton slid by the windows, until Bill turned the car onto a muddy track under a tunnel of waving branches. We'd never been down this road before, so I might have asked how we knew where we were going, but this was Bill, so I didn't.

After a while, we emerged onto a flat under the bright gray sky. In front of us, the sloping levee rose.

"Should we park and climb? Or look for a road?"

"Let's climb," I said. We left the car and cut a diagonal across the grassy, treeless slope. Bill, his long legs taking him ahead, waited for me at the top. He offered me a hand up and I took it. His palm was warm in the chill of the Mississippi morning. Holding hands, we crossed the levee's flat top and looked out over the slow-flowing river. Cypresses with their tangled roots shadowed the shoreline. Beyond them, the water glittered silver.

"What's on the other side?"

"Here, Arkansas. Farther down, Louisiana."

"I've never been to those places, either. I know so little about the South."

"You know a lot more than most Yankees, now."

"Maybe so. But still. Listen." I watched the water flow. "I want to stay around until Leland's funeral. I think Pete would like that. Then maybe we can see some more of Mississippi? Some of those big mansions. Natchez, maybe, and go to Jackson and meet Frank's kids? Get to know the family a little."

"Sounds good, but you sure you want me around? I'm not family."

"Well, you sort of are."

"Tell that to your mother."

"I will. I've been thinking. About relations, and people not knowing each other, and people giving things up. Giving each other up. And poor Leland, dying on a day that wasn't supposed to be different from any other day. I think I just figured out we don't have all the time in the world. I know, it's a giant cliché, go ahead and laugh at me."

"I would never."

"You would."

"Well, okay. But not now."

"So what I'm thinking is, when we go to Natchez, maybe we can find a warm, Christmasy bed-and-breakfast? With one cozy room and a big soft bed?" I turned to look at him, and added, so he wouldn't have to ask, "Yes, I'm sure."

I could read surprise and wonder in his eyes; then he leaned down. I stood on tiptoe to meet him halfway, and we kissed under the gray sky beside the silver river, in this Mississippi that wasn't at all what I'd expected.

35